Memento Amore

by Alice Greene

To Kara, who always held space for my imagination to run wild.
And to little me, who always dreamed of being an author. You did it!

Trigger Warnings

Sexual assault/Rape

Death

Dead bodies

Violence

Blood

Murder

Kidnapping

Abusive/Toxic Relationships

Hard Kinks

Memento Amore deals with dark topics and includes a myriad of adult themes. Please be mindful of your limits and take care of yourself. Your well-being matters.

Playlist

Waiting For the End- Linkin Park
Swan Upon a Leda- Hozier
My Body's a Zombie For You- Dead Man's Bones
Francesca- Hozier
I Will Never Die- Delta Rae
Howl- Florence + The Machine
bury a friend- Pomplamoose (cover)
I Died So I Could Haunt You- Stars
Pet Sematary- Ramones
Running Up That Road- Kate Bush
(Don't Fear) The Reaper- Blue Oyster Cult
Rain- Sleep Token

Act 1

Oberon

Fall, 1885

I ghost my lips along the curve of her neck, careful not to wake her.

Leda sleeps soundly, her heat spreading into my chest, warming me more than the sputtering fireplace across from our bed. I tuck some loose strands of dark hair behind her ear, wafting her sweet cocoa scent into my nose.

Her eyebrows wrinkle slightly, her wine-stained lips parting to yawn.

"Shhh, precious girl." I stroke her hair. "Morning is still hours away."

Leda wriggles closer to me, soft curves molding against my field-hardened body. Her ass presses against my groin as if pulled by a magnet, stirring my cock to life.

It throbs with every little move she makes. I will myself to stay motionless.

She's had a long day and needs to rest, not get ravaged.

We'd spent most of the day in the garden, her cultivating herbs and vegetables, and I sparring with both weapons and wiles alongside my older brothers.

We toil away most of our time learning and practicing the art of magic, honing our specialties and cultivating our relationship with the Source. My magic has nearly surpassed my middle brother, Algernon, and I'd knocked him on his ass more than once.

Leda had beamed with pride and thrown a turnip or two to lend me a hand during battle.

The sun had both invigorated and depleted most of our energy in that unique way it does, and after a fall feast of bread, stew, and wine, we'd unceremoniously crashed into bed.

I was certain she wouldn't stir until well after sunrise, considering she normally sleeps like the dead. But that minx had other plans.

She squirms again, grinding her perfect ass into my rapidly hardening cock.

"Leda," I warn, snaking my hand down her bare side and grabbing a handful of her traitorous derriere.

"Oberon," she coos back, glancing at me over her shoulder, brown eyes anything but sleep-laden.

My breath catches; she is so beautiful. Plump lips, warm eyes, rosy cheeks. Full, dark brows and lashes. A wicked, sinful smile playing at the edges of her mouth.

I frown at her, despite the cloying need for her eclipsing the rational part of my brain. "You need rest, baby."

She turns over and swipes her tongue along my jaw, trailing upwards to nibble at the tender shell of my ear. "I need you," she whispers, gently taking my hand off her backside and dipping it between her thighs. She was soaking, dripping with need.

Fuck.

I flip on top of her, pressing her down into the mattress and capture her lips in mine, savoring the soft cushion of her mouth and her tongue's silken slide. We kiss slowly, decadent and sweet.

Love burns in my chest, making my heart pound. No matter how many times our lips met, it still left me breathless.

I kiss her harder, grazing my teeth along her bottom lip.

She moans into my mouth, fingers twining into my hair and pulling me closer. Our tongues dance together until she captures mine with her teeth. She sucks on it gently, teasingly, running her nails along my scalp in the way she knows I like.

Devilish girl. I slide my hand up her body, deliberately skating around her pearled nipples and grasp her delicate throat, leaning back to look into her eyes. Fire blazes behind them. Her heart thrums under my fingertips, the wings of a hummingbird. Our magic pulls towards each other, yearning to become one, all-consuming power.

With all energy, like calls to like. Magic is no different. The Source inside of us calls to the Source inside others, eager to combine and grow stronger. Source is our stabilizing energy, our well of strength. It craves nurturing and community, the things that make all of us stronger.

Leda's magic is relatively weak because her family had lived in isolation for generations after the Witch Trials, like many of us did. Periods like that, those dark, panic-filled days always left a lasting scar on the magic community, one that could only be remedied by a long stretch of peace and prosperity. Unfortunately, those seem to be few and far between.

My magic reaches for hers, coaxing it to life, fanning her flame. The connection has my cock aching, reaching for the liquid heat radiating from her core. I dip my head down and lick along her velvet breasts, lightly sucking one of her pink nipples into my mouth before shifting to the other, stoking the fire I knew was already raging in her core.

"Husband, please," Leda mewls, straining against my hold. She bucks her hips, gasping with her need for friction.

"So impatient, darling. When have I ever left you unsatisfied?" I release her throat and pepper kisses along the length of it, scraping my teeth against her earlobe. I capture her lips again, hungrily taking in her wine and sleep-soaked taste.

I tease her scalding entrance with the head of my cock, resisting the impulse to plunge brutally into her, wanting to draw her arousal out to the breaking point, make her a beautiful mess for me.

A thunderous bark sounds from outside, making us both jump.

Our mastiff, Grim carries on like a dog possessed, and is quickly joined by the distressed bray of our donkey and clattering of hooves in the stable.

"Don't move." I roll onto my feet, pulling my discarded trousers off the floor. I grab my gun from beside the door, ignoring the tremor in my hands.

Leda stares at me, fearful.

I close my eyes and will the animals to silence while scanning the property and checking my wards. The animals quiet, and I don't detect an intrusion.

All seems well.

I listen for another moment, then let my shoulders relax. I turn back to Leda, a mischievous smile already pulling up the corners of my mouth. I set the gun down and prowl toward her.

"My hero," she hums, reaching out to me from the nest of our bed.

Five, maybe six steps away from her, her eyes widen. Her smile vanishes.

Leda's scream is the last thing I hear before pain snuffs out my senses.

Something sharp plunges through my chest, shimmering with blood. My blood. It was so fast, I barely registered the pain.

I drop to my knees, unable to look away as a dark shadow approaches her. She screams and screams, but I can barely hear her. The world muffled by blood pounding in my ears.

"Oberon!"

Stay awake. She needs you.

I reach out towards her, and the world slips away.

My body rushes back to me out of nothingness. Blinding agony electrifies my deadened nerves, pressure explodes in my chest as my heart desperately pumps blood back into my veins. My head roars as life slams into me. I scream, my bones grinding out of rigor mortis.

I stagger to my feet, clutching at my bare chest. No blade, no blood. All that remains is a jagged, white scar that mars my sternum.

"Leda!" I scream, terror squeezing in my chest.

The room is torn apart, gutted like a corpse. My favorite chair turned to kindling. Her bookshelf a carcass on the ground, books heaped into the now raging fireplace. Our clothes are in tattered piles on the floor. The portrait of us on our wedding day, sliced and splashed with dark blood. The bed is ruined, stained with gore and torn to shreds.

I'm standing in a pool of my own blood, the lake of it wider than my wingspan. I nearly slip in it running to the bedside.

A deer antler rests on her pillow, a braid of dark hair wrapped around it like twine. The points were fractured and stained with blood.

I clutch the antler to my chest, reaching for my magic to find her. We are blood bound; she's my wife. I can find her anywhere in the world.

My soul reaches for hers and is met with numbing silence.

The air is forced from my lungs, leaving me gasping, retching on the scratched floor. Grief carves out my insides, turning every happy thought and memory into a fractured version of itself, leaving a trail of rot and ruin across my psyche.

I've done the unthinkable, the strictly forbidden in the magic community, the darkest of the dark arts: Necromancy. I willed myself back from the brink, condemning me to a life of immortality, of *wrong*ness.

Heaviness clings to me, a dark weight that places a vignette over everything I see, everything I think. I can feel the delicate thrum of life around me: skittering mice in the walls, crows in the oak trees, chickens and goats in the yard. I can feel the frigid void of death, too. Grim, our Guilds cemetery, our rose bushes struggling to withstand the oncoming autumn. They're all tethers in my hands, harp strings all around me, mine to play with.

I have more power than I ever dreamed possible. More than I ever dared want. And I still can't save her, not without her body. Hair and blood weren't enough, I need flesh and bone as well.

Algernon and I search everywhere. Hours turn to days with no sign of Leda. No amount of magic can track her down, can recover what has been well and truly lost.

Besides my brother, the rest of our Guild refuses to help, disgusted with what I've become and frightened by the omen of the antler.

I knew what it meant, we all did. Evil had set its sights on us, the Arcanum growing impatient with our Guilds refusal to submit. They'd sent their most powerful weapon, Keanu, whose familiar was a great, black stag.

It was only a matter of time now before our leader, my father, Absolon Raith, gave into their demands. Gave over the centuries of sacred knowledge we'd collected. Gave over to the darkness. And in a way, I already had, albeit unintentionally. I'd done Necromancy, the darkest magic a witch could do, and would be cursed by it forever.

If they could have killed me that night, they would have.

Banishment was their only option.

A few weeks after her disappearance, I lay on the front steps and nurse a nearly empty gallon jug of elderberry wine. There were no stars tonight, only clouds and the bite of October wind. Drinking was the only way to keep the noise at bay, the constant tug of my power. It was impossible to focus on anything beyond the clamor of life and death, the energy of the world around me. Everything, from the smallest insect to the tallest tree called out to me.

I'd only used my power once, excluding my own resurrection, to save Grim. Bringing him back put me out for nearly two days. All I could do was sleep and sip broth, ladled in my mouth by Algernon, who was fighting dutifully to keep me sane as the weeks pass.

Now, the mutt snored vigorously to my left, very much alive.

I took another pull of wine, close to that beautiful blurry nothingness where all the noise faded away, when the air shifted and grew unnervingly still. A new energy has stepped into my periphery, a life, albeit dark and strange.

I can't say if it was my power, or plain intuition, but I knew immediately who had arrived.

"Keanu," I seethe, getting to my feet.

"Hello, Oberon," he replies, stepping out from the shadowy tree line. He's wearing a black tunic and heavy leather armor, a white antler collar gleaming from around his neck. Dark charcoal is smudged across his eyes and stains the tips of his willowy fingers.

Normally, his presence would strike fear, but now all I felt was blistering rage, and the thick cord of his life. Most have threads like cotton yarn or horse hair. Particularly strong souls, like my brothers, have a heavier band, like braided leather. I've never encountered anything like this, black and thick as my wrist, solid as steel.

"What do you want?" I cross my arms over my chest, using my energy to test the bounds of his tether.

"You, my friend." He glides closer, seeming to hover above the grass. "You have turned out to be so much more interesting than I thought, my raven-haired prince." He pauses a few feet from the porch, sizing me up, a hungry gleam in his black eyes.

I heft the weight of his tether, growing more sure that I could sever it with enough time. The more energy I directed to it, the more brittle it became, shards of black crumbling under my fingers like obsidian until it revealed a sliver of something else, a core of bone.

But I could already feel the strain of my magic, the strength slipping away just as I get a hold of it.

"Think of what we could do together, Oberon." He's only a few paces away now. I can make out the thin scar on his nose, the strange tattoo under his eye. "You could be my Grim Reaper. The world would be ours. Every King on their knees, we'd be worshiped like Gods-"

"You killed my wife!" I snap, delivering a hard blow to his energy, sending him staggering backwards.

I can tell it surprises him, but he recovers quickly.

"Oberon, I swear to you, I had nothing to do with Leda's murder. I had no ill-will towards either of you."

I send another blast his way, nearly knocking myself over with the effort. "Why should I believe you?"

He doubles over, blood dripping from his lips. "Believe what you want." He spits, straightening. "Think about it, at least. With us, you'd never be alone. You'd have a family. Your family is afraid of you, turned their backs on you. We accept you, *I* accept you, Oberon."

For a moment, he almost seems genuine, almost seems like he truly believes his own lies.

"I'll die first," I snarl, fighting to keep conscious.

"We'll see." He smirks. With a wave of his hand, he disappears into the night, as if he'd never existed at all.

I sink to the ground, exhaustion and despair smothering the adrenaline in my system.

Come back to me.

Please, come back to me.

Olivia

Fall, 2023

"Fuck, fuck, fuck, fuck," I mutter to myself, pulling dress after dress out of my closet. "Where are you?!" I shove hangers loaded with graphics tees and sweaters aside. "Aha!" I see it in the very back of the closet, my lucky green skirt.

I pull it on over my black turtleneck bodysuit and cinch a black leather belt around my waist. The skirt is a deep emerald satin with delicate pleats and hits just below the knee. Modest, but flattering.

It's my first day as a Mortuary Apprentice at Alder Bridge Funeral and Mortuary Services, and I'm losing it. It's the last funeral home I wanted to be sent to; everyone in my graduating class breathed a sigh of relief when I was the unlucky soul selected to apprentice under Ben Raith. It's one of the most respected establishments in the area, but Raith has a reputation for being less than approachable.

This is the first year he's agreed to take on an apprentice, so I have no idea what I'm in for. But I'll be damned if I don't make a good first impression.

I put the finishing touches on my makeup, simple brown liner, blush, brows, and mascara. My dark curls are swept back into a low ponytail, save the pesky face-framing pieces that hang in my eyes. I opt for contacts on the first day, save some of the dorkiness for later. I slip on low-heeled black boots, grab my purse, and scurry out the door.

It's drizzly in Alder Bridge today, just a few days after the fall equinox, and of course, I forgot my jacket. Too late now, if I turn back I may never pluck up the courage to leave again.

I can't believe this day is already here, the day I've been working towards since I was nine years old. I'd be working in an *actual* funeral home.

To most it hardly sounds like a dream come true, but for me, it's a life mission and over a decade of work finally bearing fruit. I graduated top of my class in high school, college, and mortuary school at Folke University, dedicated my life to the science of death and the psychology of grief. I've even dipped my toes into true crime, the occult, and witchcraft. I was fascinated, some would call it obsessed, with death.

Often, I dream about my own death.

It's always the same, I wake up in an unfamiliar bed, a heavy hand clamped over my mouth. There's a man standing at the foot of the bed. His face obscured, but I know that I know him, somehow.

Just before I see his face, a shadow rises behind him and stabs him through the chest. Then, I'm swallowed up by darkness, dragged through the forest, and thrown into a deep hole. I can see stars, hanging there in the night sky like apathetic bystanders.

Dirt pours over me, rushing like water, filling my nose and mouth. All I can do is scream in that hoarse, strangled way you do in dreams.

My therapist thinks I'm attempting to control the uncontrollable, tame the unknown, and maybe she's right. But what's so bad about that?

Suddenly, I'm in front of the building, the walk flying by as my thoughts swirled. I check my watch: 7:45.

Is that early enough? Too early?

Shops are opening all around me, folks heading into work or grabbing coffee across the street at Keaton's. Rain turns the street to glitter, a haze suspended in the early morning sunlight.

The funeral home sits in shadows, ivy crawling up the black siding. It's a gorgeous craftsman home with a spacious front porch and warm wood accents. A well-tended, if a little full, garden fills the small front yard. Flowers grow along the cobblestone path leading to the richly stained front door. A plaque to the left reads "Alder Bridge Funeral and Mortuary Services, opened 1934 by Oberon Raith in Alder Bridge, NY."

I try the door. Unlocked.

I push into the cozy foyer, all dark wood and plush rugs. Lively plants adorn the space, along with familiar local artists, newspaper clippings, and old photographs. The scent of teakwood and white flowers envelop me.

Voices drift across the quiet, coming from deeper in the home. I head that way, taking note of the copious amounts of overstuffed furniture, books, and greenery.

I turn a corner and find what must be the main parlor. Mr. Raith is sitting at the end of the aisle on the black velvet stairs leading to the podium, conversing with an older couple. Fresh flowers fill the space, and the woman is dabbing her cheeks with a handkerchief.

I'd only seen the singular photo of him on the website, an overly formal, grouchy-looking head shot that captures none of the energy exuding from the man at the end of the aisle.

He's graceful, delicate in the way he speaks to the clients, his body language oozing comfort, reliability, and intelligence. His hands are soft on the mug he's holding, raising it slowly to his lips. Soft stubble lines his jaw, snags the dark waves falling just past his ears.

He's wearing black trousers and a white button down, clean and professional.

His eyes catch mine over the rim of his mug. Blue, because of course they are, lined with lashes I'd have to sacrifice an entire paycheck for. His eyebrows raise just slightly, as if he's surprised to see me, then shifts his attention back to his clients.

My feet feel glued to the floor, but I will myself to take a few more steps down the hall and sit on a settee nearby.

I take a few breaths and rally my nerves. I cannot be thinking about how hot my new boss is right now, I haven't even spoken to him. But, *fuck*, he is so hot, like book boyfriend hot.

The instant attraction makes me a bit queasy, as if I wasn't nervous enough. I've never handled relationship-py feelings well, the rare occasions I caught them. I prefer my romance in book form.

A few more minutes pass steeped in my indecision. Do I stay and see how this plays out? Or run for the hills and avoid the collision all together?

I lean forward to stand at the same moment they move out into the hall, and I drop awkwardly back onto the bench. They pay me no mind.

Mr. Raith shakes the guest's hands and bids them farewell, guiding them out the front door and down the steps.

He shuts the door, turns on his heels, and once again his eyes land on me.

I stare at him dumbly, and he stares right back, almost confused. Then he shakes his head and approaches, hand extended.

"Ms. Hunter?" he asks.

I scramble to my feet and shake his hand, probably a bit too firmly. Several rings decorate his long fingers, along with a vintage looking wristwatch and a perfectly polished gold armband.

"Yes, but please call me Olivia, or Liv. It's such a pleasure to meet you, Mr. Raith." I try to discreetly wipe my sweaty palms on my skirt.

"Alright, Olivia, do you like coffee?"

Sweeter words have never been spoken. "I love coffee!" I reply a bit too loudly.

He smiles, although it doesn't reach his eyes, and gestures to a room at the end of the hall. "I've got a fresh pot in my office. Right this way."

I follow him down the hall, kicking myself for acting like a dazed schoolgirl. He's my boss; I'm a professional. I need to get it together.

His office is decorated similarly to the rest of the funeral home, with plants, art, and dark walls. One of the walls is lined with floor-to-ceiling bookshelves overflowing with tomes, a comfortable leather couch resting in front of it. There's a neatly organized desk topped with double monitors and stacks of files. A coffee machine and mini fridge sit by the door, neighbors to a wooden coat rack, where a black leather jacket hangs.

He pours me a cup of coffee then tops up his own.

I recognize the mug from a local diner, and suddenly I can imagine sharing a tray of fries with him, laughing about the day we had. I take a sip to clear the embarrassing image and he gestures for me to sit on the couch. I expect him to sit in the large executive chair behind the desk, but he sinks into one of the guest chairs positioned in front of it, eyeing me expectantly.

"I'm really excited to get started, Mr. Raith. And thank you so much for the opportunity. I know you don't usually take apprentices, and I'm so eager to learn from someone with such a long history in the field. Did your grandfather open the service?" I ask, trying, and failing, to speak at a measured pace.

He sips his coffee. "My grandfather opened the home in 1934, then it was passed down to my father, and now me. What brought you into the field?" His tone is clipped, not quite harsh, but not warm and fuzzy either, certainly not compared to the gentle way he spoke to the clients earlier.

My nerves return. He's assessing me like a specimen, blue eyes chilling. I opt for honesty, I have a feeling that he'll know if I give him some fluffy, bullshit answer.

"I, uh, lost my sister when I was young." I take a deep breath, bracing myself. "I remember being so comforted by the funeral director. Even my own parents couldn't console me, but she took me to her office and read me a story, the Little Prince, actually. She let me ask any questions I wanted, no matter how macabre, and answered with a smile. It was such a gift, and helped me take those first steps of my grieving process. It only felt right to pay that forward."

He nods and takes another sip. "It seems most have a story like that." He pauses, scratching under his chin. "I'm glad you followed your intuition."

I try to hide my blush by taking a long sip of coffee. What is wrong with me? That was barely half of a compliment.

He sets down his cup. "Ready for the grand tour?"

"Please! This place is incredible."

He smiles, just a little, and strides out of the room.

I have to hurry to catch up with him, his long legs taking him down the hall in a blink.

"This is the main parlor, as I'm sure you guessed." He gestures to the room I initially encountered him in. It's dripping in black velvet, greenery, and warm wood. It feels lush and comfortable, moody in all the best ways.

He turns to the right. "Down this hall is the display room and meeting space." We pass an organized room with rows of coffins, urns, flowers, and fabric swatches, and another room with a large oak table and comfortable looking red chairs. "And here—" we approach a heavy metal door with a key card lock— "is where the fun happens." His tone is so dry it takes me a second to realize he's told a joke.

"I certainly think so," I giggle.

He smiles again, eyes searching my face. A beat passes, his gaze lingering.

Warmth kicks up in my belly, heat rising in my cheeks.

He clears his throat and turns to swipe his card. "I'll have a key card made for you tomorrow."

I guess that means I passed the entry test. Relief loosens some of the anxiety still clogging my lungs.

The cold of the morgue immediately bites into my skin. We walk down a short hall leading to the double doors of the morgue and autopsy lab.

It's by far the cleanest morgue I've ever stepped foot in. The stainless steel gleams, throwing our distorted reflections around the room. The open shelving showcases an assortment of chemicals and cleaners, meticulously arranged in alphabetical order. Each drawer has a label and internal organizers to keep things straight. Not a single paper is out of place. It's immaculate and nearly makes me giddy.

"I'm very type A," he mutters, almost looking embarrassed as he trails behind me.

"This is incredible. I've never seen such a well-kept facility. Most feel more like slaughterhouses than medical spaces." I walk slowly around the room, taking mental notes of where everything is stored.

"Yes, well, thank you, Olivia. I hope it helps your training go smoothly."

I pull open drawers, check bottles, and explore. I feel his eyes trailing my movements, and can see in his reflection that he's frowning slightly.

He crosses the room, collects the files from the refrigeration units, and then waits for me by the doors to finish ogling.

My hands are nearly twitching with excitement to get to work. The thought of sharing the room with him, working together, completing exams, and even paperwork makes my heart leap.

I've never felt drawn to someone like this before, why does he have to be my boss? This is too good of an opportunity for me to throw away by pretending I'm in a romance novel.

I need to get it together.

I meet him at the door and he hands me the stack of manila files. "These are our current residents, go into my office and read over these while I finish setting up for the service this afternoon."

He leads us back towards the lobby. "I'm just going to have you observe today. I know this is a lot to take in and I don't want to overwhelm you." He sets the paperwork on his desk and gestures for me to sit in his chair. "Help yourself to coffee or the fridge, and take a lunch break at some point. Come find me if you need anything."

"Okay, Mr. Raith. Thank you!" I sink into the supple leather, perfumed by his sweet, woody cologne.

"Just Ben is fine," he says, meeting my eyes before stepping into the hall and closing the door behind him.

"Ben," I whisper to myself, cheeks heating up.

I'm in so much fucking trouble.

A few hours pass in comfortable quiet, sipping coffee, reading through autopsy notes, and fetching lunch at the French cafe a few doors down. We eat together in amicable silence on the couch in his office: crusty bread, cheese, and spinach quiche. After, I clean up and settle back at his desk.

Ben rises to leave, but lingers at the door. He walks back over to the desk, displeasure like a smear across his face.

"Something wrong, sir?" I ask, worried I messed something up.

He bristles at that, and pauses mid-stride.

He snatches my coffee mug from the desk, drops it into the sink, and grabs a water bottle from the fridge. He holds it out to me expectantly.

I see tattoos peeking out under his shirt sleeves and thick veins spidering across his hands. His rings catch my eye, a silver signet ring with onyx on his thumb, and a Celtic braid around his middle finger. No wedding band.

"Enough coffee, Liv."

I take the water bottle and offer a weak smile, not trusting myself to speak with the ripple of heat spreading from the pit of my stomach to the tips of my ears. Three words, all he said were three words, and I'm about to leave a wet spot on his fucking chair.

He turns briskly and shuts the door behind him.

Fucking hell.

I take a sip of water and try to cool off. There's something about him, even though we just met this morning, I feel like I've known him for a lifetime. It's like I know what his hands feel like, his touch, his mouth. There's something so familiar in his eyes, his smile.

No, I have a job to do. *Focus, Liv.*

I escape back into the paperwork, easing into the familiarity of embalming procedures and tox screenings.

Soon, I hear the front door open and guests start filtering into the lobby. Ben greets them warmly and ushers them into the parlor room. After about an hour, the door closes for the final time and the service begins.

I peek out the office door and see the parlor doors are closed, and Ben leaning against the wall beside them. His head is resting against the wall and his eyes are closed. Listening.

"How's it going?" I whisper, taking a few steps towards him.

He doesn't open his eyes, but a corner of his mouth quirks up. "Good, it's a family we've served for a long time." He drops his head to peer at me. "How are you?"

The question feels loaded, even though his tone is casual.

"Honestly? This is going so much better than I anticipated. I meant it when I said I was excited."

He smiles openly at that, sending a bolt of electricity to my heart. "And what did you anticipate?"

"I didn't anticipate...well, you," I answer honestly, fiddling with the ends of my hair.

"I didn't anticipate you either, Olivia."

My mouth dries up, butterflies bursting to life in my chest.

Conversation suddenly starts up again in the parlor, and the service has concluded.

"Duty calls," he says, but doesn't move, doesn't shift his gaze. The parlor door opens, making me jump. He nods towards his office, and I take that as my queue to retreat.

I shut the door behind me and slide down to my butt. Am I crazy, or does he feel some tension too? No way, that's ridiculous. He's a grown ass man, not a lusty frat guy. He has better things to do than pay any attention to me.

He's a smoke show, and I'm nervous about my first day. That's all. No feelings to speak of. What kind of idiot catches feelings on the first day?

I only half believe myself, but it's enough to get me back to the desk and back to work.

The guests leave and some time ticks by, but Ben doesn't reappear.

I slink back out of the office and find him sitting in the front row of the parlor. I walk down the aisle and approach the casket. I hadn't seen who the service was for until this moment. It's a woman, likely in her 70's, with graying curls in a white dress. He'd done a beautiful job setting her face and applying makeup. She looked peaceful, content.

I reach out and hold her hand gently. "Hey, I'm Olivia, the new Mortician's Apprentice here. I only heard bits and pieces. but just know you were so loved and will be missed dearly." I gently place her hand back to its resting place and go sit beside Ben, a familiar mix of thoughtful melancholy settling over me like a blanket.

"I always like to take a moment before bringing them out to the hearse. Let them process what was said undisturbed," he says, leaning back in his chair.

"That's very kind of you, Ben."

"I want you to go home early and do the same." He tilts his head towards me.

Anxiety spikes. "What do you mean?"

"I want you to process everything that happened today and commit to this, or don't. This is not like your classes, and I'm not like your teachers." He looks over at me, blue eyes loaded with emotions I can't even begin to decipher. "There's no half-way. I need to know that you're in this with me."

I raise an eyebrow. "Respectfully, sir, I know exactly what I'm doing. But, thank you."

He stares me down, eyes calculating. "I'll walk you out."

My stomach plummets. I fucked this up already by being too eager, just like everything else. I collect my things from his office and we walk silently to the front door. He opens it for me and watches as I descend the stairs.

"Olivia?" he calls.

"Yes?" I turn, my heart leaping into my throat.

"I hope I'll see you tomorrow."

"You will." I smile, desperately trying to play it cool while my stomach does somersaults. I start walking back towards my house, not trusting myself to stay a minute longer, lest I melt into a puddle of lovesick goo.

I am so thoroughly fucked.

Oberon

I sat in my office for hours last night, head in my hands, replaying the moment I saw her over and over and over again. The name I never let myself think nearly fell from my lips when she came into view: Leda. My murdered wife was standing there, just down the aisle, looking so achingly beautiful I would have fallen to my knees if I wasn't sitting down.

But Olivia isn't Leda, that's impossible. At best, she's a descendant. Even more likely, she's just a girl who happens to look just like her, and I'm losing it.

But things only got more confusing as we spent the day together. She's so familiar, her voice, her laugh, her smile. She even *smells* like her, chocolate and campfire.

I almost sent her away, told her I changed my mind on taking on an apprentice. I *should* have sent her away, but I couldn't bring myself to do it. Instead, I practically begged her to come back.

As soon as she was gone, I ran to my office and called Algernon.

"Brother!" he answers, chipper as usual.

"What do you know about reincarnation?" I ask, impatient.

"C'mon, how about a 'Hello, Algernon! Sorry I haven't called in a month, I've just been so busy brooding and scaring the general public of Upstate New York. How are you?'"

I groan. "How are you, Algernon?"

"I'm fabulous, thank you for asking," he replies dryly.

"So, reincarnation?"

"Aren't you the Necromancer? That feels like your area of expertise. I just turn shit to gold."

"Al," I warn.

"Okay, okay, fuck. I forgot your sense of humor died with you."

At that, I chuckle.

"So, reincarnation. Soul is reborn after the body dies, may or may not return in the same form or species. Usually, it's an indication of *unfinished business*," he says with inflection. "Hold on, Ayla's yelling—" he covers the mouthpiece with his hand— "Will you just come here and talk to him!" He shouts to his wife, who is infinitely more knowledgeable than us about pretty much everything. If the three of us had 12 brain cells to share, Ayla has at least 10 of them, maybe 11. And that's not just because she's a seer.

"Oberon." Her honeyed voice comes over the line.

"Ayla," I reply.

"What did you do?" she asks.

"So presumptuous," I counter. "Nothing, I just didn't feel like digging up the books myself."

"Mhm, how's your new apprentice?"

That fucking card-reading, fortune-telling, smart ass. Of course, she knows about Olivia. I hang up, the sound of Algernon's laughter ringing in my ears.

I dig through the internet, finding nothing particularly interesting besides fantasy smut and fan-fiction. I turn to my extensive book collection, finding a few things that confirm my thoughts and Algernon's limited knowledge, but nothing more concrete. I do find a copy of Dracula, though, and lose myself in vampire romance and a bottle of Cab.

I wake up on my office couch with the book open on my chest, early morning sunlight streaming in. I check my phone at 7:30. *Shit.* I scramble into a fresh shirt, throw all my books back on the shelf, toss the empty wine bottle, and try to get my hair under control.

Then I feel it, the tiniest shift in energy. The front door opens with a delicate chime.

"Mr. Raith- er, Ben? I brought some coffee and breakfast!" Olivia calls.

I walk over to my office door and brace my hand on the top of the frame.

She's wearing tan slacks and a cream colored sweater tucked in at her waist, showing off those delicious curves. Her dark hair falls in loose waves around her shoulders, shining like chocolate ganache.

Gods, how could I forget just how beautiful she was?

"Welcome back, Olivia." I smile, hoping I come across like a normal boss, not a touch-starved maniac that wants to rip her clothes off.

She holds up the box of pastries and a tray of coffees with a shy smile. "Hungry?"

I lick my lips. "Starving."

I move out of the way so she can set everything down in the office. She opens the box, wafting the smells of warm sugar and bread into the room

.

"I wasn't sure what you liked, so I got you a mocha latte," she says, still seeming a bit bashful as she hands me a coffee cup.

"My favorite," I say, taking a sip. "So, did you think about what I said?"

She sinks into the couch and takes a small sip of her coffee. "Yes, I did. And I'm committed. I want this. I can't explain it, but I feel like I'm meant to be here." She takes another sip of coffee, cheeks flushing pink.

This girl is so cute, it's going to fucking kill me.

"Good, I'm glad." I pick up a chocolate croissant and break it in half, an old habit. Almost everything Leda and I ate, we shared. Crusty baguettes, slices of cake, bowls of pasta, it was one of the little things I missed most.

Instead of returning it to the box, like I would normally do, I offer it to Olivia.

She accepts with a small smile and takes a bite, powdered sugar dusting her rose-painted lips.

"So, did you grow up in Alder Bridge?" Maybe I can trace back her lineage, see if she is a descendant or not.

"No, I'm originally from Albany. My dad was offered a position at Folke University after I graduated high school. He got sick last year, so I relocated to take care of him. He left me his house," she replied. "I fell in love with the area and decided to stay."

"Do you have any other family?"

"No, my mom left a few months after my sister passed. My dad raised me on his own."

"I'm sorry for your loss, Liv," I say, fighting the old instinct to reach out and touch her hand.

"Do you have family?"

"I have two brothers, Al and Gideon. My parents passed a long time ago."

"Are you close with them?"

"Al, yeah. He and his wife live in Maine. Gideon, not really. I haven't seen him in years." Twenty years, to be exact.

She nods, thoughtful. "Are you seeing anyone?"

The question catches me by surprise, and a familiar sadness swirls in my stomach. No matter how much time passes, her name will always rise to my lips whenever someone asks me that. "No," I reply, habitually rubbing the place my wedding band used to rest with my thumb.

Her eyes catch my movement, quick little thing. "Were you, um, married?"

I hesitate.

"You don't have to talk about it, I shouldn't be prying."

"I was," I find myself saying, wanting to dispel her anxiety more than avoid my own discomfort. She'd been vulnerable with me, it's only fair to return the favor, at least a little bit.

She must catch something behind my eyes and asks a question that feels like a blow to the chest, "What was her name?"

"Leda," I whisper. I haven't said her name aloud in years, the pain unbearable. Guilt clutches at my throat, threatening to swallow me whole. I used to chant her name like a mantra, now I guard it like a secret. Keep her locked away in the darkest recess of my memory. But I can't shake the feeling that she's right here, sitting right in front of me, just with a new name.

"That's beautiful. I'm so sorry you lost her." Olivia places a hand gently over mine, empathy dampening her eyes.

I nod, not trusting myself to speak.

"Like you said, we all have a story." She releases my hand and takes a sip of coffee.

I follow suit, wrangling my emotions back down and pivoting back to the reason we're having this conversation in the first place. I need to dig into her subconscious, the places that retain memory as instinct, that may be carried along with the soul. Maybe there's something hidden in her subconscious that will confirm my suspicions, or disprove them entirely.

"What are you afraid of?"

She raises her eyebrows, clearly surprised by my question. "Um, being buried alive, actually," she chuckles, finishing her half of the croissant and grabbing a chocolate chip muffin. "Spiders, too."

Was Leda buried alive? I can't think about that right now, the thought alone makes my stomach turn and rage spike. "Being buried alive?"

"My therapist says it's because I struggle with control." She pauses mid-bite, "Is that too personal?"

I find her honesty endearing, it was always one of my favorite quali-ties in Leda. "We spend every day surrounded by death; nothing is too personal. You know as well as I do that time is too precious to waste on pleasantries." I take another sip of my coffee, wondering how the chocolate would taste on her tongue.

She smiles and holds up her cup, "Cheers to that. Politeness and pleasantries are overrated."

I tap my cup against hers, smiling back.

The front door chimes, and heavy boots stomp through the lobby. I hold out my hand, indicating to Liv to stay seated, and step out into the hall.

"Raith!"

"Detective Radcliffe, how can I help you this morning?" I hide my loathing behind a half-smile. Randall Radcliffe makes my skin crawl. He's brash, crude, and cruel, with no trace of empathy or kindness. He's a power-hungry pig, and can't seem to stop seeking me out. I've gone so far as to set wards against him, but no luck. His will is greater than my effort.

I think about unbinding my power in moments like these, just so I can eviscerate him off the face of the earth.

"College kid got drunk and fell into a pool. Jacob Smith." He hands me a police report. "The guys are bringing him around back. No family, so go ahead with cremation," he drones, apparently bored by the death of this 18 year old kid.

"Sure, I'll send over the paperwork when I'm finished—"

"And who is this?" he asks, his voice falling an octave.

My neck prickles and I clench my teeth.

"Olivia Hunter, Mr. Raith's new Mortuary Apprentice." Olivia holds out her perfect hand to that slime ball.

Radcliffe takes it too eagerly. "Randall Radcliffe, *Detective* Randall Radcliffe. It's about time Raith got some help around here, and the place needed a little sunshine."

I resist the urge to suck his soul out of his beady eyes. "Olivia, could you handle intake down the hall while I wrap up with Detective Radcliffe?" I don't even try to mask the displeasure in my voice. It's pointless, I know anger is coming off of me in waves.

"Yes, sir," she says, dropping his hand to take my card and hurrying down the hall.

"Lucky you, Raith. Got yourself a little treat." Radcliffe smirks, watching her walk away.

"Are we finished?" I snap, crossing my arms over my chest.

"For now," he says, heading towards the door. "Appreciate your time."

I glare until the door shuts behind him, then practically run to the morgue.

Olivia is alone, standing over a body bag on a gurney. She's put on a white lab coat and black latex gloves, her hair twisted up in a claw clip.

"I apologize for him," I say, pulling on my own coat and gloves.

"A friend of yours?" she asks, moving to get blank paperwork from the filing cabinet.

I chuckle darkly. "I wish it were him in this body bag instead of some kid."

She gapes at me, "Ben!" But I see the smile threatening to escape.

"Like you weren't thinking it," I tease, opening up the bag. "Okay, Jacob, let's get you taken care of."

I go slow so Olivia can watch and process what I'm doing. I remove the body bag and wash his body with disinfectant solution, massage the muscles to relieve rigor mortis, and stretch to limbs to ease stiffening in the joints. "Read the coroner's report out loud," I ask her.

"There isn't one," she replies.

I look up. "What?"

"There's no coroner report, just the police record."

"That's not possible," I take the paperwork and flip through it, but she's right. And that means something is wrong.

"I can see he has bruises and lacerations. He drowned, right?" She asks, looking at me inquisitively.

I nod, moving to check Jacob more closely. He shows the clinical signs of drowning, vascular marbling, discoloration, but also has obvious bruising on his arms, face, and chest. And a clean cut across his breast bone. I grab a syringe and draw a blood sample.

Olivia is diligently taking notes as I work, worrying her bottom lip with her teeth.

I put my hand over her clipboard. "I'm going to run a tox screen, don't document it."

She nods, and I feel a flush of warmth at her implicit trust in my instincts.

I run the screening via immunoassay and set it aside to process.

"Hey, Ben?" she calls me over to the computer on the desk.

I walk up behind her and lean over to look at the screen. She has Jaco' social media pulled up.

"He was popular, an honor student, and a star athlete. You're sure they don't want to have a service for him?" she asks, clicking through photo after photo of a much livelier Jacob surrounded by friends. "It doesn't seem right..."

"He has no family, and no one wants to foot the bill for a service." I note her down-turned eyes. "But no, it doesn't feel right."

"What do you want to do?" She turns to look up at me.

Kiss you, I think, trying and failing to not look at her lips. "I haven't decided," I answer honestly, or mostly honestly.

"Is it okay if I examine him?" she asks, her chest flushing a bit.

"Whatever you want, Liv," I say, imagining sinking my teeth into the tender skin of her shoulder.

She looks at my arms, and I realize I have her caged against the desk. I take a step back, shaking my head. I watch her put gloves on and begin examining the boy. She's gentle, but thorough and I find myself getting lost in her process.

I drag my eyes away and turn to the computer, continuing to dig into his history.

He was an incredibly accomplished student and athlete, with a bright future in theology. He specialized in ancient religions and the occult. Whether he was also a student of the Old Arts would be harder to determine. But he was definitely one of my borther's students, and an alarm bell rings in my head.

Gideon has worked at Folke University for nearly a century as a Religion Professor, and was one of the founding members.

Music kicks on from the small speaker by the door, drawing me out of my head. Kate Bush. Olivia dances back over to the body, lost in her head.

I watch her sway and spin as she works, softly singing the lyrics to herself. She is ethereal, haunting almost, in the way she moves. And a bit macabre, dancing in the morgue as she works on a body. *My wicked little thing*.

No, not mine. But now, more than ever, she echoes Leda, who loved nothing more than to dance while she worked in the garden. I was never much of a dancer, but with her, I'd dance for hours, just to feel her body close to mine. Just to see her smile. We danced into the early morning on our wedding night, until our feet were sore and blistered. Then we took our shoes off and danced some more.

Leda's wedding gown had been the lightest green, with hand-embroidered flowers and leaves. Barely a slip of a thing, but it didn't matter, the ceremony was just us and our closest friends and family down by the waterfall. She had wisteria braided in her hair, and a crown of baby's breath.

I could picture Olivia in it, kissing me under the willow tree, just as I could picture Leda dancing around the morgue. They were blending together in my mind, and I was becoming more and more convinced that Olivia and my Leda were one and the same. Had her soul come back to find me?

It was insanity, but stranger things have happened.

I'm rising out of the chair before I realize it, the opening notes of "Running Up That Hill" spilling from the speaker. She has her back to me, swaying slightly, rolling her shoulders to the music.

I'm a breath away from her when she turns suddenly and we're chest to chest. My heart is pounding, and I can feel hers doing the same, her energy thrumming along her tether like a live-wire.

I know the truth then. I want her, desperately. And she wants me too. She feels it too. It's insane, and so, so, stupid, but the attraction to her sings through my blood like a siren song, defying all reason.

"Ben," she whispers, barely audible.

"Oberon," I respond. "Call me Oberon."

"Raith!"

We jump apart, Radcliffe's voice booming through the home.

I barely swallow the growl that bubbles up from my chest before he's banging on the door to the morgue.

Olivia runs to let him in.

I pause the music.

Radcliffe saunters into the room, Olivia trailing nervously behind him.

"Shouldn't he be dust by now?" he asks, gesturing to Jacob.

"Shouldn't you have brought him to a coroner?" I snap back, barely containing the rage smoldering in my chest. I feel the arm band, my power binder, tremble and grow hot, struggling to contain the surge of energy.

Radcliffe frowns. "A coroner? What for? He drowned, case closed."

Olivia opens her mouth to speak, but I shoot her a firm look and compel a single word into her head.

Silence.

Her mouth clacks shut, eyes blown wide.

"What are you implying, Raith?" Radcliffe takes a few steps closer to me, his hand moving to rest on his side arm. A clear threat.

"Nothing, Detective. Just doing my due diligence." It takes every ounce of willpower to back off. I can't help Jacob with Radcliffe breathing down my neck, or worse, snooping around.

"Yeah, well. Whatever. Just do your job, alright?" he sneers, turning to Olivia. "Being down here doesn't bother you? Doing this nasty work?"

"No, it's an honor to provide care and compassion to those that have passed," she answers coolly.

His eyes roam over her shamelessly, but she doesn't wither under his gaze. She tilts her chin higher.

"We were about finished, so if you wouldn't mind giving us space to work, Detective Radcliffe," she says, gesturing toward the door.

"Fine, fine. I'll see myself out." He walks over to the door. "And Raith, I expect that paperwork by this evening."

I nod once, and he shuts the door behind him. Neither of us breathe until we hear the bell signal his departure, and his car pulls away.

"What a creep," Olivia says with a disgusted shiver. "Are we actually going to cremate Jacob?"

"Of course not. Set his face, I'll get the equipment ready."

"Yes, sir," she replies, putting fresh gloves on and getting to work.

I start gathering equipment and play the music again.

I make a small incision near the collarbone, careful to preserve the natural appearance of Jacob's body.

Using a mixture of formaldehyde and other embalming fluids, I begin the process of arterial embalming, injecting the solution into the arteries to replace the blood and slow down the decomposition process. We work methodically, ensuring an even distribution of the fluid throughout the body.

Once the arterial embalming is complete, we gently massage the limbs to encourage better fluid distribution.

Next came the cavity embalming, where Olivia carefully aspirated any remaining gasses and fluids from the internal organs. She replaced them with a preservative fluid, taking care not to disturb the internal structure.

Throughout the process, we spoke softly to Jacob, as if he were still alive and listening. It was a personal ritual, a way to honor the person as they prepare for their final journey.

Finally, I carefully sutured the incision and began the process of restorative art. Using cosmetics, I gently applied color to his features, subtly enhancing his natural complexion. It was a delicate balance between making him look presentable and maintaining the essence of his unique character.

As the hours passed, we worked diligently, creating a serene and peaceful image of Jacob. Olivia and I work together like a well-oiled instrument. Intuitively mirroring each other's movements and anticipating each other's needs and questions.

Around 6 pm, I notice her energy dip, and she starts to yawn.

"Alright," I approach her and slide the coat off her shoulders. "You're done for the day, go home, eat some food, and get some rest."

"Are you sure?" She seems reluctant to go, but I can see the heaviness in her eyes.

"Yes." I slip off my own coat and move Jacob into a cooler. "And I'm walking you home."

She perks up a bit at that, making my heart go fuzzy. "Okay, Oberon." She rolls her eyes.

My knees turn to liquid hearing my name, my real name, on her lips. I want to hear it again and again and again. I want to taste it on her tongue and brand it on her heart.

I send the fake paperwork over to Radcliffe quickly, then shut everything down.

We leave the morgue, gather our things, and head out into the evening, the sun just starting to dip below the trees. String lights and shop signs blink to life, casting a warm glow over the street. There's a chill in the air, and the leaves have just begun to soften their green hue. Autumn is upon us.

I notice she's nibbling something as we walk. "Did you sneak a croissant?" I tease, grabbing her wrist to inspect what she's holding.

"We skipped lunch!" she protests, trying in vain to pull her arm back.

I take a bite of the flaky pastry and release her, savoring the buttery taste on my tongue.

"Rude!" she laughs, "All you had to do was ask." She breaks the pastry in half and passes it to me.

My chest aches at the sweetness of her gesture, and a sharp pang of both fear and hope. Could she really be my Leda?

We nibble our bits of croissant in silence, enjoying the bustle of the evening.

Too soon, we reach her door.

It's an old house, but clearly beloved, with green siding and a black front door. The lawn is overgrown with native species, crowded enough that a few have survived deeper into the season than usual. There's small bowls of water on her porch and bird houses strung on almost every tree.

It suits her perfectly.

"Thank you, Oberon," she says, turning towards me.

"My pleasure, Olivia," I respond, swallowing the impulse to press her against the door and devour her.

She unlocks the door and with a shy wave, disappears behind it, closing it with a soft click.

I turn and head back the way I came, head reeling, licking croissant crumbs off of my fingers.

Olivia

Two weeks have passed since I started at Alder Bridge Funeral Home and Mortuary Services, and I've loved every minute of it. And not just because I get to spend everyday with Alder Bridge's most interesting man. The work has been incredibly fulfilling, spending hours preserving, honoring, and celebrating life in death, getting to support my community in such a vital way.

We've fallen into a comfortable routine, a morning debrief over coffee and pastries, followed by a few hours spent in the morgue or working with clients. Then a working lunch as we set up any services that afternoon. And finally, a few more hours in the morgue until he sends me home around dinner time.

As we march toward mid-October, the Halloween spirit has infected the town, well everyone except Oberon. Every store front is decorated with ghosts and bats, jack-o'-lanterns and hay bales, cornstalks and goofy inflatables.

I've busted out my seasonal sweaters and spiderweb leggings, and have been playing my favorite indie Halloween playlist while we work. Oberon tolerates it, sort of. More like he begrudgingly indulges me because he was tired of my whining.

But I'm not satisfied yet. The funeral home remains decidedly un-festive, and of course we can't decorate inside, or so Oberon says, but the front porch is just too darling to remain jack-o'-lantern-less.

So, I'm dragging two large pumpkins with me to work this morning in hopes of convincing him.

He opens the door as I climb the stairs. "Absolutely not," he says, crossing his arms and baring my entrance.

"Come on! We have nothing to do today, nobody has died in like a week!"

"So, we clean. Or, if you'd prefer, I have plenty of books you could study." He counters.

"I will clean the entire morgue if you carve a pumpkin."

"No."

"I'll even do the incinerator!"

"No."

"I'll dust the display room."

He looks offended. "There is no dust in the display room."

Stubborn fucker, time for the big guns. "I'll clean your office."

His eyebrow quirks up.

"Including organizing the bookshelves and stocking the fridge."

He lets out a dramatic, long-suffering sigh. "Fine. Now let me carry those before your arms fall off." He takes the pumpkins from me and heads back inside, smug.

Let him be smug, I got exactly what I wanted.

I follow him, practically skipping, into the morgue.

He sets the pumpkins on the embalming table. "Did you bring carving tools?"

I pick up a fresh pack of scalpels from the labeled drawer, "Not necessary." I grin.

He shakes his head at me. "You're insane." He turns, smiling to himself, and grabs a bone saw and some bio-hazard bags.

I put on a spooky playlist and grab my tools and a pumpkin. I start sketching out my design with a sharpie on the rubbery skin. I'm not particularly artistic, but I did pick up a thing or two sketching models in my anatomy notes. Line by line, an anatomical heart starts to come together, bloody ventricles and all.

I feel Oberon come up behind me to watch, his delicious woody cologne wafting over me. I resist the urge to lean back into his chest and focus on the final details, tongue between my teeth.

"At least it's not a skull," he chuckles, using his sharpie to correct an error in one of the arteries.

I shove him away, "I did that on purpose!"

"Mhm." He smirks, walking back over to his pumpkin, which he turns to reveal a human skull so perfect it looks straight out of a textbook.

"Show off," I grumble, adding my last line. "Now, the guts." I grab the bone saw and start sawing off the back of the pumpkin.

"Easy, killer." He takes the saw from me. "You'll lose a finger." He saws off the rest of the pumpkin and pushes it back to me with a bio-hazard bag, then starts on his own.

The sweet smell of pumpkin fills the room as we work, seeds and pulp sticking to everything as we fill the bags with guts, occasionally flicking seeds at each other. It's all fun and games until we actually start carving, both of us slipping into hyper-focus, surgeon mode.

That being said, I can't help but pause to watch him work, as I often find myself doing.

His dark brows are furrowed in concentration, his hand steady as steel as he shaves away layers of orange flesh. His forearms flex under the scarred and tattooed skin, healthy and strong. He's a near perfect specimen, as my anatomy professors would say, well-built with lean muscle and bright eyes.

I could admire the slope of his nose, the bow of his lips, the architecture of his torso, for days. He's built like a lethal machine, with the precision of a master artist. I can picture him painting the Sistine chapel, or carving David from the marble. There's something divine about him, ethereal and graceful, but strength ripples just below the surface, a power I can't put my finger on.

His eyes flick up to meet mine and my heart skips a beat.

"Don't neglect your heart," he says, as if he could read my mind. Then he points at my pumpkin, and I remember what the hell we're doing.

I shake myself and get back to work.

An hour passes in comfortable quiet as we carve away at our pumpkins.

"Done!" I yell, a bit too loud, dropping my sticky scalpel with a clatter on the table. It's not a perfect heart. It's a bit crooked in places, carved too deep or too shallow in others, but it's mine and it's exactly how I pictured it.

Oberon comes around to look and smiles approvingly. "Well done, Liv."

The compliment fills me with warmth, making my cheeks heat. I scurry over to his jack-o'-lantern so he doesn't see me blush.

It's perfect, of course, all clean lines and smooth shading. Those hands are gifted.

"Okay, da Vinci," I tease, rolling my eyes at him despite the stupid grin I know is plastered across my face.

"Far from da Vinci, I'm afraid. Let's put them up front." He picks them up and nudges me to the door with his elbow.

We set them on either side of the steps and I clap my hands together. "They're perfect!" I squeal, "Now we just need some mums and corn husks, and oh! Ghosts around the banisters and bats on the door!"

"Settle down, one thing at a time." He chuckles, putting his hands on my shoulders and turning me to face him. "I believe we had a deal?"

"But can't we just—"

"Ah, ah, we had a deal. Better get started." He smirks. "I'm going to run a few errands, I expect progress when I return."

"Yes, sir." I roll my eyes and stick out my tongue.

Quick as lightning, he catches my chin.

"And a pleasant attitude," he says, a breath away.

I put on the sunniest smile I can muster, ignoring the liquid heat pooling in my panties and the shake in my knees.

He turns away, reaching the bottom of the stairs in a stride. "I'll be back in a few hours."

I stick out my tongue to his back and head inside.

Two hours fly by in the blissful cocoon of his office. The smell of him is everywhere, and his personality is reflected in all the little odds and ends around the room. Like his favorite mug covered in tiny botanical drawings of mushrooms, or his worn collection of Gothic classics, like Frankenstein, The Castle of Otranto, and the Strange Case of Dr. Jekyll and Mr. Hyde. Or his favorite olive green cardigan with elbow patches draped over the back of his chair, or the giant dog skull on his bookshelf.

I've gotten all the paperwork sorted and filed, and cleared all the clutter off of his desk and coffee table. I had just started reorganizing his books, *so many fucking books*, when I hear the door chime.

Oberon's familiar footfalls head towards the office and he surveys the room. Apparently pleased, he gives me a nod and produces a white bag from inside of his coat, tossing it to me.

I peek inside. "A donut!" I cry, pulling out my favorite apple cider donut from a bakery across town. I take a big bite and moan, cinnamon sugar exploding over my tongue. "Thank you!" I mumble, mouth full.

He smiles at me, "You earned it, keep going and there will be more where that came from." He takes a sip of his coffee, turns, and heads back out.

My heart feels like it might explode, his sweetness rivaling the sugary donut. I had hoped all that was drawing me to him was simple attraction, a physical thing, but as the weeks pass, more and more I'm finding myself seeking out his company, hanging on his every word, noticing the tiniest quirks in his mood, doing everything I can to make him smile, make him happy.

Things are just getting more and more complicated between us, and the worst part is that I have no idea if it's all in my head or not. Maybe I'm just reading too many romance books and none of this is real.

It doesn't matter anyways, nothing can happen, I remind myself, a strange sadness unfurling in my chest. Just because my head knows that nothing can happen, doesn't mean that my heart is willing to move on. It's only a matter of time before I have to break my own heart.

I toil on despite my lingering melancholy, and at six o'clock on the dot, Oberon returns.

"How'd I do?" I ask, putting the last water bottle in the fridge and closing the door. His office is immaculate, everything clean and in its designated space, but still cozy and warm, the way he likes it.

He pretends to inspect the room closely, even having the audacity to swipe his finger along one of the bookshelves to check for dust. "Acceptable work, Olivia." He grins at me, clearly pleased. "Now, let me show *you* something." He takes my hand and pulls me towards the front door and out into the crisp night air.

Warm light engulfs the porch. The banisters are wrapped in fall leaves, with little paper bats and ghosts hanging from the eves. Orange lights are strung along the ceiling and fresh mum's fill the pots on either side of the front door. Our pumpkins flicker with soft candle light, with a few more gourds of varying colors and sizes keeping them company.

"Oberon," I gasp, brushing my fingers along the garlands.

"Do you like it?" he asks, sounding a little bashful.

I turn towards him, tears threatening to surface. "Thank you," I say, moving towards him and wrapping my arms around his middle in a tight hug.

He keeps his arms open for a beat, unsure, before letting them wrap around me gently. "Of course," he mumbles into my hair, letting out a held breath.

I release him before I get carried away, not trusting the wave of emotion that washed over me in his arms. I want nothing more than to climb him like a tree, which is my queue to head home for the night.

"Get home safe, okay? I'll see you in the morning," he says, rubbing the back of his neck. I could swear there was sadness in his eyes.

"See you in the morning," I wave, fighting the urge to pull him in for another hug, instead turning and heading out into the night towards my house.

I slide into my desk holding a glass of wine and flip open my laptop, typing in the same search I did right before starting the apprenticeship: "Oberon Raith".

The same results pop up, the funeral homes website, two obituaries with the name, and a few local articles from when the business opened.

I click the first obituary, for his father, and scan through it.

Oberon Raith Jr. passed away on December 15, 1998 at his home in Alder Bridge, NY. He is survived by his three sons, Gideon, Algernon, and Oberon III. As per Oberon's request, no funeral or memorial service will be held.

It was odd for a Mortician and Funeral Director to not have a service, but it sounds like the family isn't particularly close, so it probably wasn't worth the expense.

I click on the picture of him included with the obit, an old picture from when he must have been in his 20's or early 30's. Oberon is a spitting image of his father, the only things differentiating them being his father's coke bottle glasses and coiffed hair. They have the same intense eyes and sculpted face, even the same brooding expression.

I open his grandfather's obituary, and it's identical, save 'Sr.' instead of 'Jr.' and the absence of a picture.

I navigate over to the record from Newspapers.com, but it's only a few words and a picture of the funeral home.

Alder Bridge Funeral Home and Mortuary Services opened today on Church Street. It is owned and operated by Oberon Raith Sr.

The search is extremely unhelpful, just like it was the first time.

I top up my glass and try a new search, "Algernon Raith". The same obituaries pop up, along with a metric ton of articles about Flowers for Algernon, which I promptly set the search to filter out. That leaves the obituaries, a few records from Newspapers.com, and a few articles from other historical sites.

The headlines immediately catch my attention: *Raith Debuts Amazing Machine that Converts Lead to Gold at the 39' New York's World Fair!*

I click the link and am greeted by a .pdf of an old newspaper. Algernon must be a family name as well. The article is brief, but compelling.

Algernon Raith, resident of New York City, debuted his incredible electromagnetic machine that converts lead to gold with just the flick of a switch. However, just before the gates opened, the machine was found mysteriously destroyed. Rumors claim that Raith destroyed the machine himself to avoid failure on the world stage, a claim he vehemently denies. I guess we'll never know if Albany's beloved mad scientist truly cracked the golden secret. Better luck next time, Al!

Next to the article, there's a black and white picture of a smashed hunk of metal and a blurred man crouched beside it. I zoom in, but can just barely make out his face. He has incredibly sharp features, with a curled mustache, full beard, and slightly mussed hair. He seems remarkably tall, with long legs and massive hands, like he'd been stretched just a little too long on a taffy puller. His hair seems lighter than Oberon's, as far as I can tell from a black and white photo.

Good looks must run in the family. I email the article to myself and poke around a little bit more, but find nothing interesting. If anything, the complete *lack* of information is more compelling than the little bit I do find.

I try Gideon next and am shocked by what I find. Hundreds of search results all for Dr. Gideon Raith, Head of the Religious Studies Department at Folke University. I click on his school biography and am greeted by easily one of the best looking men I have ever laid eyes on.

"Bet that's a popular major," I mumble to myself.

He has Oberon's same dark hair, shot through with gray at his temples and extremely tidy facial hair. I can't help but think he looks like Oberon and Doctor Strange smashed together. He has that same severe expression, and if it's possible, looks even more grouchy than his brother and superhero doppelganger.

His bio is brief, and pretty much exclusively mentions his numerous accreditation's, publications, and accolades. *Snore.* I keep searching, by passing all the boring professor stuff.

There's a link to a Reddit page deep in the search that catches my eye, in the subreddit r/cults from a few years ago.

Has anyone heard of Gideon Wraith?

There's only a few replies.

"Nah"

"Who??"

"That cannot be a real name, what is he, a super villain?"

"My grandfather knew someone named Gideon at Folke, he tried to get him to join some secret society on campus. The Arcane or something. I think his son teaches there now."

Very weird, but barely credible. I shoot a text to a friend of mine that works as a Teacher's Assistant in the English Department at Folke, Gin.

"Hey, do you know a Dr. Raith?"

I check the time, 11:30 p.m., way past my usual bedtime. I plug up my phone and take a shower, then climb into bed. I grab my phone and see a characteristically vague response.

"Sure do. Let's talk over lunch?"

"Sounds great, tomorrow?" I text back quickly, before letting my eyes finally close.

Oberon

I am as good as putty in Olivia's hands.

She's already got me wrapped around her little finger, and no matter how much I try to fight it, I know I'm falling in love with her at breakneck speed. And the strangest part of all, I'm not just falling for the parts of her that remind me of Leda, but for the parts that make her uniquely Olivia. Her playful sense of humor, her insatiable curiosity, her quick wit, and macabre interests.

She's nothing short of extraordinary, and I have no fucking idea what to do.

I turn back to my computer, scrolling through this morning's news. It's about two weeks until Halloween, but instead of reporting on local haunted houses and hayrides, the headlines are focused on one thing, the four missing college students from Folke.

The first student disappeared about a week after Jacob was brought in, and the disappearances have only accelerated. The first was a biology student, Marta Ruiz, next was a psych student, Jack Porter. The most recent is a couple, Victor Lewis and Tiana Hamilton, two gifted language students. The police are claiming to have no leads.

It's entirely possible that the kids just went off on their own, but when this many go missing from the same university in less than two weeks, people take notice. And Folke is putting in the work to ensure no one can accuse them of brushing anything under the rug.

I look over at my phone and not for the first time consider calling Gideon. But I'd doubt he'd appreciate the interruption, or the implied accusation, I'd bring.

It's been decades since I last spoke to my brother. Our relationship had always been a bit tense, but after the Arcanum unraveled, we never really recovered.

I've done a lot of things I'm not proud of, but joining the Arcanum is by far the most shameful.

It was right after the beginning of World War 1, and the world was teetering on the edge of ruin. I could feel it hanging heavy in the air, it dragged me down, turned me into a shell of myself. I was angry, and lost, and being swallowed whole by the power cloying inside me. I'd sworn off using magic at the turn of the century and it was tearing me apart to try and break free, to release.

Gideon had found me passed out drunk at a memorial, surrounded by dead grass and flowers. We had still been close then. He took me back to his house and put me through a grueling detox, using Psychomancy to keep me from leaving.

Over the next few weeks, he slowly introduced me to the Guild he was a part of, who were able to help me hone my skills and practice without undue harm to others. I was brought in to teach a course on Black Magic at the burgeoning underground magic school at Folke.

They made me a part of something bigger, a part of the important work to preserve Source in our society.

As the 20th century marched on, magic was becoming weaker by the day. Our communities were dying, all of us flung to the far corners of the world, hiding in secret to avoid persecution. Out of this need, and the fear of complete extinction, the School of Old Arts was born in the bowels of Folke University.

I found purpose in nurturing future generations of witches. The School provided safety and community and created an environment of learning. I could come to terms with what happened to me, with what I'd become, in the bosom of family.

But like all good things, it didn't last

He waited three years, waited until I was bought in, indebted, before he told me the truth. The School was created by the Arcanum, and their leader, Amadeus and Keanu Kennedy.

I was livid, but couldn't deny how much they had helped me, how much power they had, how much power they showed me that *I* had. Instead of wine, they were getting me drunk on grandeur, wealth, and influence. I wanted more.

Gideon brought Keanu to talk to me, and agreeing to hear him out was the greatest mistake of my life.

For 10 years I served him, 10 years we were inseparable. For 10 years, I helped him commit unspeakable acts of cruelty and greed. I helped him topple governments, raise empires, and build monopolies. There was nothing and no one that could stop us. He was a God, and I was his Grim Reaper.

But the Great Depression struck, the Second World War looming, and his greed only grew. I watched him build an empire on the back of a dying world, and had enough.

I resigned from the Arcanum and Folke, and cut all ties with Keanu. He didn't let me go easily, but there was nothing he could do to stop me, and he knew it. By then, my power nearly surpassed his, and I was struggling under the weight of it. If anything, I was becoming a liability, a hairpin trigger.

As far as I knew, Gideon had left the ways of the Arcanum behind and turned the School around, turning it into the safe haven it always should have been. Gideon had found solace as a scholar, power in knowledge. He directed his energy towards Academia, leaving lesser pursuits behind. He sold his million dollar home, his fleet of cars, and designer wardrobe. He donated his millions to charity, used it to build schools in impoverished areas, and established scholarships to bring wayward witches into the safety of Folke. Our relationship never healed, but we both found contentment elsewhere.

There's been no sign of Keanu for decades, but that doesn't mean much.

Something about these disappearances and Jacobs death raised my hackles. I couldn't pinpoint why, but something in the current of the town's energy had shifted.

The front door chimes, Olivia arriving for work.

"Morning, Liv," I greet her at my office door. Immediately, I can tell something is off. She looks beautiful, and impeccably dressed, per usual, but even makeup couldn't cover the dark circles under her eyes, and the absence of light within them.

"Morning," she passes me my coffee and a bagel with lox and sinks into the couch.

I have a feeling I know why. The service today is a special one, for a little girl that passed after a long battle with brain cancer. She was only 8.

Olivia had handled the embalming process and client meetings in stride, but I had a hunch that the service would be more challenging. I knew she'd put undue pressure on herself to show up for the family, and probably neglect her own grief for her sister.

I give her some space while we set up even though I wanted nothing more than to bundle her up in my arms and take her far away, where pain and grief can never touch her. I considered sending her home, but decided against it. She'd refuse, anyways.

As the service begins, she helps me greet mourners and get everyone settled. She even stays through opening prayers and a slideshow of Julia's bright, brief life, but as soon as the mother steps up to the lectern, Olivia disappears.

After the mothers eulogy, the service wraps up quickly, people in a hurry to escape the crushing sorrow in the room. I ask the coroner to handle transport to the cemetery, and go find my girl.

"Liv?" I open the door to the office and find her curled up on the couch, knees to her chest. Tremors wrack her body, her hand over her mouth to try and stifle her sobs.

"Hey, hey." I rush over to her side and pull her into my chest. "Shhh, shhh. I'm right here. You're safe." I rub her back and whisper reassurances in her ear.

Her muscles stay locked up, frozen in terror, but she clings to my arms like a lifeline.

I continue to rock her and speak gently, slowly coaxing her to relax into my arms and breathe. "That's it, breathe with me."

We breathe deeply together, her lungs stuttering as she continues to cry. I hold her face and draw her red-rimmed eyes to mine. I wipe her tears away with my thumbs. "I'm right here, baby, I'm not going anywhere. I've got you."

She nods weakly, taking a deep breath, her hands fisted in my blazer.

I lean my forehead against hers. "I've got you, Liv."

I hold her for awhile, letting myself sink into her sweet scent and the gentle rhythm of her heartbeat as she relaxes. I trace shapes onto her back and arms, just feeling her, indulging in the closeness of our bodies despite the circumstances.

"Oberon," she whispers, barely audible.

"Yes?"

"Do you feel it?" she asks, going still as a held breath.

I try desperately to cling to my resolve, to reason, but the way she's looking at me unravels any semblance of control I thought I had. "You know I do," I breathe, sliding my hand into her hair to cup the back of her head. "But Liv, I—." How could I possibly tell her everything that's in my heart? How can I tell her the truth in a way that doesn't ruin this fragile trust we've built.

"I know, you're my boss. You don't have to do this." She pulls back, gets to her feet and wipes her eyes with the back of her hand.

"No, listen—"

"It's fine, Mr. Raith. I'm a big girl, no worries." She grabs her purse. "I'll see you tomorrow." She turns her back to me and walks out.

I almost chase her out, but a wave of grief steals my breath and roots me to my spot

Coward, I'm such a fucking coward.

I can't keep acting like this isn't happening. I can't just pine for her in the shadows and hope that nobody gets hurt. I have to make a decision; either I open up to her and take the risk, or shut everything down completely, which would mean sending her away.

My chest aches at the thought, how disappointed she would be. How lonely this place would feel without her music and laughter. I never minded being here alone, and I still don't when I know she'll be back in a few hours. But the thought of her being gone forever, it's agony.

I'd be grieving the loss of my love all over again. I barely survived the first time, let alone now, knowing I had her within reach but was too much of a fucking coward to claim her. If I let her slip out of my grasp again, I could never forgive myself.

Honestly, I'm naive to think that I ever had a choice in the matter.

Olivia

"I'll be honest with you, Olivia. I've been dying to hear about how your apprenticeship is going," Dr. Khan says, ushering me into her office. "I half expected you to ask for reassignment. Anyone else would have."

"I'm not one to back down from a challenge." I smile, sitting down in the familiar orange chair across from her desk. She was my advisor during my Mortician program, and we'd grown quite close over the few years. I wasn't really in the mood to meet with her after my episode yesterday, but I already had coffee scheduled with Gin, so I was going to be on campus anyways. Might as well get it over with.

"So, spill." She steeples her fingers and looks at me expectantly.

I rack my brain, trying to find something to talk about that doesn't have to do with my unhealthy infatuation with my boss. "It's going a lot better than expected. He's very good at his job, both the Mortician aspect and the Funeral Director aspect. I've never seen someone host guests with such ease. I've learned a lot from him so far."

"I'm surprised to hear that, I've heard he can be quite a pill from local suppliers and the police."

A bristle of anger spikes. "He's extremely kind and compassionate. Any-time I've seen him be obstinate was in defense of residents or myself. I witnessed some tension between him and Detective Radcliffe, but frankly, Radcliffe deserved it."

Dr. Khan snorts. "Now that I don't doubt. I heard he's been on call for the missing kids. Did you help with Jacob?"

"Yes, it was the day after I started. He handled it with tremendous grace despite being pretty upset at the way the police handled his death."

"Oh?"

"Ben wanted to have a service for him, but Radcliffe demanded he be cremated, even without a coroner's report."

Her eyebrows quirk up. "Ben?" She smiles.

"Oberon is a mouthful and he doesn't like to be called *Mr. Raith*." I backpedal, realizing that I'm talking about him entirely too much.

"I'm surprised they didn't do a coroner's report," she said thoughtfully. "I've always heard it was standard procedure."

"That's what we thought as well, but apparently not." I need to change the subject, I don't want to get Oberon in trouble. "But anyways, I've embalmed a little over 20 bodies and have helped him direct 17 funerals. He says that I'll direct one on my own soon."

"That's great! He gets a pretty high volume compared to some of the other funeral homes in the area. I figured that was why he requested an apprentice."

"Probably. Although, it hardly seems like I've taken any work off of his plate. I can't imagine how much he worked before if I'm seeing the reduced version." I chuckle.

We chat for another twenty minutes or so, gossiping about town-goings-on and how my peers are fairing in their apprenticeships.

I bid her farewell and head over to the campus coffee house, Folkepour, to meet up with Gin.

The cafe is quiet, with only a few students lingering around the counter. It's a small cafe, only a dozen or so tables, with a small kitchen in the back.

An orange and red garland of leaves is strung around the counter, with tiny fairy lights giving off a violet glow. Each table is decorated with black table cloths, a dripping pillar candle, and ghost shaped salt and pepper shakers. Paper bats are glued to the columns and entryways, flapping lazily in the gale from the heater.

The menu is decorated with chalk pumpkins and spiderwebs, showcasing their seasonal offerings: a Cherry Mocha Latte and Pumpkin Pie Cold Brew. I opt for the latte, and order a caprese flatbread to eat. It was always my go-to in between classes, and I hadn't had it in ages.

I wait with the other patrons, all of whom entirely too cool to be within ten feet of me. Young, rich kids wearing designer coats and wielding their parents credit cards. I shift from foot to foot, looking down at my own jacket, an oversized black peacoat I thrifted three seasons ago.

Yikes. When did my youth get away from me? It feels like yesterday I was one of them, just old enough to drink, coasting on caffeine and dreams of academic grandeur. Desperate to be exactly where I am right now.

"Olivia!" The barista calls out, setting a Folkepour signature wide mouth mug on the counter, piled high with whipped cream, chocolate bat sprinkles, and a chocolate dipped cherry on top. "Your flatbread will be right out if you want to take a seat."

"Thank you!" I take the mug and find my favorite table in the corner, up against a large window that overlooks the manicured courtyard. Students are littered all over the green lawn and marble benches, bundled up in their coats and scarves against the October chill. Leaves drift to the ground around them, landing on their books and in their hair. I can see a couple reading aloud to one another, and a group holding sheets of paper act out a scene. Other groups laugh and gossip, others study in amicable silence.

"Liv!"

I look up and see Gin waving at me across the cafe. I beam and wave back, a flush of warmth washing away my melodrama.

She looks breathtaking, as always. Parisian-chic from her aubergine beret to her platform loafers. Her perfectly tousled bob accentuates her round cheeks, the textured bangs framing her round hazel eyes. She's wearing a plaid skirt and black tights, with a darling cream sweater and a brilliant blue scarf.

I'd despise her preppy perfectness if it wasn't for her sailor mouth and uncanny ability to make men cry.

She places her order and hurry's over to me, sliding into the booth with a dramatic hair flip.

"Guess who's my teaching supervisor this semester?" she grins, slapping her hands on the table.

"Who?" I laugh at her theatrics, realizing how much I've missed her.

"Gideon motherfucking Raith."

"Shut up, you're joking." My mouth falls open.

"I am most certainly *not* joking, babe." She interlocks her fingers and rests her chin onto them.

What are the odds?

"My apprenticeship is with his brother!"

"I know! So weird, right?"

A waitress comes over and sets a massive iced americano and charcuterie tray in front of Gin, and my flatbread in front of me. We smile at them in thanks before resuming gaping at each other.

"What's he like?" I ask, taking a bite of food, too distracted to savor the melty mozzarella and bright pesto drizzled on top.

"A giant, pretentious, douche bag cocksucker."

I nearly choke. "Is that all?"

"He's also so beautiful I've cried and or masturbated myself to sleep every night for the last month," she sighs, making a brie, apple, and cracker sandwich. "I had to buy a new vibrator, Olivia. I blew out the fucking motor."

"Jesus Christ." I can't help but laugh. "You haven't been this torn up over a guy since Pietro—"

She holds up a hand, "When I tell you he makes Pietro seem like country fried cunt, I mean it." She gives up on the crackers and starts nibbling a wedge of Gouda.

"That's rough, babe. And I happen to know exactly how you feel."

She drops the cheese. "You *what*?"

"I am beside myself with lust for this man."

"Excuse the fuck out of me! You, Miss Olivia pure-as-Sandra-Dee Hunter, is hard-up for her *boss?*"

"Yes." I take a sip of my drink, letting this sink in for her, and myself.

"Don't they have a third brother?"

Mocha latte nearly comes out of my nose, laughter bursting from my chest.

"Fucking ridiculous. This shit shouldn't be allowed in decent society," she tuts, swapping a piece of my flatbread for some pepper jack and Club crackers, my favorite. "Tell me everything."

"I wish there was more to tell. We flirt, he broods, we work, we flirt, on and on. I have no clue where he's at with this, but I know for sure that he feels something." He has too, right?

"He'd be an idiot not to. You're the baddest bitch in this backwoods town."

I laugh. "Yeah, well. We'll see."

"Oh, no, no, baby." She wags her french-tipped finger at me. "You don't wait, you bring him to his *knees*." She takes a decisive bite of a small pepperoni log. "Either he worships you, or you kick him in the head. Period."

I lean back, pondering this. I've always been passive in relationships, waiting with bated breath for him to make the first move. What if I forced his hand?

"You know, I think you have a point." I smile.

"Duh." She smiles back.

"So, what are you going to do?"

"I was thinking I might suck him off after class," Gin muses, taking a sip of her drink, leaving a dark red lipstick print on the straw.

"Romantic," I tease.

"But I don't know. That's what all the other girls do, throw themselves at him. I don't want to be just another hook-up, y'know?"

I nod. Gin was never one to be on the sidelines, she was your entire world, or she was gone.

"I'll figure something out." She polishes off the last bit of cheese.

"You always do." I chuckle.

We finish up our drinks while reminiscing about our school days before she has to rush off to her next class, where she'll be assisting Dr. Raith with a discussion on *Paradise Lost*. Before she leaves, she pulls out a headband with a fluffy white halo attached to it. "Too much?" She asks, swapping it with her beret and striking a few poses.

"Entirely. It's perfect."

She hops up, drops a tip, and blows me a kiss. "See you soon, my love!"

I wave and shake my head as she scurries out, already 5 minutes late.

I leave my own tip and head out to my car, an unremarkable Volkswagen my dad left me. I rarely drive it because everything in Alder Bridge is close, but I didn't want to chance the weather.

As soon as I slide into the driver seat, the sky opens up, dumping buckets of heavy rain.

I crank up the car and flip on my windshield wipers. The radio cuts in at the tail end of a Billy Joel song. I drive home to the sound of inane announcer chatter and thunderous rain, and park as close to my front door as I can. Rain soaks me as I dash for the door and follows me into the foyer, leaving a puddle on the floor.

I shed my wet clothes right there in the hall and stalk to the bathroom, craving a hot shower.

The scalding stream washes away the cobwebs and lets me think clearly for the first time in days.

I'm falling in love with my boss, and I don't think there's a way to stop it from happening. Both my body and soul ache for him in a way I've never experienced, with a certainty that is more than a little bit alarming. I've never been certain about anything in my life, besides becoming a Mortician.

Is it a coincidence that the two things coincide?

I've waited for this my entire life, not just the job, but the feelings. The wanting. The completeness.

I've pined for love for as long as I can remember, am I willing to let it slip by?

Act 2

Oberon

The main campus building looms before me, full of foreboding and memories. There isn't a soul in sight, the last class ended over an hour ago.

It's pitch black tonight, storm clouds swallowing up the meager light of the new moon. I approach the twelve foot Gothic doors, guarded by wrought iron and mats of ivy. I hold my hand about the padlock and concentrate, rotating the internal mechanism and popping it open with a hollow click.

The doors screech in protest when I pull them apart and step inside. I shine my flashlight around the lobby, illuminating the marbled floors and gallery walls. Statues are scattered throughout, looking too realistic in the darkness. Display cases hold treasures from the University's history, old tomes and inkwells, typewriters and portraits, even the crooked skeleton of the black cat that used to wander the grounds.

I was three sheets to the wind the first time I stepped into these hallowed halls. They'd been basically brand new then, not that I noticed much with the room spinning around me.

Gideon had dragged me there after finding me passed out somewhere, my power spilling outside of my control. He guided me through the halls, one arm wrapped around my middle to keep me standing, and brought me to the very back of the building.

"This might feel uncomfortable," he warned me, before stepping clear through a massive portrait of Amadeus Kennedy, the Founder of the Arcanum, Folke University, and the School of Old Arts.

We emerged in a nearly identical lobby, only this side was littered with magical relics instead of historical ones, and was lit by floating candelabras instead of gas lamps. The statues depicted deities instead of historical figures, Hekate, Lilith, Hades, and Diana. The portraits were of famous witches, their Grimoire's and personal effects displayed in crystal cases. A pyre dominated the center of the room, ever burning coals glowing at the base.

A haunting reminder of what they did to our mothers, and will inevitably do again.

"What is this place?" I asked him, disoriented and fearful.

"It's a sanctuary, Oberon," he said. "It's home."

I walk the same path we did then, the beam of my flashlight landing on Amadeus' permanent scowl.

I'd only met Amadeus a handful of times before he was killed by his son. He'd been cruel and domineering, a masterful manipulator with a fatal temper. Keanu had told me he killed him to protect the Arcanum, that his father was threatening to destroy everything they'd built, but I didn't believe it then and I believe it even less now. It was a power grab, end of story.

I walk past the portrait and out into the courtyard. The only sounds are the preening of crickets and the wind through the bare Oak branches.

This was always my favorite spot on campus when I was a Professor. Students would often find me reading under the trees or grading papers at the fountain. On warm days, I'd even hold classes out here, let them practice defensive spells without fear of breaking anything.

I approach the fountain. It's been drained, leaving a thick film of algae covered coins and decaying leaves at the bottom. I sit on the edge, cold seeping through my clothes and into my skin.

This was where Keanu had found me after I took my first life.

One of my younger students had a stalker, a local priest determined to prove she had the devil inside of her so he could justify over a decade of sexually assaulting her. He had followed her through the portrait, discovered our secret.

Any other professor would have killed him as well, but I was unlucky enough to find him first. She had come screaming into my office, pale and petrified. I grabbed him by the throat and reduced him to ash the second he rounded the corner. Only his golden cross remained.

He deserved it, I knew that. But I had never taken a life before, and it sat poorly on my psyche. If I'd only known that he was just the first of *many*.

I sat in this spot for hours, replaying that moment over and over again. Keanu had found me a little after midnight.

"My prince," he had said, crouching in front of me and taking my face in his hands. "Your heart is so heavy."

I remember thinking he looked ethereal in the moonlight, otherworldly. His dark eyes soft and down turned with sympathy, his coal-black hair a little messy, like he'd gotten out of bed just to find me. He made me feel special.

"I can make the pain go away," he murmured, wiping my tears with his thumbs. "Can I take your pain away?"

I nodded, and his lips ghosted against my cheek, licking the salty tears from my skin. He had kissed me all over, my eyes, my nose, my forehead, my jaw, my neck. His lips were scalding, branding me as his with every touch.

At some point, I had grabbed him by the hair and kissed him, full of heartbreak and hunger. I had poured in every bit of self-loathing and fear, every bit of doubt and greed. It was our first kiss, one of ruin and rage, and I'll never forget it for as long as I live.

That was the night he knew he had me, and I knew I had sold my soul. After I had gotten a taste of him, felt the burn of his mouth and magnetism of his touch, I would crave it every waking moment.

He became my drug, the poison I used to numb the never ending pain of losing her. We spent every night together, tangled in one another, kissing, touching, sucking, fucking, until we were to exhausted to feel anymore. We were obsessed with each other, completely addicted in mind, body, and soul.

He owned me, and I thought I owned him. But I was naive. So naive.

I wanted to be loved by someone. He needed to control everyone.

I shake myself and stand up, wiping away angry tears with the back of my hand. I came here for a reason, not to relive the memories I worked decades to forget.

Back inside the building, I traverse the halls until I find Dr. Sondra Khan's office door.

This lock is a breeze compared to the padlock, and I quickly step inside and flick on the lights.

Dr. Khan keeps an extremely tidy office, apparently. Not a single paper out of place. It's also remarkably colorful for the Head of the Forensics Department. The furniture is brightly painted and pop art hangs on the walls. Even the bookshelves are organized by color, creating an eye-catching rainbow.

Not exactly my style, but I can appreciate the attention to detail.

I walk over to her desk and find exactly what I'm looking for.

"Thank you, Dr. K," I mutter, flipping open the pink file with Olivia's name on it.

On top is her transcript. I skim through it, proud to see high marks across the board. My smart girl. Beneath that is the notes from their meeting today.

* *Balanced workload, Mentor trusts Apprentice with limited responsibilities and enables independent work*

* *Apprentice enjoys her work with Mentor and a healthy working relationship*

I grin, pleased, and keep reading.

* *Apprentice notes the Mentor is "extremely kind and compassionate", seems protective over Mentors reputation*

* *Notes tension with local authorities over recent string of disappearances, mentions Detective Radcliffe and the death of Jacob Smith.*

* *Refers to Mentor on a first name basis*

* *Would recommend Mentor for future apprenticeships, particularly those with an interest in criminology*

Warmth blooms in my chest at Olivia's kind words, clearly she spoke quite highly of me. I chuckle and shake my head, removing the piece of paper from the file and crumbling it up. My sweet girl also revealed entirely too much for my comfort.

I head out of her office, locking the door behind me, and exit the building, tired of the uncomfortable pull of nostalgia.

Outside, I take out a lighter and ignite it, holding the flame up to the crumpled paper ball. It goes up quickly and I drop it into a nearby trash can, setting the entire thing ablaze.

I walk back across the quad to where the hearse waits patiently for me, letting the fire roar, and hoping the smoke will cleanse away the grime of my dark memories.

Olivia

I schlep out of bed nearly 30 minutes after my alarm goes off. I take a quick shower and get dressed in the outfit I had laid out the night before, a white blouse, black skirt, and stockings. I'm in a shitty mood, and I'm hoping that dressing like a bad bitch will make me feel more like one.

I haven't seen Oberon since my panic attack, and I'm struggling to not feel embarrassed about the whole thing. I hadn't meant to bring up our relationship, it just sort of slipped out while my guard was down, which only made the whole situation more awkward.

I was vulnerable with him, and he didn't return that energy. He knows where I stand, and now the ball is in his court. I just have to be patient, which I'm terrible at.

So, I'm hoping I can force his hand a little bit.

I keep my makeup light and glowy, then swipe on an oxblood red lipstick. I pull my curls into a half-up pony, tied with a black ribbon.

It's a chilly morning, and I wore the thinnest bra I own that could still hold the girls up. We're pulling out all the stops. I want Oberon to be drooling. And if he isn't, I'll know for sure whether or not our connection is all in my head. All the cards, and assets, are on the table.

When I arrive at the building, Oberon is puttering around in the front, pruning the dying rose bushes. His black shirt sleeves are pushed up to his elbows, displaying his motley of tattoos to me for the first time. It's a patchwork of black-and-white flora and fauna. I see a dark snake coiling on his inner forearm, and nightshade crawling from his wrist to elbow. A cardinal taking flight. A doe grazing in a field of poppies.

He's collecting the pruned roses in a basket by his feet.

"Morning, Oberon," I say, coming up beside him, feigning cheerfulness.

"Good morning, Liv," he says, pushing dark hair out off his forehead and smiling at me, eyes skating quickly over my body. Dark circles have collected under his eyes since I saw him last, his fingers dry and cracked from working long hours in the cold.

"You look like you need a cup of coffee." I take the shears from his hands. To my surprise, he doesn't protest.

"That bad?" He smirks, gaze trailing from my eyes, to my lips, and down my neck.

My skin tingles under his gaze and I can feel wetness collecting in my panties, nipples pearling in the cold morning air.

"Did you work all night?" I put my hands on my hips, frowning at him.

His eyes darken, zeroing in on my mouth. "Maybe."

"That decides it." I grab his wrist, my fingers barely closing halfway, and drag him across the lawn and onto the street. "We're getting coffee, and a pastry, stat."

He chuckles and allows me to haul him across the road.

The coffee shop, Keaton's Beanery, is busy but orderly. The shop is lit with strings of lights and vintage sconces, nondescript folk music drifting from the speakers. The warm scent of espresso and cinnamon perfumes the air. Garland's of autumn leaves are strings around the windows and counter, giving the space a distinct autumnal vibe.

I release his hand to drool over the pastries in the display case, danishes, muffins, cupcakes, and croissants. Festive pies and slices of cake, even brownies with orange and purple sprinkles.

"Morning, Liv!"

I look up to find Keaton leaning on the other side of the display case, smiling merrily at me. He's handsome, with russet-colored hair, impish freckles, and hazel eyes. His shop crew neck is pushed up at the sleeves, and the navy color of it makes his hair seem extra coppery.

"Morning, Keats, I love what you've done with the place." I smile, genuinely impressed with his decor skills.

"Aw, thank you. It's my favorite time of the year," he says, eyes wandering my face.

"Mine too!"

"No kidding." His grin widens. "Then let me get you a pumpkin pie latte to celebrate the season."

"Oh perfect!" I feel Oberon come up behind me, the heat of his body enveloping me, and Keaton's smile falters just the slightest bit.

People get nervous around Oberon outside of the funeral home, as if he carries death like a shadow.

"Mr. Raith! Is there anything I can get you?" Keaton turns on the charm.

"Mocha latte, please. And a few danishes."

His tone is short, but polite. I chalk it up to the growing number of people in the cafe.

"Course! I'll get that started for you guys." Keaton sends me a wink before turning to start brewing the drinks.

"You know him well?" Oberon asks, taking a step closer as the crush of people grows. His chest is nearly touching my back, the proximity electric.

"We went to college together, and I do a lot of studying here—" someone jostles me to look at the baked goods and I stumble backwards into his arms, his hands locking on my hips. The touch is scorching, his fingers a brand against my skin. My heart ricochets against my chest and my cheeks heat, desire coursing through me.

I feel a rumble rise from deep within his chest and the pushy patron scurries away, mumbling apologies as they go.

"Here's those drinks!" Keaton calls out, placing them on the counter. "And some danishes."

I move away from Oberon and back up to the counter to grab our order, the absence of his touch leaving me cold.

"Plus a brownie, my treat," he whispers to me.

Oberon hands Keaton his credit card, the plastic held casually between his middle and pointer finger.

Keaton takes it and starts ringing us up. "So, Liv, do you have any plans tonight?"

Oberon stiffens behind me.

"We'll probably be working pretty late, but nothing planned," I reply, trying to keep my voice even despite the growing nerves in my chest.

"Would you want to grab a drink with me?" Keaton asks, passing me a receipt and a napkin with his number on it. If he can detect Oberon's anger, it doesn't register on his face. But I feel it like a smoking gun at my back.

"I'll text you, okay?" I say nervously, unsure of what to do. Did I take this too far?

"Sure, have a good day. You too, Mr. Raith!" Keaton says, but I barely hear him as Oberon drags me out by the elbow.

"That was rude!" I scold, pulling away once we step outside. But the look in his eyes makes my mouth clamp shut, and heat pool between my legs.

"You think I give a shit, Olivia?" He's nearly crushing the pastry bag in his other hand, muscles flexing under the tight button down.

"You should! He's my friend." I pout.

Flames lick behind his eyes.

I don't know what makes me say it, but the heat in his eyes makes me bold. "And maybe I want to get a drink with him later! Now he's going to think I'm not interested!" I stomp the rest of the way to the funeral home and throw open the front door.

Impossibly fast, he catches up to me. His hand closes on my arm and he spins me, sending my back colliding into the wall.

"You're not interested in him," he hisses, kicking the door shut with his foot.

"Oh no?" I set the drinks on the foyer table and cross my arms. "Says who?"

He grabs my jaw firmly, sending my heart skittering to a halt. "I do."

"And why should I listen to you?" I'm not sure why I continue taunting him, we both know I want him so bad I'd fall to my knees and beg. But there's something about the feral look in his eyes that makes me want to see just how far he'll go. To find his breaking point.

He releases me and shakes his head, stalking back toward the morgue.

"Oberon, don't walk away from me!" I follow him, despite my legs feeling like poorly set jello. "Hey!" I shout, catching the heavy door just before he closes it in my face. "Now you're really being fucking rude. What's your problem?"

"Olivia..." he growls, leaning over his hands on the embalming table, the corded muscles along his back flexing with tension.

"Don't 'Olivia' me. What, are you jealous?" The words are out before I can stop them.

His spine straightens as if he was struck by lightning, then he's on me.

He presses me against the cold marble counter, chest heaving with anger, eyes dark and pupils blown. "Very," he snarls, grabbing a fistful of my hair and dipping my head back, exposing my neck. "Don't provoke me, darling. You have no idea what you're asking for. When you deal in death, there is no half-way. It's all or nothing. I will take *all* of you." His lips hover just above my throat, close enough to feel his hot breath along my pulse.

Suddenly I feel very much like prey, a sacrifice displayed for consumption. My entire body is an exposed nerve, vibrating with tension.

"So, what do you want, precious girl?" He releases my hair and meets my eyes, raw emotion like I've never seen churning in the sea of blue.

"I want you, Oberon," I manage to whisper, nearly choking on my own desire, all bratty-ness evaporating, surprising myself with just how much I mean it.

There's a moment of conflict on his face.

I wrap my arms around his neck, pulling him closer. "I want you," I whisper against his lips, moments away from begging like a dog.

His hands slide to the back of my thighs, and then I'm in the air. I wrap my legs around his waist, digging my fingers into his thick hair.

We're sharing breaths, tension coiling like a snake around us.

"Liv," he whispers, groaning as if he's in agony. "This is your last chance to run."

I shake my head. "Please, sir."

Then his mouth crashes into mine, devouring me like a man starved. I kiss him back, getting swept away in the current of his tongue. The kiss is searing, our bodies melting together like heated iron.

His teeth skate along my lips, I moan into his mouth. He drinks me in and I do the same, actively trying to drown in one another. He pulls my sweater over my head and casts it aside, hands all over me, trailing his lips in a scalding path down my neck and across my collarbone. His fingers deftly pluck at my hardening nipples, sending spikes of pleasure to my swelling clit.

He turns us around and walks until cold burns into the back of my thighs. He's moved us to the embalming table, setting me down gently on top of it. The cold steel does nothing to quell the heat erupting from my core, if anything, it sends my nerve endings to space, heightening every touch, lick, and kiss.

His hand closes around my throat, and he pulls back slightly. His lips are deliciously red and wet, eyes wild.

"Lay down," he orders.

I obey instantly, despite the shocking bite of the icy table on my flushed skin. My breath is coming out in erratic pants as I watch him stride around the table, fingers ghosting over my goosebump-covered skin. He stops behind my head, just out of sight.

"Tell me how you feel," he says, voice low.

"I don't know," I stammer.

Suddenly he's leaning over me, forearms resting on either side of my head and eyes directly over mine. His woody scent fills my lungs, making me dizzy with desire.

"Liar." His thumbs brush against my throat, teasing, like he can't resist touching my skin.

I can't stop the words as they come bubbling up. "I feel...frustrated, and confused, and so horny I can barely see. I feel afraid of you, but also safe. Like I've known you forever. Like I hate you, but would do anything you said. Like I want to eat you alive, or I want you to eat me alive, or both. And more confused because your my mentor and-"

His hand clamps over my mouth and he presses a kiss to my forehead. "Good girl." He releases me and I exhale, tears burning behind my eyes.

Why did I say all of that?

He circles back around to my side, a fresh scalpel in hand. The cold steel glints in the fluorescent lights and I shiver.

"I won't lie to you," he says, running the dull back of the blade along my arm. The cold feels like it singes me, leaving a bright tingle in its wake. He's barely touching me with it, tickling me with an instrument sharp enough to turn flesh to ribbons. "I'm not nice, or easy-going. When I said all or nothing, I meant it." He turns the knife quickly, the point pressing against the tender flesh inside of my forearm, parallel to the veins running just under my skin. "Trust is paramount." He leans down to whisper in my ear, hot breath tickling my skin. "Do you trust me, Olivia?"

I swallow thickly, feeling the blood in my veins thrumming against the sharp edge of the scalpel, of his words. *Do I trust him?* A resounding yes answers me, like every cell is screaming for him. I've never felt anything like this before. I've never acted like this before. I don't understand what's going on, but I know that I trust him. Completely.

"Yes, Oberon. I trust you with my life," I gasp, the knot of anxiety in my chest releasing at my confession.

He hums happily, nibbling on the shell of my ear. The scalpel continues to descend along my arm, across my palm, up every finger. He kisses my neck, bringing the scalpel up to follow his mouth along the curve of my throat, pressing harder now. Not hard enough to break skin, but enough to pinch, enough to freeze the air in my lungs. His mouth continues exploring, trailed by its more sinister shadow across my collarbones and down my sternum.

I'm gasping for air, the pain swirling with pleasure turning all my thoughts to goo, my muscles to liquid. A moan leaves my lips, a strangled whine trying to take the shape of his name.

Oberon pauses over my navel and looks up at me.

"Getting impatient, love?"

I squirm in response, feeling the blade bite into the soft skin of my stomach. A sharper pinch of pain blooms. He sucks in a breath as I let out a long moan. I don't have to look to know that he's broken skin. Or rather, I did, marking myself for him.

The scalpel clatters to the ground and his tongue is sliding over my soft stomach. His mouth covers the wound, his tongue lapping at the rubies of blood welling to the surface. He moans against me, a shutter wracking through his entire body.

"Wicked little thing," he growls, standing to his full height over me.

I can see a drop of blood on his bottom lip, my blood. A fresh wave of pleasure sends my pussy into spasms, and I try to feel bad about it, ashamed of being so turned on by something so morbid, but the feeling doesn't come. All I can think is *more*.

Oberon moves to the bottom of the table and grabs my ankles, yanking me roughly down towards his hips. I can feel his granite cock straining against his trousers, pulsing against my sopping core. With one hand, he tears my tights at the crotch and moves my panties to the side.

His thick fingers slide along my center, collecting the nectar that's gathered there.

Moans are falling like a song from my lips, any semblance of control lost. I spread my legs wider and grind against his hand, desperate.

"Such an eager girl," he praises, continuing his agonizingly slow exploration. "I want it all, Olivia. Don't hold anything back." He slams two fingers inside me and I let out a cry loud enough to wake the dead.

He finger fucks me ruthlessly, eyes sweeping from my tear-streaked face to my dripping pussy. Lewd, wet sounds fill the air, but the pleasure is too intense for me to be embarrassed.

A familiar coil is building in my stomach, but it grows beyond the usual breaking point, mounting and swelling and cresting until I feel like I could explode.

His thumb finds my swollen clit and massages it in slow circles.

"Come for me, baby. Give it to me," he growls, biting the meat of my left calf slung over his shoulder, the sharp pain of it giving me that final push over the edge.

The coil snaps and I come undone, screaming and thrashing. I'm blinded by pleasure, my whole body bursting into starlight. My cries echo off the walls and return back to me, as if to punctuate where I am, and who exactly just gave me the most intense orgasm of my life.

He gently massages me through it, coaxing the shattered remains of my soul to come back together. "Good girl, Liv," he purrs, running his free hand along my legs and stomach to relax my twitching muscles.

I return to earth, feeling more than a little starstruck. A smile plays at my lips, and giddiness overwhelms me.

He pulls his fingers out of me and licks them clean, moving back around the table as I sit up. With a knuckle, he tilts my chin up and kisses me softly, all urgency gone. Just pleasure. Languid, unhurried indulgence.

I reach down and cup his erect cock, stroking it slowly. It's long and veiny, heavy in the palm of my hand, with a slight upwards curve. My mouth waters at the thought of it splitting me open.

He catches my wrist and brings my palm up to his lips, pressing a kiss into my hand. "Don't worry about me, darling. Ready for breakfast?" He asks, smiling lazily at me, the cat who caught the mouse.

I pout, but acquiesce. "You better hope my latte is still warm," I tease, pushing him backward so I can get to my feet and pull my sweater back on.

"Enjoy it. It's the last latte anyone else will ever make you." He smirks, tucking my hair behind my ear.

"Yes, sir," I laugh, standing on my toes to kiss his bristly cheek.

He smiles, but I'm not sure that he's kidding.

He takes my hand and we walk back out towards the lobby where we left our breakfast, just in time to see a police cruiser park out front. His hand tightens on mine. I swear the metal band around his wrist grows hot, hot enough that I involuntarily yank my hand away. *What the hell*?

But before I can ask about it, Detective Radcliffe is pushing open the doors, and he doesn't look happy.

"Do you have that boy's ashes?" he snaps, nearly coming chest to chest with Oberon.

"Why?" he responds coolly, giving me a look that has me tiptoeing backwards to his office.

"Chief wants me to take them into evidence, in case we can eventually track down the family."

"My storage is safer and more organized, I have the space to keep him here."

The air in the room grows thick with their charged energy, I can almost feel it licking along my skin. Even the plants in the hall seem to shiver under its intensity.

Oberon's hands are clenched in tight fists, and for a moment, I think he might punch him. Something deep in my brain cries *danger* at the sight of him, making the hairs on my neck stand up. He looks almost otherworldly. And I know with inexplicable certainty that Oberon could wipe this man off the face of the earth should he choose to.

It's an alarming thought, but heat begins to stir in my belly again, wetness collecting on the inside of my thighs.

"Are you disobeying direct orders from the Chief?" Radcliffe snarls, leaning into Oberon's face.

"Not at all, let me give him a quick call to discuss the best option for Jacob." Oberon takes a step back and pulls out his cell phone, his casual tone bone-chilling.

Radcliffe reacts quickly, trying to snatch the phone out of Oberon's hand, but Oberon is quicker, catching his wrist mid-air.

"Ah, ah." Oberon flexes his fingers, sending Radcliffe to his knees with an anguished cry. "I think you should *go*. This conversation never happened."

Immediately, Radcliffe stands, cradling his already bruising wrist, and leaves without another word.

"Oberon, what the fuck was that?" I ask, completely flabbergasted.

He jumps like he forgot I was standing there. "Radcliffe is a liar, and I called him on it." He moves over to me and places his hands on either side of my face, the same hands that sent a cop the size of a bear to his knees, the hands that brought me to a mind-shattering orgasm less than 10 minutes ago. "I have a few calls to make, could you take the 10 a.m. appointment with the Carter's?"

"Uh, yeah. No problem," I respond, my heart sinking. We finally cross that line, then he sends me away?

He pulls me in and presses his mouth to mine, parting my lips with his tongue. I kiss him back, unable to resist the intoxicating taste of him. "We'll talk later, okay?" He mumbles against my lips, eyes locked on mine.

"Okay." I nod, feeling a bit better. We still have work to do, death waits for no man.

The day passes quickly as work inconveniently piles up. I'm finishing up paperwork in the meeting room for the Carter's funeral service tomorrow when Oberon finally pokes his head in.

"Busy?" he asks, holding up a bottle of wine and two glasses.

"No, just wrapping up." Heat spreads across my cheeks.

He sits beside me and opens the wine, pouring us each a generous glass.

"How'd it go with the Carter's?" he asks, taking a sip of the burgundy Malbec.

"I thought we didn't do pleasantries?" I counter, taking a deep swig of liquid courage to steady my nerves.

He smirks and sets his glass down. "Did you like the way I touched you?"

A roaring blush erupts on my face and I nearly spill. "I, uh—"

"You wanted to skip pleasantries, Olivia." He leans back in his chair and crosses one leg over the other, ankle resting on his knee.

"Fine. Yes, I did," I say, looking him in the eye. I've never been one to back down from confrontation. "Did you?" I wasn't about to be the only one on the spot.

His head falls back, and his eyes flutter shut as if recalling the memory. His Adam's apple bobs in his throat, then he drops his chin to look me dead in the eyes.

"I could eat you alive," he growls, expression darkening.

Arousal floods my senses, the surge making me squeeze my thighs together.

"Oh?" Is all I can manage, my heart thundering behind my breast.

"But you'll have to be patient with me, Liv," he trails off, looking down at his hands.

A sharp pang stings my chest, I hadn't thought about his late wife. No wonder this has been so difficult for him.

"Oberon." I place my hands over his, "Don't feel like you have to do anything or we have to rush into something—"

"Oh, Liv." His hands tighten around mine. "You misunderstand me. I know exactly what I want. It's just the journey to get there that I'm unsure about."

"And what do you want?" I ask, swallowing thickly.

"More of you than I'm willing to take right now." He exhales, releasing my hands and taking a long drink of wine.

What the hell does that mean? "I don't understand..."

He gets up and perches on the table in front of me, taking my face in his rough hands, the cold of his rings biting into my heated skin. "I know you don't, but you will. Trust that you're safe with me. Trust that I'm yours."

His eyes are so sincere, and I know deep in my soul that I trust him. I meant what I said before, I trust him with my life, even if I don't have a good reason for it. It isn't him that has me terrified, it's the connection blossoming between us.

"I do," I whisper, and he leans in to capture my mouth in a breath-taking kiss, washing away all my reservations.

"Thank you, baby." He places a few feather-light kisses along my cheeks and jaw, making me giggle. "Let me walk you home." He finishes the rest of his wine in one swallow.

I raise an eyebrow, then follow suit, pouring the luscious red down my throat. "I'll allow it," I say with a smile, then hiccup, feeling the wine tingle all the way down to my toes.

Oberon

I drop her off at her door, and despite wanting to carry her across the threshold and fuck her within an inch of her life on the kitchen counter, I kiss her forehead and nudge her inside, alone.

I've already gone further than I intended, but she's irresistible, the smell of her like a drug.

For the first time in days, I go home. It's nothing fancy, an old brick house built in the early 1900's with odd character and a sagging foundation. The neighborhood kids claim that it's haunted, which it is, but not because of me.

I pour myself a glass of wine and sag into the worn leather couch, letting the quiet sounds of the early evening wash over me.

Thoughts of her creep in, the delicate curves of her body, the sounds she makes, the way her mouth falls open when she comes. My cock stirs, remembering the way her pussy clenched around my fingers through her orgasm, the way she gave herself over to me completely, and the wicked grin she flashed me when I lapped up her blood.

My cock is hard as steel, straining against the confines of my trousers. I undo the buttons and free it, precum already gathering at the head.

I imagine her on her knees in front of me, big brown eyes blown wide with hunger, those wicked lips wrapping around me and sucking gently, tongue running along the thick vein on the underside of my cock, pulsing with need.

I smear the precum around the head and spit into my palm, lubricating the shaft, imagining it was her drool coating me. I start stroking my cock with urgency, drowning in filthy thoughts of her, until an orgasm roars through me, and I come in ropes all over my chest, her name on my lips.

"What the hell am I going to do," I mumble to myself and swallow the rest of my wine. I strip, tossing my ruined shirt into the hamper, and slip into an ice-cold shower, trying to shock her out of my system so I can think clearly, but it's useless. She's got her hooks in me without even trying.

I shower, towel off, and fall into bed, flipping through my worn copy of Frankenstein until I succumb to restless sleep.

I dream of her running through the poppy field behind our cottage, naked skin glowing in the early afternoon sunlight. I can't tell anymore if I'm dreaming of Leda or Olivia. In my subconscious, they're the same.

Jogging to catch up with her, I tackle her into the grass, her peals of laughter making my heart thud. She pulls me in for a breathtaking kiss, her tongue tastes like sunshine and spring, her lips soft as flower petals.

I spread her legs and dip my fingers into her pussy, slippery and hot, begging for me.

"Oberon," she whispers in my ear, over and over again, as I massage her walls, coaxing her to orgasm.

A shadow falls over us, and her voice changes. "Oberon." Her lips move, but Keanu's voice falls from them, low and full of malice.

Then, I'm lying on top of her desiccated corpse, the putrid smell of rotting flesh filling my nose and mouth. My hands and chest are covered in gore, and I hear Keanu laughing.

I jerk awake, a scream dying at my lips. Retching, I fall to the floor, pressing my forehead into the cold hardwood to bring myself back to reality. Tears threaten behind my eyes, but I swallow them down and sit up.

Pink light is just starting to break over the tree line. I drag myself to the kitchen for a cup of coffee, then sit out on the back porch and light up a cigarette.

I don't usually smoke, but I need something to relax. The smoke burns my throat, but loosens the knot in my chest, though my hands are still shaking slightly. I conjure Olivia's image in my mind, imagine her puttering away in my office, tapping away at the computer, shuffling through papers. Alive.

Without realizing it, I reach for my phone and press her number, needing to hear her. It rings twice, then her voice drifts through the speaker.

"Morning, Oberon," she yawns, throat still scratchy with sleep.

My heart lurches with relief. "Good morning, Olivia."

"Everything okay?" She asks, sounding slightly concerned.

"Yes, of course," I reassure her while racking my brain for an excuse to be calling so early. "I just wanted to tell you not to worry about breakfast. I have a few things to pick up for the service today and will grab it on my way."

"Oh, okay!" She exhales quietly. "I'll see you in a bit, then?"

"Course." I smile, something resembling peace settling over me.

We hang up and I get ready in my usual service attire, a navy suit and black button down with a black silk tie. I wrangle my hair into a low bun and head out, anxious to see her.

I stop by the flower shop and grab a single violet rose for Liv, along with the order for today, and then the post office before getting coffee and breakfast sandwiches. A dirty chai with pumpkin spice syrup, and egg and cheese on an everything bagel, just the way she likes it.

She's waiting for me on the front porch when I reach the Funeral Home, reading on her Kindle amidst the Halloween decorations. She's wearing a satin, navy dress with a high neck and lantern sleeves. Black tights stretch along her gorgeous legs, disappearing into black-heeled boots. Her hair is pulled back into a sleek ponytail, and her makeup is done to perfection.

I find myself at a loss for words as I approach her, although she doesn't seem to notice, too engrossed in whatever she's reading. Her tether snags me, wraps around my soul and drags me in.

I set my bags and the coffee down quietly, then snatch the device from her hands.

"Hey!" she shouts, trying in vain to get it back from me as I hold it just out of reach. I skim the page, my jaw falling open. *Dirty girl.*

"Vampires, darling? I could have guessed." I smirk, letting her snatch the Kindle back, taking the opportunity to grab her instead, emboldened by the feisty glint in her eye. I pull her close to me, breathing in her decadent, sweet perfume. I nibble along her neck, making her squirm and stirring my cock to life.

"Oberon," she whines, nuzzling closer to me, grabbing at my suit jacket.

"I can be Dracula," I hum, sinking my teeth into the fragile skin below her ear, enough to create a small flare of pain. I feel her arousal spike, sending a wave of pleasure down her tether directly to my heart, and cock. I use my tongue to soothe the bite, turning her to mush in my arms. "Later," I whisper in her ear before stepping away, not wanting to get carried away right here for the neighborhood to watch, although I secretly hope Keaton caught a glimpse from across the street.

She pouts, but brightens when I hand over her coffee and the rose. "Tease." She grins, inhaling the delicate scent of the rose while I unlock the door.

It's an early service today, so we eat quickly and move into set up. I step back and let Olivia handle most of the preparations, testing to see how she juggles all the different elements that go into planning a service. And as I suspected, she's a bit frantic, but executes her vision perfectly.

The morning flies by, and the first mourners arrive at 11:00 a.m. on the dot. I fall back, nodding to her that she'll be the one greeting them. Her eyes go wide with fear, a wave of anxiety rolling down her tether, but she shakes it off and runs to open the door.

Guest after guest filters in. Olivia greets each of them and helps them settle into the parlor room. She glides around the room, elegant and composed as a swan. Breathtaking. The guests are enamored with her, the energy of the room higher than usual, and I'm more than happy to let all the attention be on someone else for a change.

A few guests approach me and we chat quietly, but for the most part, they steer clear.

After about an hour of socializing and mingling, the pastor approaches the stand and everyone takes their seats.

I send her a wink and slip out of the room and into my office, shedding my jacket and tossing it onto the couch.

A few minutes later, I hear her heels click down the hallway. I fling open the door and grab her before she can touch the handle, lifting her into the air and kicking the door shut behind us. I crush her into the bookcase, capturing her mouth in mine in a sloppy kiss.

She wraps her legs around my waist and runs her fingers through my hair, unraveling the messy bun I had it in. Her soft moans against my mouth are intoxicating, and I can't help but rut my hardening cock against her core.

Our mouths feast on each other, desperate for more. She sucks on my lower lip and I nearly crumble to my knees at the intense wave of pleasure it sends coursing through my body. I feel her grin at my reaction and attempt the move again, but I'm faster, wrapping my hand around her throat and pulling my head back.

"And you call me a tease," I chuckle darkly, running my tongue along her jawbone and up to her ear, relishing the way she trembles under my grip, her warm chocolate scent making me drool. "I'll bet there are a lot of things that pretty mouth of yours can do besides tease," I whisper, my lips brushing against the shell of her ear.

I slip my fingers under her dress, ghosting my knuckle over her soaking pussy, shocked when I don't feel any fabric, just dripping, hot skin. I pull back to look at her, and she's got that wicked little grin on her face.

"Surprise," she sings, raking her fingers through my hair.

I nearly come on the spot.

"That's my girl," I growl, plunging two fingers inside her and tightening my grip on her throat so she can't make any noise. I fuck her slowly, curling my fingers each time I sink all the way to my knuckles. "No panties with all those people around? Parading around like a whore during a funeral?" I pick up the pace, adjusting my hand to cover her mouth instead of her throat.

She writhes in my arms, biting into my palm to keep herself quiet. The pain is exquisite, making my cock jump with excitement.

"You wanted me to touch you so badly, didn't you? Wore these just for me?" I press my thumb against her clit and feel her muscles contract around my fingers, getting closer and closer.

She nods, grinding down against my fingers the best she can while still holding herself up. My other hand can barely contain the lewd sounds she's making.

"Such a little slut, Liv. Is this what you wanted?"

Her pussy spasms around my fingers, her body starting to stiffen as her orgasm looms.

"Come for me, baby. You can do it." I release her mouth and capture her lips with mine, drinking down the profanity that rips from her throat as she comes around my fingers. "Atta girl, that's it." I massage her clit through her orgasm, getting softer as she begins to come down.

"Fuck, Oberon," she pants, skin glowing red.

I pepper kisses along her cheeks and ease her onto the couch, her legs shaking with aftershocks. "Open," I murmur, feeding my soaked fingers into her pretty mouth.

She sucks them clean, giving me a taste of what exactly that mouth can do.

I smile and bend down to kiss her forehead, withdrawing my fingers with a pop and patting her cheek. I grab a water bottle from the fridge and pass it to her, which she drinks down greedily.

She will most certainly be the death of me, or at least the death of my self-control.

"I think I better get back out there," she says, smoothing her skirt with a coy smile. "Thank you for a restful break, *sir*." She kisses my cheek before sauntering out of the room.

I flop down on the couch, taking deep breaths and willing my hard-on to subside.

"Gods save me," I mutter to myself, finishing off the rest of the water bottle. I gather my composure and step out to join her as the service comes to a close.

Guests filter out, seeming almost reluctant to say goodbye to Olivia. She'd charmed the hell out of them, and I had to admit that I was impressed.

She shuts the doors behind the final guest and leans against them, letting out an exasperated sigh.

"You did it!" I smile, walking over to her and bracing my hands on either side of her head.

"Was that really only 3 hours?" She rubs her forehead, looking drained and a bit dazed.

"Sure was." I nod, knowing exactly how she feels. It can be exhausting, having to be emotionally available but composed enough to keep things running smoothly. Especially when you can feel every energetic shift from every person, their lives like gnats buzzing around my ears.

"I feel like it's been 10 years."

I place a kiss on top of her head. "I'll do the cemetery part. You stay here, clean up, listen to your murder podcast, and decompress."

"But—"

"No buts. I'll see you in a bit." I snag the keys from the bowl by the front door and slip past her. "Lock the door behind me," I say, stern, before shutting the door.

After leading the procession and delivering the casket to the Sexton and gravedigger, I stop by a quaint chocolatier downtown. I order a dozen chocolate covered strawberries and a bottle of a special edition sparkling red by her favorite label.

I park the hearse and unlock the front door, pleased that she did as she was told.

"Liv?" I call, walking through the lobby. I approach the double doors of the parlor and spot her at the end of the aisle, sitting on the velvet altar surrounded by paperwork. Her shoes are kicked off and her hair is down in loose waves around her face. For a moment, I forget how to breathe.

Her headphones are in, so she doesn't hear me approach. I crouch down in front of her, a parishioner kneeling before their goddess, and hold up the offerings I procured.

She startles, then grins. "Oberon!" She squeals, snatching the heart shaped box out of my hand and tearing it open. "How'd you know they're my favorite?"

"Lucky guess." I smile, watching her select one and take a bite, eyes rolling back with pleasure. "I wanted to get you a little treat for a job well done."

"Thank you." She blushes, strawberry juice dripping down her chin. She holds out the bitten strawberry, a wicked glint in her eye.

I indulge her, taking the sweet fruit between my teeth and biting down, imagining what it tastes like on her tongue.

She pulls her hand away and leans forward, gently pressing her lips against mine, and I don't have to wonder anymore. I lace my fingers through her dark hair and pull her close, deepening the sweet kiss into something more indulgent.

I lean her back onto the altar and crawl on top of her, refusing to let our mouths separate for a single breath. My hands roam her body, trailing over every inch of heated skin.

She reaches up to run her hands over my chest, quickly undoing the buttons and raking her nails over my bare chest, sending a shiver along my spine. Distantly, I worry about the ugly scar on my sternum, but her touch is far too distracting.

My hands are all over her but it isn't enough. I trail my lips along her neck and start massaging her soft breasts over her dress, flicking her hardening nipples gently as she arches into my touch.

The tiny sounds falling from her lips are making me delirious, chipping away at my self control. It takes everything in me to move slowly, but I refuse to rush this.

I move down, down, pressing open-mouth kisses onto her silky inner thighs, inching her dress up to pool around her hips. The black garter tights leave her completely bare to me, her glistening pussy practically begging me to dive in, to eat her alive.

With a flat tongue, I lick one stroke from her knee to core, stopping just before tasting her. My mouth waters at the heady scent of her arousal.

She shivers under my ministrations, grabbing fistfuls of my hair, trying to drag me closer.

"Greedy girl," I groan, teasing everywhere but where she needs me with my tongue and teeth. "Beg for it." I flick my eyes up to see her expression. She looks positively radiant, cheeks flushed with arousal, panting with need.

Her eyes meet mine, glittering wickedly. "Please, sir. I need you."

I shift and hover my hand over her pussy, raising an eyebrow. "Tell me exactly what you need, Olivia."

"I need your tongue," she mewls, squirming under my arm.

I deliver a sharp slap to her pussy, relishing in the surprised yelp that falls from her lips.

"I need your tongue, sir!" she cries.

"Good girl." I smile, licking a long stripe from her opening to clit, her taste like sparkling honey on my tongue. I tamp down my need to devour her and savor her instead, licking languid swirls and patterns over every inch of her sweet cunt. I dip into her entrance, then along her lips, up and around her swollen bud, pausing to circle it a few times before moving back down.

She's a mess of moans beneath me, grabby hands searching everywhere for purchase, finally settling on my forearm that's bracketed across her hips so she can't escape from the pleasure. Her nails bite into my skin, and my control starts to unravel further.

I lash her clit with my tongue, sucking it between my teeth while running a finger around her opening, collecting her wetness before sliding into her. I add another quickly, encouraged by the ravenous way her pussy sucks on my fingers. I match the pace with my tongue, and soon I can feel her orgasm building, the walls of her channel fluttering with delicious tension.

She's chanting my name, clutching desperately to my arm and head, bucking wildly against my face.

I don't relent and send her hurtling over the edge into an intense orgasm, the force of it gushing down my hand and chin, sweet and sinful.

I lap up every last drop, slowly easing her down, before sitting up onto my knees and looking down at the gorgeous mess I made of her.

Mine.

She props herself up on her elbows, shivering with aftershocks, dark waves falling in her face. A shy smile graces her swollen lips.

"On your knees, darling," I say, standing up.

She pushes herself up, resting shakily on her knees, eyes never wavering from mine despite the submissive position.

I walk in a circle around her, feeling predatory. I remove my shirt and toss it aside, then bend down to unzip the back of her dress. The material is silken against my fingers, warm from the heat of her skin. I push it off her shoulders, the navy fabric pooling around her legs. A lacy black bra barely contains her heavy tits, flushed and heaving from her orgasm.

I pick up the box of strawberries.

"Look at you. So beautiful," I whisper, moving around to her front, brushing her hair out of her eyes and gathering it in my hand, tilting her head up. "The most beautiful creature in the world."

I take a bite of a strawberry, sweetness exploding on my tongue and mingling with the taste of her, then trace her lips with the crimson juice.

She parts them immediately, tongue dabbing at the dripping flesh.

I pull the fruit away and replace it with my thumb. She sucks the digit into her mouth, doe eyes blinking up at me. *Gods.*

"Take what you want, baby. I'm yours," I say, removing my thumb to unbuckle my belt.

Eagerly, always so eager, she makes quick work of my pants and pulls my throbbing cock free, rock hard and leaking precum. She pumps it twice, sending tingles of pleasure through me, and I can see the gears turning in her little head, calculating the best way to approach my cock.

"You think too much, pretty girl. Let me show you what it's like to be brainless." I pull her head forward, driving my cock most of the way into her hot mouth. Stars explode behind my eyes, and my knees turn to liquid. I hold her still, a breath away from coming already. Her wicked tongue laps at the vein on the underside of my cock, making my hips to buck deeper into her throat.

I move slowly, sliding my cock in and out of her throat, relishing in the tiny gasps and moans falling from her. I hold her head still as I fuck her mouth, picking up the pace as my balls start to tighten.

"Such a good girl," I growl, watching her eyes roll back and drool drip down her chin. "My perfect little slut." I withdraw my cock before I get carried away and bend down to capture her abused mouth in a searing kiss.

"Fuck me, please, Oberon," she begs, trying to grab my shoulders and pull me down. "Please, sir."

How can I resist that?

I let her pull me down and settle on top of her, hiking one of her legs up with my arm, lining up my pulsing cock with her needy core. I tease her, sliding the head along her soaking lips, just for a second, before notching into her entrance.

She stares up at me, eyes locked with mine. "I need you," she whispers, bringing a hand up to touch my face.

Without breaking eye contact, I push slowly into her, nearly collapsing as pleasure racks through me. Her pussy is a vice grip, tight and hot, softer than the velvet beneath us. Heaven. I feel that broken piece within me click back together, feeling whole and *right* for the first time in over a century.

I've waited so long for this, for her. Waited so long to come home.

She lets out a long moan and grits her teeth against the stretch, taking me so well.

I slowly start thrusting, letting her adjust, letting the pain morph into pleasure. The tension in her muscles finally starts to loosen, and she catches my eyes again.

"God, please fuck me."

"God, hm? He'll have to go through me." I smirk, keeping the same lazy pace on the withdrawal, but snapping my hips forward, forcing my cock as deep inside her as I possibly can. Her cunt is perfect, squeezing around me with every thrust, like she wants me to stay buried inside her forever. I keep that rhythm until she's screaming, nails digging crescent moons into my back and arms.

I feel my control starting to wane as my orgasm approaches, and then I'm fucking her savagely, ripping screams from deep inside of her. I'm feral, brutally pounding her little pussy, completely lost pleasure. In her.

"I'm coming!" she cries, her cunt gripping me so hard it stalls my thrusts, freezing me in place as my own orgasm crashes over me.

"Fuck!" I roar, pumping my release into her as her pussy milks me, both of us dragged under the tsunami of our shared orgasm.

I collapse onto her, thoroughly spent, and cover her neck and face in messy kisses.

She giggles and hugs me closer, nuzzling into my neck and licking away the beads of sweat rolling off my shoulders.

"Olivia," is all I can manage to say, my heart squeezing.

"Oberon." She presses a sweet kiss into my lips and I can feel her smile, her heart thudding against my chest.

"You're mine," I whisper, leaning my forehead against hers.

"I'm yours," she replies, grinning.

Contentment swirls around us, as if the world has finally righted itself.

Reluctantly, I get up and grab a towel to clean us up, gently wiping away the mess between her legs and down her thighs, every touch making her shiver with sensitivity.

After I finish cleaning up, she pops the bottle of wine and drinks straight from it, naked and sprawled on the black velvet altar, soft curves and blush stained skin on full display for my greedy eyes. My Goddess.

We polish off the rest of the strawberries and the bottle of wine, love drunk and giddy, but something dark begins to swirl in my gut. I try to ignore it, wanting to stay in this moment of bliss with her, but it's gnawing at me, drawing my attention away despite my best efforts.

I can't escape the cycle of grief, and cold terror. The debilitating fear of losing her holding me hostage.

She notices my energy change, and frowns.

"Are you okay?" she asks, taking my hand.

I nod, swallowing the anxiety clawing up my throat.

"I'm scared too," she admits, dropping her head on my shoulder. "I've never felt anything like this before."

I kiss her head, willing my emotions to stabilize. If only she knew. "You're safe with me, Liv."

"And you're safe with me," she responds, snuggling closer.

My resolve nearly slips, her words hitting me like a suckerpunch. *When's the last time someone cared about my safety, about my feelings?*

I've been solely responsible for myself for so long that someone else shouldering the burden feels foreign. Uncomfortable, but not unpleasant.

Reality, however, is immediately sobering. We weren't safe, not really. My secrets twist like a sword through my chest. I can almost feel my scar burn, remembering exactly how *not* safe we truly are.

I won't lose her this time. I won't fail. I'll keep her safe, no matter the cost.

Olivia

I thought I had experienced the full gambit of emotions, the duality of woman, but turns out I was dead wrong.

Is it possible to be floating on cloud nine, while simultaneously scared out of your mind?

My feelings for Oberon are developing at a rapid pace, and not just the physical ones. I've never experienced physical love and affection like he's been giving me the last few days, saccharine sweet and filthy, the kind of touch you read about in novels.

I take another pull of sparkling red wine and slip my dress back over my shoulders.

Oberon moves behind me and zips it up, his warm fingers brushing my spine.

"Are you hungry?" he asks, coming back around and holding his hand out. I take it and he hauls me up, slipping an arm around my waist.

My heart lifts a bit, I was afraid he'd disappear like the day before. "Course, what did you have in mind?"

He smiles, almost bashful. "I was thinking maybe I could cook for you? At my place?"

"That sounds perfect." Excitement swirls in my stomach. This feels like a step in the right direction, finally. I stand on my toes to kiss his cheek.

We collect our things and head out into the brisk early evening, walking the few blocks to his house in comfortable silence, our hands twined together.

Well, external silence. My mind, on the other hand, is reeling.

He's brought me more mind-shattering orgasms in the last 72 hours than I experienced in any past relationship. Truthfully, the only mind-shattering orgasms I've ever had in my life. And they keep getting *better*. He's a quick study, and evidently my body is the subject.

I burn for him. And that scares the shit out of me. My career is on the line, and more and more, it's starting to feel like my heart is on the line as well. If he hit the brakes on whatever this is, I'm not sure how I'd cope. Just the thought alone makes me feel like someone stabbed me through the heart.

Even my dreams are getting more intense, more vivid. The larger picture unfolds like a memory. Every night, I get more and more snippets of this dream life. Gardening and sun soaked kitchens, dancing around fires and wadding in waterfalls, baby's breath in my hair, green silk in a ball on the floor. Getting dragged away from my bed by my hair, watching the man I love bleed out on the floor.

I've started trying to write it all down as soon as I wake up, the images like silverfish through my fingers. But slowly, the picture is coming together, like scenes from a past life. Memories that aren't mine.

It's slightly maddening, and I've thought about bringing it up to my therapist more than once. But I've been a bit, uh, distracted. Lusting after my boss and all.

It doesn't help that he seems equally as confused as I do, a sappy love bug one second and brooding Mortician the next. I have a suspicion it's to do with his late wife, and I'm honestly not sure how to deal with that. On one hand, I would never, ever try to replace her or encourage him to forget her, that's not my style. But at the same time, the thought of him thinking about anyone else while he's touching me is unbearable. I don't want to be dredging up grief or regret, that can only complicate what is already a complicated relationship.

I'm really not sure how to move forward, but I also know in my heart that I can't be the one to stop this. I don't want to stop this.

I'm pulled from my thoughts when we arrive at an adorable cottage with whitewashed brick and ivy crawling up the walls. Old oak trees grow tall, their orange and red leaves leaving a blanket across the lawn and sidewalk.

He unlocks the front door and lets me step through, the smell of him wrapping me up like a tight embrace. It is decorated similarly to the funeral home, but it's warmer, with tons of organic texture and ambient light. There's books stacked on every surface, in every corner. Knickknacks and collected artifacts decorate the remaining space. He has several gallery walls, with some of the most beautiful landscape paintings and portraits I've ever seen. There's plenty of classic art I recognize, as well as countless pieces collected from thrift stores, flea markets, and small businesses.

His home is less tidy than the funeral home, it feels delightfully lived in, and oh so Oberon.

We settle in his kitchen and he pours us some more wine, his glassware smokey gray and amber. The counter tops are black stained butcher block, the cabinets natural walnut. It's gorgeous and comfortable, like a beloved cafe.

"Can I pick a record?" I ask, eyes snagging on what appears to be an extensive vinyl collection with a vintage black Victrola.

"Course, love." He smiles, starting to gather the ingredients for whatever he's planning on making.

I walk over and skim the shelves, grabbing one of my favorite albums and setting it up. "Don't judge me," I warn as the opening notes of "Second Hand News" fill the air.

"Never. Fleetwood Mac is mandatory listening in October." He's started chopping onions and zucchini, and has water boiling on the vintage gas stove.

We chat and dance as he cooks, and I never would have guessed that Mr. Grumpy Mortician had moves, but I stand corrected. He sweeps me into his arms and waltzes me across the kitchen, one hand lightly pressed against my back, the other cradling my hand. I nuzzle into the crook of his neck, letting him lead.

He extends his arm and spins me in a slow circle. "You are so beautiful." He pulls me back into his chest and dips me, one hand sliding down my thigh, the other holding my waist flush against his.

I let my head fall back, savoring the delicious warmth in my chest, the freedom of falling and knowing, just this once, someone might be there to catch me.

He lowers his head and presses an open mouth kiss under my jaw, right on my pulse point, then slowly lifts me back up until we're heart to heart.

"I'm so glad you're here," he murmurs, pressing a kiss to my forehead as the record comes to an end.

"Me too." I caress his stubbled cheek, absolutely floored by how natural this feels. How *right*. Nothing has ever come to me naturally, but being with him is as easy as breathing.

We reluctantly separate so he can add the finishing touches to dinner and I can pick a new record: Bon Iver's *For Emma, Forever Ago*.

He spoons luscious, saucy pasta into black ceramic bowls. Charred roasted vegetables tossed in garlic olive oil are nestled on top, followed by freshly shaved Parmesan off the block. We eat at the kitchen island, feeding each other and kissing between decadent bites. It feels so blissfully domestic, my anxieties from earlier melt away, and I let them.

No matter what happens, I can have tonight. I deserve tonight.

I watch his lips as he talks, his words fading as blood rushes in my ears. I reach out and grab his face, pulling him into a hungry kiss.

It came on quickly, but I'm on fire for him.

He kisses me back eagerly, tongue dancing with mine. In a flash, I'm in his arms, legs wrapped around his waist. His body is hard and strong, muscles built by work rather than a gym. He drops me onto the counter, grabbing my hips hard enough to leave marks as he devours my mouth.

I put a hand on his chest, stopping him. "Do you think I could, uh, take a quick shower? Freshen up a bit?"

A mischievous smirk spreads across his face. "You're in luck, I happen to have a very spacious shower." He kisses me one more time then helps me off the counter, practically dragging me towards what I assume must be the master suite.

We discard our clothes as we go and he pulls me into a gorgeous bathroom, all black marble and gold.

He turns on the water in the stone shower, jets along every wall.

I step into the hot stream, relishing the impeccable water pressure.

His arms snake around my middle, pulling me back into his firm chest. His lips travel along my neck and the curve of my shoulder, sending sparks along my skin. I lean into him, letting his touch and the water loosen my muscles, calm my thoughts.

It's almost meditative, steam enveloping us in a cocoon of safety. Just us, heart and soul.

I turn in his arms and find his mouth, water rolling off our noses as we kiss, running in rivulets down our bodies.

Oberon breaks the kiss, grabbing a bottle off the shelf and pouring a creamy, woodsy smelling soap into his palm. He lathers it between his hands and starts massaging my scalp, tilting my head back. His fingers are heaven, lulling me into a trance. Kisses rain on my skin along with the water, the steam lifting the sandalwood smell into the air.

He moves me slightly to let the water rinse away the shampoo, then grabs a different bottle, this one smelling of rich coffee and cocoa. Good enough to eat. Slowly, he starts massaging the soap into my skin, working the muscles from my shoulders, down to my arms, back, and thighs, even getting on his knees to massage my calves and feet, sore after a full day of wearing heels.

I melt under his reverence, allowing him to undo all the knots I've collected under my skin, both physical and emotional. The release is intense, an outpouring of stress and sorrow, like he's tipped over my cup of emotions and is washing them away with loving touches.

Needing to touch him, to feel his solidity under my fingers, I grab the same soap and coax him to his feet, lathering up his broad chest. I work my fingers down, down, letting bubbles collect around his hardening cock. I wrap my fingers around him, pumping him slowly.

His head falls back as he groans, his throat bobbing. He looks otherworldly, black hair clinging to his face and shoulders, water dripping from his gorgeous face.

Every moan that falls from his lips spurs me on, stoking the heat in my core into an inferno. He's hard as steel and throbbing, his arms thrown out to brace himself on the shower walls. A God, all mine to worship.

Just when I think he's getting close, that I might bring him over the edge the way he's done for me so many times, he grabs me and spins me around, pushing me against the wet stone.

In one thrust, he's inside me, stretching me sharply.

"Oberon!" I cry, the pleasure nearly sending me to my knees. His steel grip on my hips are the only thing that keeps me standing.

"How sweet are you, trying to get me off?" He slaps my ass, hard, electric pleasure shooting straight to my clit.

"Yes!"

He starts fucking me ruthlessly, splitting me open on his cock over and over again.

He grabs a fistful of my hair and yanks my head back, his hips never breaking their relentless pace. "I only come in that pretty little mouth or this perfect cunt, understand?"

"Yes, sir!" I scream, my orgasm cresting, so close.

He reaches around to pet my clit, giving me that final push over the edge. I come undone, my orgasm ripping through me, stealing the air from my lungs and the remaining tension from my limbs.

Oberon follows close behind, bottoming out and holding my hips tight enough to bruise as he finishes, my name a song on his lips.

He thrusts lazily as we come down, stroking his fingers down my spine and the curve of my ass, smoothing my hair out of my face.

Once I feel mostly steady, I turn and throw my arms around his neck, peppering kisses all over his stupid, talented, godly face. My heart soars with affection. I feel like I've been put through a rinse cycle and wrung out, leaving me clean and brand new.

We rinse off and he bundles me up in a gray fluffy robe, carrying me to his bed.

I'm drifting off before I hit the sheets, falling into blissful oblivion.

Fresh coffee coaxes me out of sleep, filling my nose and stirring my soul. I blink my eyes open, but the room is mostly dark. A soft glow spills in from the hall, haloing Oberon leaning against the door frame, twin mugs in hand.

I sit up blearily, remembering where I am and exactly what I did last night. Heat creeps into my cheeks and I fight the urge to bury my head under the fluffy duvet and hide forever.

"Morning, Olivia," Oberon says gently. He sets a mug on the end table and perches on the foot of the bed. His dark hair is tousled from sleep and he's wearing only a pair of black flannel pajama pants slung low on his hips.

"Morning." I take a sip of coffee. It's creamy with a dash of cinnamon and vanilla, housed in a mug shaped like a little ghost.

"Algernon thought the mugs were funny, they were a gift from last Christmas," he says sheepishly, running his fingers through his hair.

"I love them." I take another sip. "I have a set of skull mugs at home. And one with the Death tarot card," I ramble, failing to reign in my thoughts.

"Transformation and rebirth, my favorite card," he replies, adjusting to get a little more comfortable. He rests his hand beside my legs, his fingers just barely touching my skin.

"You're familiar with Tarot?" I ask, a little surprised. He doesn't seem the spiritual, witchy type.

"My mother was, and my sister-in-law is into it. I've gotten a lot of readings against my will." He smiles, but it doesn't meet his eyes.

This feels too intimate, too raw.

"We should probably start getting ready, gotta open in an hour." I suddenly find myself desperate for the sanctuary of work, the buoy of common ground and something to talk about.

"Sure," he says, withdrawing his hand and standing up.

I can tell something is weighing on him, but I don't press. It's probably the same thing weighing on me. *What now?*

We get ready in mostly silence. I rummage through his closet to find something I can wear, and settle on one of his black button-downs, belted at the waist, with one of his oversized cardigans. I pull on my tights from yesterday and my boots. He wears a gray turtleneck and black slacks, with shiny leather loafers.

I feel some of the awkwardness melt away, my body and mind hyper-focusing on the delicious way the turtle neck accentuates his broad chest and jawline.

He catches me staring and smiles to himself, fidgeting with his shirt sleeves and watch.

I head into the en-suite to figure something out with my hair, settling on a half-up-half-down mess and forgo makeup. His reflection appears behind me, so handsome I forget how to breathe for a second.

Oberon snakes his arms around my waist and nuzzles into my neck, sighing deeply. "You smell like me," he mumbles, squeezing me a little tighter.

Relief washes over me. We're okay. He still wants me. I place my hands over his, tracing the tattoos on his forearms with my nails. "Good."

He shivers under my touch and gives me one last squeeze before pulling back and turning me to face him. He tilts my chin up with a knuckle and kisses me sweetly, his lips soft and cinnamon flavored. "Ready to go?"

"Course," I smile, warmth spreading from my lips to my toes.

Coffees in tow, we walk out into the early morning, going over the plan for the day.

Oberon comes up short a few buildings from the Funeral Home, brows furrowing.

"What is it?" I place a hand on his arm and look around, spotting what must have caught his attention.

Detective Radcliffe's cruiser is parked out front, along with an ambulance.

"Another kid." He says, voice low.

I don't question how he knows that, I just follow him up to the front porch, where Radcliffe waits impatiently.

The men don't mince words. Radcliffe hands him a stack of papers barely contained by a manila envelope.

"We found the couple, Victor and Tiana. Turned up on a construction site," Radcliffe says, with notably less vibrato than usual. "The school wants to arrange a joint funeral, they'll have somebody call you sometime today I'd imagine."

Oberon flips through the folder, frowning. "Okay, take them around back for intake. I'm sure you'll see the obituary with more information soon," he says coolly, clearly intending it to come across as a dismissal.

Thankfully, Radcliffe just nods and walks back towards his car. I clock a slight limp in his right leg and some thickness around his midsection like his ribs are bandaged.

"Is he alright?" I ask as Oberon ushers me in, making a beeline for the morgue.

He doesn't respond.

We take care of intake quickly and get started on the first body. Their corpses are flawless, save the clean slices across their throats. Clearly foul play, and the coroner indicated it as such. I keep record while Oberon cleans, sets, and embalms them, every move he makes weighed down with reverence.

This job can be fascinating, but it's impossible to forget exactly what you're doing and what your purpose is. To preserve someone's dead child, mother, father, sister, brother, friend.

The day passes in quiet solemnity as we work, neither of us taking a break until we are completely finished preparing them both.

I set down my tools and peel off my gloves, fatigue settling on my shoulders now that the work is done. I look over at Oberon, feeling tears threaten.

"Come here, baby," Oberon whispers, setting down what he's doing and opening his arms.

Without hesitation, I run over and bury myself in his chest, wrapping my arms around his middle under his lab coat. The tang of formaldehyde clings to him, but I can still smell the traces of woody cologne on his skin. He holds me close, trailing his hands along my back, untangling the knots in my hair with his fingers. I let the tears fall, knowing it's better to feel it than shove it down.

"You did so well today, Olivia." He kisses the top of my head. "You really are gifted. Your capacity for compassion is just..." He tilts my chin up and brushes away the tears with his thumbs. "You amaze me," he says wistfully, blue eyes wandering my face.

"I just want to know what happened to them," I sniffle. "Who could do something like that?"

I feel him stiffen for a second, then sigh. "It is strange, the disappearances, and now three bodies, hardly feels like a coincidence."

I step back to retrieve the files, curiosity officially piqued. "Do you think we could do a little more digging?"

He flashes a crooked smile. "Course. I'll order pizza."

We spend hours pouring over the files, newspapers, the internet, and anything we can get our hands on from the comfort of his office.

There are obvious connections between the students: gifted, good-looking, and isolated. None of them have family or meaningful connections. The couple had each other, and Jacob had a few fair-weather friends, but that was about it. The other students were totally isolated, with only their professors taking note of their absence due to their GPAs.

There was another odd connection between Jacob and the couple, trace amounts of opium, which is hardly a common drug around college campuses. But they were killed in entirely different ways. Jacob drowned, the couple bled out.

Oberon seems fixated on Jacob, his education in particular, likely due to it's proximity to Gideon, his older brother. Folke was infamous for its secret societies and seedy underbelly, and it was entirely likely that the kid obsessed with the occult found himself wrapped up in one.

It was all we had to go on. Three dead kids and a hunch.

I polish off my glass of wine and rub my eyes, getting up to open the window. A storm is blowing through Alder Bridge, and I crave the ozonic smell.

"*Mew!*"

I jump back, startled by the sound.

"What was that?" I ask, glancing over at Oberon.

"I don't—"

"*Mrow!*"

"A cat?" We say in unison.

I'm already running out the front door by the time Oberon is out of his chair. I shine my phone light under the office window and see a soaking wet rag, no not a rag, a disheveled cat. It's curled up under the awning, lying oddly still.

"Oh, you poor baby." I crouch down and look it over. It's barely breathing, and I can see glossy yellow eyes peering at me through matted gray fur. It's a young cat, maybe nine months old. Taking the risk, I drape my cardigan over it and bundle them up, holding them close to my chest. I stand and nearly knock over Oberon, who I hadn't noticed was hovering over me with an umbrella.

We get it inside and lay it on his desk, clearing away the papers and mess.

In the light, I can see that one of its back legs is badly broken. Dirt and blood are caked in its long fur, and I can hear just how labored its breathing is in the quiet room.

I run to the morgue and back to get material to splint his leg and clean his fur, as well as a stethoscope and oxygen mask.

"Liv," Oberon says gently as I start examining his leg.

"Let me try," I plead. But the poor thing mewls in agony at the slightest touch, looking at me with wide, pleading eyes. I try the stethoscope but can only listen briefly before tears overwhelm me, and his fate is confirmed. "It's too much death," I whisper, sliding to the floor. "It's not fair."

Oberon crouches down in front of me.

"Is it too much to ask to save one life?" I peer up at him, eyes bleary and burning with tears.

"No," he whispers, taking my hands. "Olivia, I—," he clears his throat. "There are some things I haven't told you, haven't really told anyone. But I need to tell you because, I—"

Anxiety coils in my belly. Is he about to tell me that he loves me? That he's married? That he's a criminal?

Does he love me?

"What is it, Oberon?" I ask, the words pinched with anxiety.

"It might be easier to show you." He stands up slowly and goes over to his desk, stroking the cat gently. It immediately relaxes, even starts purring a bit under his touch. It's breathing slows to a stop and its eyes close, as if sleeping. Oberon's eyes close as well and he hovers his hand over the cat's chest.

The metal band around his arm flares a brilliant orange and sparks, making him grimace, but doesn't break his concentration.

What in the holy fuck?

Blood and dirt lift from its coat, leaving shiny silver fur behind. Oberon trails his fingers down its leg and the bones straighten with a crack, the leg fully mended in a blink.

Oberon continues petting the cat, brows furrowed and teeth bared. The bracelet is nearly white now, and smoke is starting to rise from his wrist. A sharp, almost sulfuric smell rises into the air.

"Oberon! It's burning you, stop!" I cry, running over to try and grab him.

One of his hands shoots out, palm facing me, and I freeze in place involuntarily, a prickle of fear climbing my spine.

"Almost," he grits out, hand shaking as it drifts over the cat's midsection one final time.

Oberon crumbles to the ground, panting.

I feel the hold release and run over to him, gathering him up in my arms. "Are you okay? What the hell was that? Your wrist!" I cry, seeing the charred skin around the bracelet.

Oberon ignores me and braces his hands on the desk. He hauls himself up to a kneeling position and looks at the cat. "Thank fuck," he sighs, before letting himself collapse back down, smiling this time.

"What the?" I sit up and am greeted by two yellow eyes, blinking at me expectantly.

The cat is *alive*.

It jumps down and crawls over to Oberon, nuzzling its head into his injured arm and purring loudly.

"What the fuck," I breathe, unable to resist touching the cat for myself, checking if it's really there.

Oberon sits up shakily and lifts the cat into his arms, holding it like a baby.

"I'm a Necromancer," he says quietly, eyes lowered and scratching the cats chest.

I'm stunned, my mind reeling. *A Necromancer?* When did my romance novel become Harry Potter?

"I know it's a lot to take in," he starts, setting the cat down.

I grab his shirt collar and pull him to me, crashing my lips against his. "You are so fucking cool," I mumble against his mouth, taking a fistful of his hair and drawing him on top of me.

He pulls back a little, a confused smile on his face. "You think so?"

My heart could burst, he looks so raw, so hopeful.

"Yes, you're amazing," I gasp, pulling him down to me.

"I knew you were a little crazy," he chuckles, submitting to a searing kiss.

"How similar is a Necromancer to a vampire?" I tease, nibbling along his lower lip.

He growls, dipping his head to my neck. "Entirely different. And frankly, I'm insulted." He bites down on the tender skin behind my ear, hard enough to bruise, then rolls off me and to his feet.

I prop myself up on my elbows, breathless, freaked out, and way too aroused by this newfound information. I always believed in magic and spiritualism, but necromancy was on a whole other, way more bad-ass level. I knew he was a little bit scary, but knowing that he's quite literally *lethal*? That he's been holding my life in his hands this entire time?

I've been reduced to a terrified, insanely horny puddle on the floor.

The cat crawls into my lap, distracting me from my filthy thoughts.

"Can we keep it?" I ask, scratching under its chin.

"I always liked the idea of a shop cat. He seems the type," Oberon replies, taking a pull directly from the bottle of wine, wiping his mouth with the back of his hand.

"Can we name him Church?" I stand up, holding the purring beast to my chest.

"Church?" he quirks up a brow at me, confused.

I gasp. "Have you never read Pet Sematary?"

"Ah, no. Didn't sound appealing," he chuckles.

"Oh my god, you *have* to. You can borrow my copy!" I prattle on, overstimulated and giddy.

He strides over to me and takes my face in his hands, kissing me hard enough to take my breath away, and shut me up.

"Whatever you want, precious girl." He smiles, kissing the tip of my nose.

I sink into his steady arms, heart swirling with emotion, Church purring like a motor in between us.

Oberon

I don't know what possessed me to tell her. Whether it was the heartbreak in her eyes, the pleading of her voice, I just couldn't deny her. There's nothing I wouldn't do for her.

It was a gamble, but deep down I knew she could handle it, could handle my world. I hadn't expected *that* positive of a reaction, but I'll take it. Hopefully that won't change if she ever learns the whole truth.

What I am is cool in theory, I guess. Humans have dreamed of magic since the dawn of time, desperate to be something more than themselves. But being human is more than enough, anything beyond that is suffering in the name of power. Of control.

But I've done horrible things, traversed the depths of cruelty and malice. I've used peoples dead loved ones like puppets, manipulating them to do my bidding, provide information, sometimes just to fuck with them. I've sent hoards of the undead to haunt my enemies, drive them insane. Showed them their dead children, their dead mother, made their corpses dance and scream and suffer for a scrap of intel, for compliance.

Sure, the majority of them were a scourge on the earth. And for a long time, I believed everyone deserved to die, that we all deserved to die. Whether in the name of punishment or peace. I sent swathes of dead slaves to the homes of warlords, legions of children to tear their abusers apart.

No amount of good can undo the harm I've caused, the nightmare I became. And for better or worse, I'm still here. Will always be here, surviving, even if I shouldn't be. Even though I would have given up everything to have never woken up that night. To have rotted in the earth beside my Leda.

But no, that's not exactly true. Not anymore. Because here's Olivia, beautiful and alive, snuggled into my chest with the kitten she loved so much it was brought back to life.

There's nothing I wouldn't do for her.

"Do you have any questions?" I ask gently, pulling back to find her eyes.

"Is your wrist okay?" She sets down Church and takes my hand, inspecting the damage. "Wait, what the fuck?"

My wrist is almost completely healed, save some redness. "Regeneration is part of the deal." I shrug.

"What is this thing? Can you take it off?" she runs her finger along the metal binder hesitantly, as if it could bite her.

"It's a power suppressor. Like a shock collar on a dog. It can't come off, it's fused to my skin."

"A power suppressor? So you can do *more*?"

I smile, wolfish. "Yes, I can."

"So, why suppress it?"

"It's a lot of power for one man. Things are easier this way," I answer vaguely.

She moves away from me to grab the bottle of wine and flop onto the couch. "How did—" she gestures vaguely to my body— "This even happen? Were you born this way?"

I sit in my desk chair to give her some space. "No." I debate how much to tell her, I don't want to pile on anymore than I have to. "For most of my life I was a regular witch. I specialized in Transfiguration. But, I died, and when I came back, I was...different. Cursed."

"Who cursed you?" Her brows knit together.

"Myself, I guess. It just sort of happened. It took me a long time to sort through it all, figure out how it worked and how to control it. I was, ah, pretty unhinged for a while. I had no idea what I was doing."

"So, you can bring things back to life and regenerate..." Her eyes go wide and her mouth falls open. "You opened this place! There was no dad or grandfather, it was always you!"

Clever girl. "Yes, it was always me."

"So, you're like...shit, how old are you? I can't do math right now."

"I stopped aging at 28, in 1885."

Her mouth falls open.

"I'm 168, technically." I rub the back of my neck. I hadn't thought about the age gap potentially freaking her out.

"So, I'm not only fucking my boss, but a *much* older man. That tracks." She takes another long pull of wine, thoughtful.

I suppress a laugh. "Dirty girl."

"What else can you do?"

I mull over how to explain this in terms she'll understand. "Basically, everyone has a cord that connects to their soul. Like how the Fates cut a mortal thread of life?"

She nods, leaning forward.

"I call them tethers because they bind our souls and our lives. I can heal the connection." I interlace my fingers together. "And I can sever it." I pull my fingers apart.

"Which would kill someone?"

"Yes." I drop my hands. "It would detach their soul from their life. Depending on how much of the connection I destroy, the person's body will shut down, be petrified like a mummy, or turned to ash. A mummy, I can bring back. A pile of ash...that's pretty much final."

"Have you ever...?" She chews her bottom lip with her teeth.

"Yes. I have." I hold her gaze. I've killed many, *many* people.

"Did they deserve it?"

The question takes me aback and I think on it for a moment.

"Mostly, yes."

She stands and walks over to me, hips loose and swaying, and bends over to place her hands on my thighs.

My cock stirs to life, all my nerves hyper focused on the warm weight of her palms.

"Take me home?" she asks sweetly, batting those dark lashes.

I smile, her acceptance glowing in my chest. "Course, love."

We gather our things and scoop up the cat, agreeing that he could stay with her after hours. We pop into an all-hours supermarket to pick up bowls, toys, food, and a litter box, and finally make it back to her house around midnight.

She unlocks the door and I follow her inside, immediately swallowed up by the warmth of her energy. It feels like sinking into a hot bath, like I'm a marshmallow in a mug of hot chocolate. Cozy and decadent. Her presence is an indulgence.

After setting up Church's new things and letting him get acquainted with the space, I start to get impatient, or rather, my cock does.

Olivia's pouring some wine for us at her kitchen island and I approach from behind, undoing the belt around her waist and worshiping the curves of her body with my hands. She's a work of art, built like Venus herself.

She turns against me, draping her arms around my neck. Something flickers in her eyes, the same look she gets at work. Morbid curiosity.

"Do you want to feel it?" I ask, twirling an energetic finger around her tether. "That tip over the edge? The maw of nothingness opening just for you?"

"Yes, sir," she breathes, energy crackling under my touch.

"You want to kiss death?"

She pounces on me, pressing a scalding kiss to my mouth and stealing the air from my lungs.

"I have, countless times," she murmurs, pulling at my lower lip with her teeth.

I grab her by the thighs and throw her onto the counter, knocking over the wine she just poured. I run my tongue along her jaw and slender neck, feeling her pulse hammering just under her skin. The hickey I left earlier blooms under her ear, and I want to leave a million more. Mark every inch of her as mine.

I undo the buttons of her shirt, my shirt, to expose her perfect tits and belly, bathing them with my tongue. My teeth graze her nipples and she moans, arching into me. I give her tits the attention they deserve, sucking and nipping until she's a squirmy, moaning mess.

"Please, Oberon. I need more," she whines, breathless.

I bite down on her right tit, sucking hard. She yelps and tries to squirm away, but my hold on her hips is iron. I travel between the valley of her breasts, leaving a trail of pink and purple across her skin until I reach her pussy.

"You understand what you're asking me to do, Olivia?" I ask, looking up at her from between her legs. I've never done something like this before, never even considered it. The feel of someone's soul, the taste of their life, each one is unique, the effect is addicting. Maybe I am like a vampire, but instead of blood, it's life I crave. I've never indulged like this before, but my body is screaming for it, raging like a wolf in a cage to taste her soul.

"Yes, sir," she pants, holding my gaze and destroying the last of my resolve.

I dip my head and devour her pussy, a man starved. Her taste is addicting in and of itself, but feeling the current of her soul along with it, it's almost maddening.

Slowly, slowly, I siphon her life energy from her, taking sips even though my power demands drowning in it. Her moans swell, cries of ecstasy, then taper off as she grows weaker, further away, and closer. She starts to look pale and feel cold to the touch, tears start spilling from her eyes. Breathy whispers start falling from her lips, words I can't understand.

She's seeing beyond the veil.

Her pelvic muscles begin tensing, her pussy spasming under my tongue despite the rest of her body as lax as a sleeping angel. She is close, so close.

With a final lash of my tongue, I break the connection and stumble backwards, wiping her wetness from my face with the back of my hand. I watch her orgasm, and life, crash into her. The scream that tears out of her is music, the greatest crescendo I've ever heard. I feel unhinged, drunk on the power she gave me.

She's flush with life, energy, passion, pleasure. I can feel it pouring off of her, doing nothing to soothe the carnal desire that tasting her life awoke in me. But she needs me, so I wrangle down my feelings and try to regain some control.

I rush to hold her as she comes down, terrified that I may have hurt her, or traumatized her. She shivers in my arms, her heart racing. It takes a few moments for her to come back to herself, and once she regains some of her senses, she clings to me, trembling and breathless.

"Liv, you did so well," I soothe, brushing her sweaty hair from her face.

"More," she gasps, shaking hands turning to claws. "Again, inside me." She digs her nails into my hips and bites my collarbone, wild with desire.

The beast seizes me again.

I throw her to the ground on her hands and knees and pull her hips back towards me, undoing my pants and taking her in a single punishing thrust. Her pussy is magic, scalding hot and slick, puffy from my viscous feasting. I pound into her as she cries, desperately dragging her nails on the checkered tile for purchase.

I massage her soul with my cock, dominating her life and body. I bring her to the brink and back ruthlessly, let her taste agonizing ecstasy, blistering pleasure, before bringing her back to reality just enough to say my name.

"Oberon!" She chants it like a prayer, like I am her God.

That thought is the end of me, and I come inside her with a roar, dragging her over the edge with me one final time.

I collapse on top of her, both of us desperately gasping for air, slick with sweat.

Holy shit. What did I just do?

"Fuck, are you okay?" I fly off of her, suddenly wracked with concern as she sprawls out on the floor, boneless. I hadn't meant to take her that far. But when I brush the hair out of her face, I can see that she's grinning, tears still running in tracks down her flushed cheeks.

"Oh, baby. That's my brave girl." I beam with pride and relief, kissing away her tears and gathering her up in my arms.

A few minutes pass as she comes back to herself, violent tremors weakening to a slight shiver.

"It's bliss," she whispers, voice hoarse with emotion. "Death, I mean." She nuzzles into my neck. "I've never felt peace like that."

I press a kiss to her damp forehead and try to settle my racing heart. "Anything for you, my love."

She falls asleep almost immediately, her body and soul completely spent.

I carry her to bed and tuck her in. Church follows us in and hops up next to her, curling up in the crook of her stomach.

"Watch over her. I'll be back soon," I tell him, before kissing her goodbye.

I have some dirtier business to attend to tonight.

I lock up and catch a cab out to Folke University.

The night is quiet, not a soul on the street. Soon, a stone house comes into view. Smoke curls from the chimney, and a single light is on at the back of the house. A black BMW sits in the driveway.

I can feel his energy inside, warm and inviting, familiar and safe. My big brother. But I push through the glamour and am met with the cold and calculating truth, his tether black and glossy like a king snake. I know he can feel me, and he sends a warning like a whip to my frontal lobe.

"*Leave*," Gideon's baritone voice snarls in my head, sending pricks of fear down my spine.

I pick up another energy, thin as a spider's web, nearly swallowed whole by him. A girl, early twenties, practically drowning in lust.

Gross. I should have guessed he'd have company.

"*We need to talk*," I send back along his tether, where his wards can't keep me out. I climb up his front steps, feeling the protection spells clawing at me, everything in me screaming to turn around, but I push through and bang on his front door.

A white dress is discarded on the railing.

The door opens, and my brother is there, naked save for a barely cinched burgundy robe. He looks exactly as I remember him, dark hair shot through with gray, sculpted facial hair, ice blue eyes hard as glaciers. The only change is his bulk, he looks stronger than he used to, with even muscle tone and fuller cheeks. Less like the gaunt, hollowed-out phantom he'd been.

He looks at me in the same way, and I see a flicker in his eyes. I'm not naive enough anymore to think that it's anything resembling happiness. Much more likely distaste.

A pretty blonde pops up behind him, wearing a white button-down and nothing else. Her hair is mussed, eyes a bit wild.

"Zoe, I expect that essay on my desk in the morning. See yourself out," he says coolly, not even turning to look at her.

She obeys immediately, although I can't tell if it's because he compelled her, or she's that submissive. Just the way he likes them. She gathers her things and pushes past us, head down, and starts walking towards the dorms.

"You could at least give her a lift," I say, watching her trudge pitifully down the sidewalk.

"Wouldn't want to give her the wrong idea," he says briskly, turning and heading back inside.

I follow him and try to avoid being impressed by his eclectic but modern home.

He leads me into his living room, a dark, tidy space with a roaring fire against the far wall. Books and minimalist art decorate the walls, and an Irish wolfhound with a sugared snout sleeps soundly on the patent leather sectional.

Gideon goes to the bar cart and pours two glasses of Basil Hayden's, my favorite. I ignore the warm feeling that flickers in my chest and sit beside the dog, Dorian.

Dorian picks up his head and thumps his thick tail, nudging my hand for pets.

I remember when Gideon got him, back when wolfhounds were first brought to the country. He'd wanted a guard dog, something to, quote-un-quote, strike fear into the hearts of anyone that came near. Instead, he got Dorian, a lovable lump who'd follow anyone with a biscuit. He pretended to be disappointed, but I knew the dog was everything to him, and vice versa, even though he'd never admit it.

He hands me a glass and sinks into an armchair beside the fire, taking a sip of his own.

"What do you want, Oberon?" he says, locking eyes with me.

"Your students are disappearing," I reply, throwing back the whiskey and setting my glass heavily on the glass coffee table, deliberately avoiding the coaster.

"That sounds like an accusation, little brother."

"Just a question. Radcliffe has been sniffing around and I'm getting tired of it."

Gideon pulls out his phone and sends a quick text before tossing it onto the couch. "What makes you think I have anything to do with that imbecile?"

"Gideon," I warn. I can tell he's lying and he knows it.

"He's working the case, albeit poorly. I'm trying to have him removed as we speak," he relents, taking another pull of whiskey. "I know you think so little of me, but I do care about my students."

"Clearly," I sneer, nodding towards what appears to be an eyelash Zoe left on the coffee table.

Gideon plucks it up and tosses it into the fire. "She loved every second of it, even being sent away like a dog. I made sure of it," he smirks, patting his knee. Dorian hops up and lumbers over, sitting obediently by his master's leg. Gideon scratches behind Dorian's ears and offers him the last few drops of whiskey, which the dog eagerly laps up.

"Tell me what you know, brother."

"I know you have a pretty new assistant." He gets up to refill his glass.

"And?" I feign disinterest, despite feeling another prickle of fear. Olivia being on his radar can't be good.

"Come now," he sits back in his chair and spreads out the picture of arrogance. "If you want information, you'll have to offer some."

"She's irrelevant," I scramble for a piece of information relevant enough to keep his attention, but doesn't leave me vulnerable. "I have Jacob's body embalmed in the morgue, Radcliffe didn't order a coroner's report despite obvious signs of struggle."

Gideon rubs his chin, processing. "I thought he'd been cremated?"

I shrug.

"The disappearances are connected, I'm not sure how. Clearly, you think Radcliffe is involved, which I'm inclined to agree with," he takes another sip of whiskey, then looks at me, really looks at me, his mouth pressed into a serious line. "I also know that Keanu is in the area."

The air is squeezed from my chest. *No, not now.*

"How do you know?" I ask, rising to my feet.

"Tell me about Olivia," Gideon responds, the corner of his mouth pulling up.

Everything is a game to him, every person a pawn in his never-ending game of chess.

"There's nothing to tell," I growl.

"Liar," Gideon hums, ruffling Dorian's ears.

I storm over to him, slapping the glass out of his hand and hauling him up by the front of his robe. Anger coils like a serpent in my stomach.

"Are you working with him?" I spit in his face, nose to nose.

He flicks his wrist and sends me flying over the table and crashing to the floor.

"Of course not, you idiot," Gideon says, adjusting his robe. "He's a guest lecturer for the Kineticism department this semester. I'm not sure what his angle is, but I have no part in it."

"You expect me to believe that? You're basically the fucking Dean of the Old Arts," I snarl.

"Just Head of Psychomancy and Religion, I'm afraid." He clicks his tongue. "Believe what you want, it doesn't matter." He comes up to me and offers a hand. "I left the Arcanum behind, Oberon."

I slap his hand away and climb to my feet. His response was oddly sincere for my brother, and I found myself wanting to believe him, despite everything. But that's how it is with family, isn't it? Despite all the evidence of the darkness within them, you still cling to the light, or the hope that someday there will be light. Because if there's goodness in your brother, then there must be goodness in you.

"I have no interest in playing God, unlike Key." He drops back into his chair, rubbing his forehead.

"No, you only care about yourself." I sigh, swallowing the last of my drink.

"Makes life so much simpler."

A hot blast of rage wells up inside me. How can he be so fucking blase? I grab hold of his tether and it immediately kicks back, lashing like a viper, but I bear down and Gideon starts seizing, spit dripping from his mouth. My wrist is bright with pain, but my anger pushes it to the back of my mind.

"A simple fucking life, huh?" I shout, throwing the glass at him. "Kids are dead, you fucking bastard. So many people are dead. So many lives cut short by our hands, and for what? So you can fuck your students and get wasted every night? So I can pretend I'm not an abomination, a monster?"

Dorian cowers behind his master, letting out a high-pitched whine.

"Oberon," Gideon grits through his teeth, veins in his neck bulging. "Do it this time, you fucking coward."

With a scream, I release him, dropping to my knees, vibrating with rage.

Gideon falls out of his chair and drags himself towards me, pale as a ghost. He grabs my face in his hands, forces me to look at him.

"You're no monster, brother. And neither am I," he says, shaking me. "Don't feel bad for what you did to survive."

He releases me and we lay there on the floor together, catching our breath. After a few minutes, he reaches his arm up and the bottle of whiskey flies into his hand. He takes a swig and passes it.

"So, are you gonna tell me about your apprentice?"

I take a big swallow of liquor and hand the bottle back to him. "I'll see you around, Geo." I stand up, exhausted, and wanting nothing more than to go back to Olivia's embrace and forget for a while.

"Oberon," he calls as I place my hand on the door knob. "If shit go's south, call me."

I pull open the door and close it behind me, not looking back.

I opt to walk back to Liv's, exhaustion clouding my thoughts. I unlock her door using an old spell and drift through the dark house, collapsing into bed next to her.

She snuggles closer to me, tucking herself under my arm. I find sleep with her hair in my face and legs tangled with mine.

Act 3

Olivia

I wake up to fuzzy paws tapping my nose. Church sits regally on my pillow, impatiently waiting for me to stir. Oberon is wrapped around me, our legs tangled together and his heavy arm draped across my waist. He snores softly in my ear.

Morning sunlight streams through my black sheer curtains, and I check my phone, 8:30 a.m. Thank god it's a Saturday.

The thought kicks up a flurry of butterflies in my stomach, we've never spent the weekend together. It feels so domestic, waking up smothered in his drowsy heat, the entire day ahead of us full of nothing but opportunity.

I give Church some scratches under the chin and marvel that he's here before me, alive. That Oberon, my grouchy boss turned lover, who is apparently a *Necromancer,* used his incredible, otherworldly gift to bring back this fur ball.

I know I should be way more freaked out, but I've always believed that there was more out there. Something greater than plain old humanity. I never dreamed that I'd come across magic in my lifetime, I was content to get my fill of fantasy through books, but I'll be damned if I let a little fear stop me from having a taste of the divine.

Oberon stirs beside me, his arm tightening around my waist.

"Morning, love," he mumbles, pressing kisses into the curve of my neck.

That small touch is enough to stir desire in the pit of my belly. I scooch back slightly, pressing my ass against his thick morning wood, swirling my hips just the tiniest bit.

I feel him smile against my skin. His fingers snake down my body and between my legs, the touch agonizingly soft, and he coaxes my pussy to open for him, unfurling like dew-dampened morning glory. His expert fingers pet my clit and tease my entrance, turning me to moaning mush.

"You've been such a good girl, Liv," he whispers against the shell of my ear, voice gravelly from sleep. "You know that you're stuck with me now?" He slips two fingers inside slowly, the stretch sharp and exquisite.

His words send waves of pleasure through me, my pussy dripping for him.

His other hand slides under me and wraps around my throat. "You're mine, little one," he growls in my ear as he slowly finger fucks me. "Say it."

"I'm yours," I whine, breathless, grinding against his palm, desperate for more.

"There we go." His hand moves away from my core to grasp his cock, pumping it against my backside. He swipes the head back and forth between my lips, teasing me, letting me feel how hard he is, and how wet I am. "Say it again," his grip tightens on my throat and he notches his cock at my entrance.

"I'm yours, Oberon," I pant, fighting to stay still.

He pushes into me, inch by agonizing inch, making me feel every bit of him.

I'm almost embarrassed by the wail that falls from my mouth, pathetic and needy, but I feel him smile against my cheek.

Once he's buried to the hilt, he pauses, pulling me tighter to his chest. His energy shifts, suddenly becoming serious.

"Olivia, you were made for me. And I was made for you. I've always been yours," he murmurs, his breath warm against my skin.

My mind short circuits, the truth of the words singing through me. My chest fills with light, burning away the shadows and hollow spaces, leaving me as full and breathless as his cock.

"Oberon," my voice wobbles with tears.

He releases my neck and adjusts slightly so his face hovers over mine, still buried inside me. Delicate kisses catch my tears.

"I've waited so long for you," he breathes, resting his forehead against mine.

"Then take me," I whisper, meeting his eyes.

I feel his cock pulse, impossibly thick, and blessedly, he starts moving.

Oberon fucks me steadily, with patience and reverence, feeling every square inch of one another. I melt into him, and him into me, until we are one being made of pleasure and light. His cock is like medicine, ridding me of every negative thought or feeling, every moment of doubt and insecurity. He's *mine*.

"Harder, sir, please," I beg, feeling the beginning spasms of an oncoming orgasm.

Obediently, he doubles his pace, like a hellhound let off his leash, and fucks me hard enough to see stars.

"You take me so well, precious girl. I just can't get enough of this perfect cunt," he growls, taking a fistful of my hair and forcing me to look at him. "You love this cock, don't you?"

I can't form the words, my mouth hanging open like a bitch in heat, his brainless doll.

"I'll take that as a yes," he chuckles darkly, grabbing my face with one hand. "Open."

I open my mouth wide, sticking my tongue out for him, my orgasm looming closer and closer.

Oberon spits in my mouth then slaps his hand over my lips. "Good fucking girl." He grins, fucking me even harder, his hips stuttering as his own orgasm approaches.

I make a show of swallowing, ensuring he sees the muscles in my throat working.

He releases me and lowers his hand to my clit, pouring gasoline on the growing fire.

"Now, come for me."

In a heartbeat, my peak crashes over me, striking me like lightning. I writhe beneath him, a woman possessed,

He releases inside me with a low moan, mercilessly pounding into me, dragging out my orgasm for what must be an eternity.

We come down from our highs together, breathless and sweaty, hearts galloping away.

"Good girl, Liv," he praises, smoothing my hair out of my face and giving me a slow, cavity-inducing kiss. He climbs out of bed and grabs a towel, cleaning us both up before starting the shower. "Go on, I'll start breakfast." He smacks me playfully on the ass and pads out to the kitchen.

I quickly shower, throw on a black t-shirt dress, and find him in the kitchen.

He's a vision, leaning against the counter, clad in only tight black boxer briefs, his hair a dark tangle of waves. He's muscular, but not Baywatch muscular, his muscles are well-worn and comfortable, like a favorite pair of jeans. His strength is obvious, and mouth-watering, but doesn't command all the attention. That's reserved for his sloped nose and piercing eyes, his full lips and structured jaw.

"Here, baby." He slides me a cup of coffee in one of the clear skull mugs. It's the perfect milky color with a dash of cocoa on top.

"Thank you." I take a sip, "Do you have plans today?" I ask, a bit hesitant.

He smiles, flipping a pancake. "Do you have something in mind?"

"Well, there's a Halloween Festival tonight that I usually go to..."

"What, I'm not scary enough for you?" He raises a brow, placing a steaming plate of chocolate chip pancakes in front of me, topped with powdered sugar and strawberries.

"Nothing can scare me if I have the boogeyman as my escort." I smile, taking a bite of a strawberry.

"Do I have to wear a costume?" He scowls.

"Duh."

He rolls his eyes but his mouth curves into a smile. "Fine. But only because I'm not letting a limpdick Ghostface hit on you."

"Deal." I wink and shove a fork full of syrupy pancake into my mouth.

We get dressed and start walking to the nearest Spirit of Halloween, travel mugs in tow. Oberon's dressed in dark wash jeans and gray henley, so casual it feels almost sinful. He interlaces our fingers as we walk.

It's a sunny morning in Alder Bridge, and everyone in town is taking advantage of the nice weather. It's one of the things I love most about living here, the small-town hustle and bustle, farmer's markets and quaint breakfast joints, football games, and apple picking. Even Oberon seems to be enjoying the excitement and energy of a bright Saturday morning.

When we arrive at the store, it's crowded but not unmanageable, and the aisles are well-stocked, if a little unorganized. Oberon looks around wide-eyed.

A loud shriek makes him jump, a spider animatronic lunging at his legs and cackling.

"Will there be a lot of that?" he asks, nervously sidestepping the dancing tarantula. Several kids laugh at his very dignified reaction, so he raises a dark eyebrow and they scatter.

"Course not," I snicker, hoping to get him close to the giant clown.

I grab a few graphic tees and some Halloween decorations that will most definitely stay up year-round while we wander, hand in hand.

I spot a Grim Reaper costume from across the aisle and run over, dragging him along behind me.

"It's perfect!" I say, holding the black cloak out to him.

"A little on the nose, don't you think?" he looks it over, incredulous.

"That's what makes it perfect," I tease, throwing it over his shoulders and shoving the scythe into his hand. "And this!" I grab a skeleton half-mask and put it on him, concealing the bottom portion of his face.

He narrows his eyes and hooks the scythe behind my head, yanking me into his chest.

A heady kick of arousal wafts through me, those intense eyes turning me to jello. He looks entirely too attractive like this, like a God of Death.

"Is this what you wanted, precious girl?" he murmurs, cocking his head and bringing the skeleton grin closer to my face.

I nod, my heart pounding.

"Your wish is my command." He tugs the mask down and gives me a quick kiss before releasing me, leaving me breathless. With a smirk, he sheds the costume and drops everything but the scythe into the basket. "So, does that mean I get to pick your costume?"

Shit, I hadn't thought of that. "I guess so," I sigh, the mischievous look in his eyes making me a little nervous.

He takes off through the aisles, a man on a mission. Apparently, he has something in mind because he heads straight toward a black latex bodysuit. It has a mock neck and long sleeves, but a high-cut waist, leaving little to the imagination. He grabs fishnet tights, black angel wings, and a pair of devil horns to pair with it.

He shoves everything into my arms. "Dressing room, now."

"Yes, sir," I blush. This is way out of my comfort zone, but I'm game. I slip into the dressing room and put everything on, ignoring my sweaty palms and inner critic. I squeeze my eyes shut as I face the mirror, doubts swirling in my head.

I force myself to look and gasp. The bodysuit hugs my curves like it was painted onto my skin, leaving my plump ass and ample thighs on full display. But I feel *good*, dare I say sexy. It's a feeling I'm not used to, one I've fought for years to allow myself. It's so wonderful, so liberating, that tears threaten to spill.

"Liv?" Oberon knocks lightly on the door. "Let me in, baby."

I flip the lock and he bursts in, then freezes on the spot.

His shocked face breaks into a wicked grin, his tongue running along his teeth. "Fucking hell, Olivia."

"What do you think?" I ask, suddenly bashful again under his heated gaze.

"I think," he scoops me up and pins me against the mirror, crumpling the feathery wings, "You are the most beautiful creature to have ever walked the earth."

My cheeks flush with heat, and a nervous giggle escapes my lips. "Thank you, sir."

I've always dreamed of someone looking at me the way Oberon is, something akin to devotion mixed with unbridled hunger.

"All mine," he groans, dipping his head to nibble at my earlobe. I can feel his cock bump against my thigh.

"All yours," I reassure, raking my nails along his scalp.

"We're going home. Now." He places me back onto the floor before practically ripping the costume off of me and throwing my dress back over my head.

We check out and race home. He wastes no time pushing me up against the wall in the foyer and undoing his belt. I'm more than ready for him as he hikes up my leg and slams into me, burying himself to the hilt and knocking the breath from my lungs.

"I almost don't want you to wear that tonight," he growls, biting down hard on my collarbone. "I don't want to share you." His grip on my ass is painful, his thrusts punishing, but I can barely hear him over the pure pleasure saturating my brain.

"No sharing," I pant, clinging desperately to his broad shoulders. "All yours. You just get to show off."

An inhuman sound rumbles from his throat, and he fucks me harder, so hard that I'm afraid we might go crashing through the sheet rock.

Suddenly, he pulls out and drops me to the ground, sending me sprawling. He yanks me up to my knees by my hair, his expression dark.

"Open," he growls, fisting his thick cock.

I barely have time to drop my jaw before he slams my mouth down his length and starts fucking my face. All I can do is take him, gagging and drooling all over my chin, the taste of my own arousal on my tongue. No one has ever used me like this, taken me in the brutal way I always craved. It's like he can read my mind, my body, and knows every limit, every dark desire, implicitly. I stare up at him as tears start to spill down my cheeks, feeling deliriously infatuated with him as he uses me.

"That's a good girl." He braces his free hand on the wall as he pounds into my throat. "You want to be shown off? Show everyone how much of a slut you are?"

I try to nod, but can barely move under his white-knuckle grip on my hair.

"I can do that, baby. But just know, if one fucking person looks at you for too long." He pulls me forward and bottoms out, his balls hot against my chin, my nose buried in dark pubic hair. "I will fucking kill them."

My pussy throbs at his words. I could come just from his filthy, poetic mouth.

He throws me off of him and onto all fours, delivering a bruising slap to my ass before kneeling down behind me and burying himself inside me once again.

I'm rendered boneless, screaming and drooling all over my hardwood floors, focused only on his cock and my rapidly approaching orgasm.

"Who do you belong to?" He snarls, gripping my hair again and dragging me up to his chest.

"You, sir!" I cry out, my orgasm crashing over me and stealing all sense of reality.

"Yes, Olivia. Fuck!" He slams into me a final time before his own orgasm overtakes him. He fucks me through it, filling me with his release, my greedy pussy stealing every drop he offers.

"That's my girl," he soothes, lowering me gently to the ground and easing out of me, a flood of cum gushing out onto the floor.

"Would you really kill someone for me?" I ask, half-joking, rolling onto my back and panting for breath.

He tucks a strand of hair behind my ear. "Darling, I would burn the world to the ground for you. There's no lengths I wouldn't go to, no lows I wouldn't stoop to if it made you smile for a single second."

My heart soars at his words, and I bite my tongue to hold back the three words that bubble up in response. *I love you*. I shake the thought away, it's too soon. I couldn't possibly have fallen for him already, how stupid can I be?

"Well, no need for bloodshed. But takeout and a movie sound great right now." I smile, trying to push down the fresh wave of anxiety at my realization.

"I think I can handle that." He grins, scooping me up and setting me down in the guest bathroom before pulling out his phone for Doordash.

We laze the afternoon away, eating sushi, snuggling with Church, and watching horror movies. Around sunset, we put on our costumes and head out into the night, quickly slipping into the buzzing crowd heading downtown for the festival.

Oberon looks deliciously frightening in his Reaper costume, and I catch more than a handful of people ogling him. But his hand is firmly tangled with mine, keeping my jealous tendencies at bay.

As we approach the front entrance, nervous excitement takes hold. Purple and orange lights are strung up everywhere, with hay bails, jack-o-lanterns, cotton spiderwebs, and dancing skeletons on every corner. Costumed actors patrol the premises, stalking unsuspecting guests and jumping out from alleyways. Chatter and classic Halloween songs fill the air, punctuated by giddy screams. I smell popcorn and funnel cake, with a little ozone from the fog machines.

We secure our tickets and dive in, making a beeline for the beer cart stationed by the front entrance.

The willowy teen behind the counter stares dumbly about 6 inches south of my face, apparently oblivious to Death standing beside me.

"2 pumpkin ales, please." Oberon orders, placing his massive hands on the counter's edge and leaning in. He taps his fingers rhythmically, counting the seconds until the teen obeys.

I know possessiveness is supposed to be a red flag, but it feels entirely too good for me to care. I snuggle closer into his side.

"Here you go, mister," an older woman pushes the teen out of the way and hands us two frosty cans. "On the house," she adds, narrowing her eyes at the kid now trying to disappear behind her.

"Thank you." Oberon nods, dragging me away by the waist.

"You are so jealous," I tease, rising up on my tiptoes to peck his cheek.

"Not jealous," he corrects, holding me tighter and surveying the crowd over my head.

"Hey." I tap his skeleton nose so he looks down at me. "I'm yours. You should pity them. All they get to do is look. You get to touch." I take his hand and skate it along my body, earning an appreciative growl from him.

"Good point." He smacks my thigh, sending a thrill of excitement through me, and takes my hand again. "Shopping or scares, my love?"

"Shopping!"

We wander around the dozens of vendors, sipping our beers and pointing out trinkets we like. There's handmade Halloween decorations, paintings, and pottery. Jewelers, bakers, candlestick makers. Tapestries and beauty products and tea blends, a custom perfumery, and a vinyl record stand. But a crystal vendor catches my eye, and I drag him over.

"Hi there! Let me know if there's anything I can assist you with," the shopkeeper calls to us as we approach.

"Thank you!" I reply, heading straight for the handmade jewelry.

The pieces are gorgeous, hand-crafted with rough stones and botanical details. She has a little card indicating what each stone is and its properties. Immediately, I'm drawn to a moonstone choker, the crystal carved into a crescent moon, with tiny beads of tourmaline strung along the gold chain like stars.

"My mother collected stones," Oberon hums beside me, picking up a smokey quartz palm stone and hefting it in his hand. "She made us all wear these leather braided necklaces with woven pouches on end. She'd change out the crystal in the pouch for whatever we were doing, usually quartz, tourmaline, or fool's gold." His eyes have a far-off look, like he has to reach deep into his mind for the memories.

I squeeze his hand. "I would have liked to meet her."

He doesn't respond, just pulls down his mask and presses a long kiss on the top of my head.

I take the quartz he's holding and the choker over to the shop owner and purchase them, making sure to grab her business card as well. I hand

Oberon the quartz, and he smiles, a genuine 1000-watt smile, and pulls me into his side, nuzzling my neck.

"Thank you, baby," he whispers.

"Course." I hug him around the middle, squeezing him hard enough that he grunts. "Can you put this on me?" I ask, releasing him and holding out the choker.

He nods, chuckling, and puts the quartz in his pocket and turns me around. He lifts my hair off my neck and places the necklace, securing it gently. He must pull down his mask again because I feel the hot burn of his lips on the top of my spine, leaving an open-mouth kiss before sweeping my hair back into place.

"I think it's time for scares," he says in my ear, voice low.

We hop in line for the first haunted house, a zombie-themed asylum, which Oberon seems to find amusing. Green fog spills from the doors and drifts through the line, carrying patrons screams through the air. People tumble out of the exit, screaming and laughing, giddy with terror, covered in fake cobwebs and green silly string.

I notice actors sizing us up as we wait, most of them deciding we weren't great targets. One giant in a Jason costume prowls close by, a blood-covered machete slung over his shoulder, but a cold glare from Oberon sends him turning tail.

"It's no fun if you don't let anyone scare us," I whine, sticking out my bottom lip.

Deftly, he catches it between his thumb and forefinger. "No one gets close to you under any circumstances, actor or not," he says, eyes dark.

This man is sin on a fucking stick.

"Yes, sir." I submit, resisting the urge to suck his thumb into my mouth while a hundred people surround us.

"Good girl." He releases his hold and resumes scanning the area, one arm firmly around my waist.

After a few minutes, we get to the front of the line and are ushered into the Haunted House. It's dark and humid, with green fog clouding the floors and ceiling. The hall is littered with discarded wheelchairs and medical equipment, blood splashed onto the walls. Ceiling tiles hang precariously, with sparking cables dangling from the holes left behind.

The first zombie lunges at us from behind a door, sickly green and covered in viscera. Oberon steps back and behind me, letting me get the full impact of the scare. I scream and fall backwards into him, his chest rumbling with delighted laughter.

"You asked to be scared," he whispers, and I can almost hear the smirk from behind his mask. He untangles my grasp and nudges me forward.

It's like Oberon and the actors are in cahoots, hitting me with scare after scare as we pick our way through the scene. By the time we tumble out of the exit, tears are streaming down my face, and I'm cackling like an adrenaline junkie.

"Another one!" I squeal, dragging him towards the next house, this one themed like a dollhouse.

He follows along happily, apparently getting enormous pleasure from hearing me scream and laugh and climbing him like a tree.

A few hours pass and we make it to the last Haunted House right before closing. It's Satanic Panic themed, with pentagrams, goat heads, and occult imagery everywhere.

"Perfect for you," I tease, but he seems a bit off-put, his shoulders stiff.

"Indeed," a deep, silken voice drifts from behind us.

Oberon whirls around, yanking me behind him. I feel his muscles coil like a serpent under my hands, his heartbeat accelerating.

"It's been a long time," the voice says. It's attached to a tall man in a black cloak similar to Oberon's, only he's wearing a plague doctor mask that fully conceals his face. Black body paint covers his neck and hands, leaving him completely obscured.

The alarm bells in my head sound off. Something about this man screams *danger*.

"Keanu," Oberon says, his voice cold as ice.

Oberon

"That's no way to greet an old friend, Raith." Keanu pulls me in for a hug, but I rebuff him, my body rigid with shock. "And who is this?" he asks, looking down the mask's beak at Olivia.

Absolutely fucking not.

I search for his tether, finding it quickly. He always tried to hide it from me but could never quite manage it. I grab hold and shove him backward, hard enough to send a normal man flying. But Keanu is no ordinary man.

He takes a singular step back, unperturbed.

"You look familiar, dove," Keanu drones, cocking his head, and I know he's trying to compel her. Thank god for the tourmaline in the choker. He could override it if he really wanted to, but I doubt he'll go to the trouble.

"We were just leaving," I snap, moving to block her from his sight.

"Pity—" he starts, but I'm already dragging Olivia away. "I'll see you soon," I hear him call, his bone-chilling laughter reaching us over the throngs of people as if carried by the smoke.

"What was that about?" Olivia asks, allowing herself to be dragged behind me.

I don't respond, focused on getting us out of the crowd and back to my house so he doesn't track us to where she lives, assuming he hasn't already.

"Oberon!" She rips her hand out of my grasp and I whirl around. "What the hell was that?"

"I'll explain later, please, let me get you out of here—"

"Oberon?" a voice calls from behind me.

I grab Olivia and yank her behind me, but relax a little when I realize it isn't Keanu.

"Gideon," I huff. My brother stands a few feet from us, dressed in all black. Confetti litters his shoulders and hair, red lipstick smeared on his neck and exposed chest.

"Gideon?" Olivia echoes, peeking out from behind me.

"Ah, this must be Olivia!" Gideon grins, coming closer and extending a hand to her, Rolex glittering under the lights.

"Yes, it's a pleasure to meet you, Gideon," she steps out from behind me and takes his hand, which he brings to his lips to kiss her knuckles. If he's surprised by her appearance, he hides it well.

"The pleasure is all mine," he hums, eyes roaming her body openly.

"Gideon," I snarl in warning, and he looks up, grinning like a devil. "A word?" I drag him a few feet away and refrain from slapping him.

"Well, that's interesting, brother." He smiles, raising an eyebrow at me.

"Not now. Keanu is here."

His gray eyes go wide. "You saw him?"

"He saw *us*."

"Ah." He rubs his goatee. "That's not good."

"No, so I need to take her home."

"I wouldn't." He pulls out a black flask, takes a swig, and then offers it to me. "He's not going to like that his competition was reincarnated."

"You don't think I know that?" I take a deep swig, gin burning the back of my throat. "Make sure we aren't followed." I shove the flask into his hand and turn back to Olivia, who's waiting impatiently with her arms crossed over her chest.

"I'll explain later, baby. I'm sorry." I extend my hand to her, eyes pleading. She stares me down, gears turning. After what feels like an eternity, she places her hand in mine and squeezes. Breathing a sigh of relief, we walk in silence back to my place.

As soon as we get inside and I lock the door, she pulls away from me.

"Talk." She crosses her arms and narrows her eyes.

"That was Gideon, my older brother." I start with the obvious.

"Who I thought you didn't speak to?"

"I didn't, until the other day."

She grits her teeth. "What changed?"

"I wanted to talk to him about the disappearances. They're his students."

She processes that. "Why didn't you tell me?"

"Nothing came of it. He knows less than we do." Not a complete lie.

"Is he..." she gestures vaguely to me.

"He isn't a Necromancer, but yes, he has power." I try to keep it vague. We were trained to be the keepers of each other's secrets from the moment we're born.

"And who was the plague doctor? A Keanu Reeves wannabe?"

Fear slithers down her tether despite her half-hearted joke, cold and clammy. I want to wash it away with my tongue. I could kill him for making her feel afraid, for even looking at her.

"He's a monster. He runs a society of Dark magic, using their gifts as a means to gain power and influence." The weight of what this could mean settles over me. My personal boogeyman has come back to haunt me. Not just passing through town, but actively seeking me out. Possibly seeking *her* out.

"Are you in danger?" She moves closer to me, placing her hands on my chest. Worry swims behind her eyes and turns the edges of her mouth down.

I take a deep breath, finding my resolve. I won't let him have power over me again. I'll never submit to him again.

"No," I say firmly, cupping her face and looking into her chocolate eyes. "He can't hurt me, and absolutely nothing will ever hurt you. Not while I'm still breathing."

She nods, but I can see the fear lingering in her bunched muscles.

I kiss her forehead, guilt eating at me. "Everything's okay, love. I'm sorry that I scared you. Let me make it up to you."

I scoop her up and carry her into the bedroom. I run a hot bubble bath with rose petals and lavender salts, lighting scented candles and setting some of my own crystal collection around the tub: rose quartz, red jasper, moss agate, and howlite.

She pads into the bathroom, nude and a little bit shy, but perks up at the sight of the bath.

I gather her into my arms, realizing I'm still in my full costume. "Do you want me to stay with you?" I ask, trailing my fingers along her spine and the curve of her ass.

"I think I could use a little alone time, actually," she says softly. "Thank you for this." She kisses my cheek and steps away, trailing her fingers through the water to test the temperature.

"Of course, pretty girl." I make sure she has everything she needs before shutting off the overhead lights and closing the door.

I change into sweats and spend the next hour strengthening my wards and being pissed at myself for agreeing to this stupid power binder. Without it, I could have razed him the second I saw him.

But I'm deluding myself, I'm not sure I have it in me to kill him. I didn't then, but things are different now. I'm different now. I'm not a naive kid, cowed by my own gift. I'm not an idiot that will make the same mistake twice.

If he threatens her, he will not walk away with his life. If anyone poses a threat to her, their soul is mine. They will be damned.

I hear the tub starts to drain, so I head into the kitchen to brew her a cup of tea. It's something my mother used to do for us.

"There's little suffering that a cuppa can't ease," she used to say in her soft Scottish lilt. "Keeps the heart soft."

Olivia pads out into the living room, wearing my gray robe, just as the kettle boils and smiles at me.

"Tea?" she asks, sinking into the overstuffed recliner.

"Blood orange and cinnamon," I say, filling her mug and handing it to her.

She takes a deep inhale and snuggles deeper into the chair. "Thank you," she says softly.

I kneel down in front of her, taking her calf into my hands and massaging the muscles there. She rewards me with a happy mewl.

"Olivia, I think it would be best if you stayed with me for a few weeks, just until this blows over," I say, a bit nervous about her reaction. It's the right move for her safety, but it's also a major step forward in what, at least for her, is a brand new relationship.

She takes a sip of tea, looks studiously around the room, then down at me. "Stay in your gorgeous house, surrounded by books, wine, and more books, where my sickeningly handsome boss-slash-lover can give me massages and baths all the time?" She smirks, setting down her tea and leaning forward, our noses nearly touching. "How will I ever survive?"

I grab the back of her head and close the distance between us, capturing her lips in a passionate kiss. She tumbles off the chair and into my lap, kissing me back eagerly. I hold her close, trying to pour every ounce of love and feeling I have for her down her throat.

No one will ever take her from me again.

We spend the rest of the weekend holed up at my house after picking up a few things from her place, including Church, who was not happy to be left alone for a few hours.

By the time we waltzed into work Monday morning, I'd almost forgotten what awaited us. Victor and Tiana's funeral service.

We set up quickly and start welcoming mourners around 11:30. By noon, the Funeral Home is packed with a line of guests down the street. It took us every ounce of energy to host this thing, make everyone feel welcome, and ensure everyone had what they needed. On the bright side, Church was a huge hit. The roommate of one of the deceased told us how much they adored cats and that they would have loved to know a cat would be a guest of honor at their funeral.

There's a pretty large number of witches in attendance, both professors and students. It's both disarming and oddly comforting, being surrounded by so many like me. Our magic coalesces in the air, amplifying the energy to an almost tangible level.

Many of them leave bundles of marigolds and poppies in their caskets, tied with black ribbon and strung with small charms. Selenite, rose quartz, and carnelian are placed intentionally around their bodies. Packets of salt and herb are tucked into their clothing, and someone has lit rosemary incense by the door.

It takes me back to when someone passed in the Guild. We would spend days erecting a pyre adorned with everything we could spare to guide them into the afterlife, and ensure they wouldn't come back or be used for ill-intent.

It was a painstaking ritual, but one overflowing with love and reverence.

I always wished I had done one for Leda, for my parents. But the grief was too big a mountain to climb.

I spot Gideon at one point, mingling with the other professors, but he paid me no mind, which was fine by me.

After what feels like an eternity, we begin ushering guests back to their vehicles to begin the procession to the cemetery.

"My feet hurt," Olivia groans, sinking onto the bench by the front door after the last mourner leaves, shaking off her black heels.

"I know." I kiss the top of her head. "But, will you come with me to the cemetery?"

"Course, we're a team." She stands up and stretches. "But I'm changing into boots."

Liv changes into her usual leather boots, then we meet in the parlor to take our customary moment with the deceased, saying our final goodbyes. I ensure all the tokens and offerings are secured before wheeling them out and loading them into the hearse.

The hearse is old but comfortable, with a black interior and rich wood accents. Olivia drapes her hand on my thigh as I pull out, affection between us starting to come as easily as breathing.

I file in line behind the police procession and start rolling.

Townspeople, old and young, begin coming out onto their porches to watch, many deciding to walk among the cars and trail behind the procession.

I hear sniffles beside me and turn to see Olivia watching them in her rearview mirror, tears spilling down her cheeks. My softhearted girl. I take her hand and squeeze three times.

It's a short drive to the cemetery. I help the usher's carry each coffin to their grave while Olivia ensures all the flowers and portraits are as they should be. Once all that's done, we stand off to the side of the crowd, watching the burial ceremony.

At the end, the crowd slowly disperses and Olivia and I are left alone. She doesn't say a word, just looks at me with an intense mix of sadness and reverie. I wrap my arm around her shoulder and pull her close as we watch the sunlight reflect off the gravestones before us.

"Can we walk around for a bit?"

I'm never one to pass up a good cemetery stroll, and it's been a while since I've visited some of the folks resting here.

We walk for a while, hand in hand, and I tell her stories about the people I've met and buried here, some going as far back as the early 20th century. As we approach the cemetery's rear, a massive statue looms up, a black slice through the magenta sky. The Grim Reaper.

Olivia approaches it slowly, mystified.

I grab her by the hips and set her onto the foundation slab, facing me.

She looks up at it, awestruck.

"Remind you of anyone?" I ask, taking the opportunity of her craned head to kiss the pulse point below her jaw.

She gasps as the realization finally hits her. "It looks like you!"

"Mhmm," I hum, sucking gently on her skin. "Technically, it's my grandfather." I travel up her neck and nibble at her earlobe, earning a giggle that makes my heart soar.

"There's a fucking statue of you!" She laughs in disbelief.

"He was a very influential man." I smile, biting down on the skin beneath her jaw.

She lets out a breathy moan. "Are you going to fuck me under a statue of yourself?"

I pull back and meet her eyes. "Is that too vain?"

"It's the perfect amount." She grins, pulling me in for a scorching kiss. She unbuttons my shirt and pushes it off my shoulders before grabbing at my belt, unhooking it, and tossing it into the grass.

I'm already hard as a rock, overwhelmed with the need to taste her. I find the slit in her emerald maxi dress and part the fabric, revealing her fleshy thighs. I dive into them, licking and sucking at the satiny skin, leaving blooms of red and purple in my wake. Marking her. *Mine.*

I run my tongue along the silk gusset of her panties, a thrill of pleasure coursing through me when I realize she's already dripping. I rip the meager fabric and lick a wide stroke from her entrance to her swollen clit, gathering as much sweet honey as I can before swallowing it down.

Her hands fall into my hair, tugging at the roots, spurring me on.

It's more than vain how badly I want to make her scream my name under a 15 ft tall statue of myself. I feel like a greedy God, demanding her orgasm as an offering.

My tongue ravishes every inch of her sopping cunt, sucking every drop of pleasure she'll give me, taking it as my own. I tongue-fuck her channel, feeling her walls clench and shiver under my touch. I insert a finger, then another, curling them in an upwards motion.

"Oberon!" she cries, throwing her arms back to grab at the granite handle of the scythe, holding it for dear life.

I can feel her orgasm mounting, her walls tightening around my fingers like a vice grip. I suck her clit into my mouth, using the tip of my tongue to roll the bud along my teeth.

Her release hits her like a bomb, my name falling from her lips like a prayer. I drink down every drop, bathing her pussy with my tongue, praising her without words.

She drags me up by my hair, a feral look in her eye. "Fuck me," she begs, grabbing at the waistband of my trousers. "Please, sir."

"Tsk, tsk. Greedy girl," I chastise, sliding my soaked fingers into her mouth. She sucks on them hungrily, my starving little whore.

I pull out my cock, red and throbbing with anticipation, precum beading at the tip. I line it up with her entrance, collecting her wetness as I tease her.

"This what you want?"

She nods emphatically, her mouth full. Her cheeks are flushed and her eyes are sparkling, too beautiful for words. I withdraw my fingers and pull her in for a kiss, tasting her arousal on her tongue, the combined flavor of our mouths.

I ease into her while our tongues dance, her tightness simultaneously resisting me and drawing me deeper.

"Fuck, baby," I groan into her mouth, pleasure overwhelming me. "I should tear this statue down and erect one of you in its place. You are divine," I pant as I drag my cock slowly in and out of her tight cunt.

She whimpers and grasps my shoulders, nails biting into my skin, telling me she's ready to get absolutely *wrecked*.

And I'm nothing if not accommodating.

I fuck her viciously, barely giving her space to breathe between punishing thrusts, rutting into her like an animal. She takes me so well, enjoying everything I'm giving her and begging for more. Soon, a second orgasm washes over her, the walls of her pussy gripping me mercilessly as she comes with a high-pitched cry.

My orgasm starts to build, coming on fast and hard. I pull out, grab her by the throat and drag her to the ground before me, bare knees on the sharp stones. I brace myself on the statue as she swallows down my cock, bobbing her head.

I grab a fistful of her hair and fuck her face, the satiny wetness of her mouth decadent, euphoric. I only last a few moments before my orgasm crests and slams into me, spilling down her hot throat.

She sucks me dry, making my legs shake, and licks her lips when I pull out with a wet pop, not missing a drop.

I scoop her up and rain kisses on her eyes, cheeks, nose, and lips, whispering praise between each one.

She's so fucking perfect, my heart feels like it could explode.

I love you.

The words rise suddenly, nearly falling from my lips. But this isn't the right time, there's still too many secrets between us. Too much she doesn't know. I won't force her to commit like that without her understanding the full picture of what I am, what we are. So I tell her with my actions instead, kissing her deeply.

The sun has dipped low beneath the trees, the cemetery will close soon. We straighten ourselves and hurry out, giggling like a pair of teenagers.

Olivia

I'm not really sure how we got here, truthfully. It feels like a whirlwind. But here Oberon is, my Necromancer, sleeping like an angel, completely unburdened.

It's hard to feel anything but gratitude and awe. It's amazing how much can change in a few short weeks, how your life can be completely unrecognizable from one month to the next. And thank god that this time, it's for a good reason.

But I wish I could shake this nagging feeling that's chittering at the back of my brain. There's something he's not telling me, details he's leaving out. I thought the undead wizard confession would finally alleviate the feeling, but it's only gotten worse, nibbling away at my joy.

The reality is I'm falling in love with him, maybe already have, and I don't know him, not really. The other night at the Halloween Festival was more than enough to prove that. He gave me just enough information to assuage me but was obviously withholding something.

I probably shouldn't trust him, but I do. I can't explain it. Even though I don't know his story, I know his soul, the essence of who he is. I know him down to the marrow, so what's a little ancient history?

My alarm blares to life, jarring me from my thoughts. Oberon groans and rolls over towards me, dumping the sleeping cat onto the bed.

"Five more minutes," he mumbles, burying his head under the covers.

I kiss his forehead and slip out of bed. I brew a pot of coffee, feed the cat, and start getting ready for the day. I put on a shin-length black dress and an oversized checkerboard cardigan. I leave my hair down, giving my natural curls a break from heat and hair ties.

Oberon rolls out of bed about 20 minutes later, throws his hair into a messy bun, and splashes cold water on his face. He puts on a white button-down and black slacks.

While I'm doing my makeup, he comes up behind me, wrapping his arms around my waist and resting his chin on my shoulder.

"You're so beautiful," he murmurs, watching as I brush mascara onto my lashes. He spots the moonstone choker beside the sink and grabs it, delicately looping it around my throat and clasping it beneath my hair.

The tiniest touch is enough to flood my chest with warmth, softening me. He can be so gentle, it makes the moments when he isn't that much more shocking, and arousing. Knowing that the hands delicate enough to embalm are the same hands strong enough to leave bruises on my hips and bring a man to his knees...*woof*.

We make our coffees to go and head out, Oberon carrying Church on his shoulder. We toil the morning away, embalming a new intake and organizing paperwork. At 1:00 p.m., Oberon takes a meeting with some walk-in clients, so I stay back in the morgue, deciding to read through some of his anatomy textbooks, leaving the door ajar so I can hear when they leave.

There's a sharp knock on the door.

I jump and look up from the desk, anxiety coiling in my stomach at the sight of the man before me.

"Hello, Olivia." Detective Radcliffe leers, stepping inside and shutting the door behind him.

"Detective Radcliffe!" I slap on a smile. "What brings you in today?"

"Just checking in on some things. Chief wanted a copy of the paperwork from yesterday's service." He walks to the edge of the desk, placing his hands on its surface and leaning towards me.

"Of course!" I hop up and run over to the other side of the room, where the filing cabinet rests, and start to unlock the drawer.

Suddenly, I'm smashed into the cold steel, Radcliffe's weight pressing into my back, keeping me pinned. His sour breath fans into my face, making me gag, his rancid body odor making my eyes water.

Ice-cold terror washes over me.

He grabs the back of my head and cracks my face into the top of the cabinet. My teeth slice into my lip with the force of it, and my mind goes fuzzy.

He holds my head down as his other hand fumbles with my skirt, moist fingers slithering up the back of my legs.

I try to kick him off, scream, do *something*, but he's too large, his strength overpowering. And with the door closed, no one would hear me anyway.

It occurs to me that I might die here, that Oberon will find my body in the morgue with the rest, cold and stiff.

Would he bring me back?

He didn't bring his wife back.

My heart lurches.

Why didn't he bring his wife back?

Radcliffe's fingers find my underwear and he balls it up in his fist before tearing it off of me.

Another jolt of terror rocks through me, making my stomach flip.

CLANG!

Radcliffe's weight is suddenly thrown off of me, the reverberating tenor of bashed metal making my teeth rattle.

Strong arms gather me up, cradling my head against their shoulder.

"Liv, hey, are you alright? Olivia?" Oberon's voice floats to me out of the fog, and my nostrils fill with his warm, woody scent and the metallic tang of blood.

I can taste it on my tongue now, feel it dripping down my forehead. I blink to clear my eyes, Oberon's anguished face coming into focus. We're on the ground and he's holding me in his lap, rocking me gently.

"Oberon?" I barely manage, a blistering headache stealing my breath.

"I'm here, baby. I'm so sorry." He uses his shirt sleeve to dab away the blood on my face, his eyes flickering between agony and murder. "I'm so sorry."

"I'm okay," I mumble weakly, reality starting to settle back in.

Radcliffe attacked me. Tried to rape me. Is lying unconscious a few feet away, blood dripping down his face, my underwear trapped in his fist.

Oberon continues to fuss over me, but my skin is crawling, my stomach churning. I push myself off of him, crawling into the corner and pulling my knees up to my chest.

"Just, please." I hold my hand out to him, keeping him at bay, feeling tears start to run down my cheeks.

He nods and gets up, grabbing the first aid kit and sliding it across the floor to me.

I pull out some gauze and hold it to where I assume the wound on my head is, trying not to vomit.

Oberon turns to Radcliffe, anger rolling off him in torrents, the beautiful blue and whites of his eyes swallowed by black ink. It's bleeding out into his eyelids and cheeks, discoloring his veins. Smoke rises from the binder on his wrist, the metal so white it's nearly blue.

My nerves are too shot to react, my brain barely registering what's happening.

Radcliffe stirs, turns his head a fraction, then Oberon is on him. He delivers blow after blow to Radcliffe's face, the sickening crunch of bone echoing through the otherwise silent morgue.

Oberon hauls the larger man up by his shirt collar, throwing him onto the embalming table.

"Wait, please," Radcliffe babbles, his words garbled, choking on his own blood.

Oberon says nothing, just grabs the police badge out of Radcliffe's breast pocket. He holds it above Radcliffe's face, then squeezes his fist. Slowly, then all at once, the badge disintegrates into ash, covering the pig's face and mouth in fine, gray powder.

Radcliffe coughs and sputters, dust clogging his eyes and nose. Oberon slaps the hand full of ash over Radcliffe's gaping mouth, forcing it down his throat and trapping it there. Radcliffe kicks and grunts, trying to throw Oberon off, but he's unmovable, solid as a mountain.

I can do nothing but watch.

"Shut up," Oberon hisses, leaning down to look him in the eye. "Which hand did you touch her with?"

Radcliffe shakes his head, moaning, tears carving tracks through the ash.

"His right hand," I speak up, surprised by how raw my voice sounds.

Oberon glances back at me, pride flashing in those demon eyes. He releases Radcliffe's mouth and grabs his right wrist, dragging him off the table and onto the floor. He drags him several feet, leaving a trail of gore.

I don't realize what he's doing until he flips some buttons on the incinerator and opens the latch.

Radcliffe's eyes go wide with terror. "No, please!" he sobs, desperately trying to crawl away. But Oberon just drags him closer.

I can feel the heat of it from here, 1400 degrees blasting into the frigid room. It's enough to make me wince, the heat stinging my eyes. But I don't speak up to stop him. I *want* this, I realize, want him to suffer for what he did.

Oberon lurches forward, shoving both of their hands into the flames.

All three of us scream, Radcliffe and I in terror, Oberon with glee.

He rips their hands out and throws Radcliffe to the ground, the detective's hand a melted monstrosity of flesh and bone, charred flesh dropping to the floor. Oberon's hand, however, knits itself back together in moments, not a trace left behind.

Oberon seals the incinerator, then grabs Radcliffe up by the hair, muttering something under his breath. It's a language I can't make out, but their power sends a ripple of energy through the room.

"I've bound your life to this secret," Oberon growls. "Utter one word, and you're mine. I will end you and revive you, just to torture you again. Your existence will be a never ending cycle of pain. There will not be a single moment of peace in your life or death." He throws Radcliffe aside, who's barely holding on to consciousness, his body going into shock.

Oberon glances up at me, the darkness receding from his irises, leaving that shocking blue in its wake. "She's mine, in this life and the next."

I find myself nodding, mesmerized by the display of raw power I just witnessed. By him.

Radcliffe finally loses consciousness, his body going slack as It succumbs to shock.

Oberon grabs his legs and hauls him out to the loading bay, throwing him into the alley and locking the door.

He returns and kneels a few feet away from me, like he's approaching a wounded animal.

"Can I take care of those?" he asks softly, gesturing to my bleeding face.

I nod, trying to push myself to my feet.

He's by my side in a flash, scooping me up gingerly and setting me on the counter, the same one that started all this between us what feels like an eternity ago. He rummages through the cabinets for disinfectant and bandages, then removes the gauze from my forehead to assess the damage.

I don't feel the pain anymore, my nerves deadened by shock and disbelief.

"It's not bad, baby. No stitches required," he whispers, reassuring himself as much as me. He uses dabs of antiseptic on it, cleanses residual blood, and then ensures it's closed with a few wound strips. I can feel his hands shaking, like the strain of lifting them is almost too much. His face looks shallow, almost sick.

"You can't heal it with your powers?"

He meets my eyes, the corner of his mouth turned down. "I wasn't sure if you'd want me to after..." The tremor in his voice breaks my heart. Does he really think I'm afraid of him?

"Do it, please," I whisper, touching his bound wrist. "If you can."

He nods and removes the wound strips, then ghosts his fingers over my forehead. I feel a momentary pinch and a soothing warmth, then nothing as he drops his hand away. He tilts my chin up with his knuckle and brushes his thumb along my lower lip, the same sensations rising and fading away after a second, but his hand lingers.

"I'm so sorry."

I can see tears gathering on his lower lashes.

It's probably a bad time to ask this, to dredge up the past, but I can't seem to focus on the present. The pain is too great.

"Why didn't you bring back Leda?"

He drops his chin to his chest, exhaling like he was punched in the gut. "I couldn't find her," he whispers, tears dripping from his eyes onto my lap.

I start to cry, again, my heart shattering for him. I can't imagine the torment, knowing he has the power to bring her back but being unable to. It's unimaginable torture.

"How long ago did she...?"

"138 years, 1 month, and 6 days. The same day I died." He staggers and falls to his knees, trembling and cold to the touch.

I grab his chin, force him to look at me. The heartbreak in his eyes almost breaks my resolve, but I have to know.

"What happened?"

He slides all the way to the floor, resting his back against the legs of the embalming table. I climb down and sit across from him, waiting.

"It was fall, it had been a normal day on the farm," he begins, voice wobbly. "We had gone to bed, but I couldn't sleep, so we..." he trails off. "Our dog started barking, and then the rest of the animals joined. I checked it out, but there was nothing. Or, I thought there was nothing. I turned to get back in bed." His hand absently trails along his sternum, the same place as that silvery scar. "I was stabbed. The last thing I heard was her screaming." His voice clogs in his throat. "By the time I came back, she was gone."

My mind is reeling. It's the exact same story as my dream, like he pulled it straight from my subconscious. As he describes it, the images come rushing back to me, clear as if they'd happened yesterday.

I turn over and retch, the feelings and memories rushing back with a new intensity, overwhelming me. The agony, the terror, the cold shower of soil over my face, the itch of bugs crawling over my skin.

"Olivia, I'm sorry I didn't say anything sooner," he whispers, crawling over to me and brushing the hair off my cheek.

I look up at him, tears streaming down both our faces.

"I don't understand."

He wipes the tears from my cheeks with his thumbs. "I don't either, but I know it's true."

"I'm..."

"You are Olivia," he says firmly. "But in your past life..."

"I was Leda," I breathe, understanding settling over me like a blanket. All the unknowns and unexplainable things in my life, between us, clicking into place. "Your wife." I meet his eyes.

He nods, staring at me like I'm the most inexplicable thing he's ever seen. He strokes my cheek with his knuckles, tucks my hair behind my ears. Ghosting the pads of his fingers over my eyebrows, lashes, the bridge of my nose, my lips, he murmurs, "I finally found you."

I fall into his arms, sobbing.

He holds me close, rocking me back and forth. We found each other after over a century of being separated. He waited for me all those years.

I was always his, and he was always mine.

And it would take an act of divine intervention to separate us now.

Oberon takes me back to his house, where I sleep for the next 16 hours. I feel like a shell of myself, my insides scraped clean. It's strange to have a part of you die and another part reborn.

I walked into work Olivia and left...someone else. Not quite Olivia, not quite Leda.

My head hurts.

Oberon's been following my lead: giving me space, keeping me fed and watered, letting me cry and scream. He's stayed nearby, never going further than the store down the block. The Funeral Home's been closed for days. I'm not sure how he's managed that.

I can't think about it too hard, or things get hazy.

I can't think about much at all.

A week has passed, and I'm starting to feel solid again, like a person. I can feel the afternoon sunlight slanting across the bed, warm against my skin. I sit up, stiff and achy, and stretch, relishing in the pop of joints and pull of muscles.

The pain inside feels more like the scratch of a scab than the burn of a blade, and that's enough to get me out of bed.

I pad into the bathroom and turn on the shower, jumping in before the water heats up. The cold is deliciously shocking, like a power washer to the grime left by days of rotting in bed. I lather up head to toe with every soap I can find, scrubbing away at my scalp and skin. As I rinse away the suds, tears start to fall, but this time, they're different. They're tears of release, of processing, rather than despair. The pathways of healing have begun to line up. I know the journey will be long, but this shower is the first step, and for that I'm grateful.

I hear the door open slightly as Oberon peaks his head in. I meet his eyes through the steam covered glass, full of hope. I hold out my arms in invitation.

He climbs in, not even bothering to remove his sweatpants, and gathers me up, crushing me to his chest. I sag into him, melting at the feel of his skin, the thud of his heart. It feels so right, so safe.

"Thank you," I whisper.

"Don't thank me, Liv." He kisses the top of my head and tilts my chin up, searching my eyes. "There's nothing I wouldn't do for you."

Standing on my tiptoes, I kiss him, soft and slow. He kisses me back, sighing against my lips, the muscles in his shoulders unwinding.

"I love you," I mumble against his mouth, running my fingers through the wet strands at the nape of his neck. It feels silly to hold the words in now, after everything.

"I love you endlessly," he breathes, capturing my lips again in a slow kiss. His tongue dabs at my bottom lip, tasting me. I let him in, sliding my tongue along his, lapping up the honeyed taste of his affection.

His hands travel down my sides and slide around my hips, scooping me up in his arms and pressing me against the cool wall.

Wetness starts to pool between my legs as his tongue laps at the streams of water running down my throat, moving lower to gently suck a pearled nipple into his mouth. I tug him closer, needing to feel him, needing his touch.

"Oberon, please," I gasp, feeling his hard cock scrape against my unfurling lips.

"You sure?" he asks, pulling back to look in my eyes. "I don't want to rush you." He cups my cheek and brushes his calloused thumb along my flushed skin.

"I need to feel you," I whisper, pleading. "To know you're here with me."

"Always, little one. I'm not going anywhere." He leans in for a blistering kiss, notching himself at my entrance. Slowly, he lowers me down onto him, splitting me open, leaving no room for fear or doubt. Only love.

He starts to move me up and down his impressive length, his hold on my hips tender but strong. My head falls back, the stretch intense after a week. But it quickly morphs into decadent pleasure, his cock sliding effortlessly in and out of my slick walls.

Our breathy moans echo against the shower walls, floating up with the steam. We stay like that for a long time, feeling the slide of each other's wet skin, relishing in the fullness of our connection.

"I love you, baby," he whispers in my ear, placing sloppy kisses along the slope of my shoulder as he picks up the pace, fucking me against the wall. "I love you so much."

"I love you," I gasp, my orgasm rapidly approaching. "I'm going to come," I cry, digging my nails into his shoulders, my muscles coiling with delicious tension.

"I feel it, baby. Come on, come for me. Let it go," he pants, sinking all the way to the hilt and grinding his pelvis into mine, hitting every needy inch.

My peak crashes over me, shattering me apart, ecstasy blasting away all the darkness for just a moment, letting me float in blissful oblivion. Oberon slowly fucks me through it, praise pouring from his lips.

"That's my good girl, Olivia. I love you so much," he coos, holding me tight as I come down, shivering with aftershocks.

I try to hold them back, but tears overwhelm me, emotion crashing down as the bliss from my orgasm fades away.

"Shhh, love. It's okay. I'm right here." He eases out of me and lowers me to the ground, turning off the water. He grabs a towel and bundles me up, carrying me back into the bedroom.

'No, no." I stop him, placing a hand on his chest and sniffing back tears. "I don't want to get back in bed."

"How about something to eat?" He sets my feet gently on the ground, wiping the tears from my cheeks.

I nod, pulling the towel tighter around myself.

"Okay, get comfy in the living room and I'll throw something together." He kisses my forehead and backs out of the room, leaving the door ajar behind him.

I take a steadying breath and fish some clothes out of the dresser, an oversized tee and bike shorts, and head out to the living room. Church makes some space for me on the couch and I snuggle in, putting on a comfort film, Practical Magic.

Halloween is only a week away.

Oberon

Slowly but surely, Olivia is coming back to herself. She was up and about on Friday, went with me to the store on Saturday, and now insists we go into work.

I'm reluctant to let her throw herself back into work and distractions, but she's as well versed in the psychology of grief and trauma as I am, if not more so; she can make the decision for herself. I'm beyond proud of the steps she's taken, my warrior.

She slips into a comfortable swing dress and one of my black cardigans, I opt for a gray sweater and slacks.

Before heading out the door, I pull her into my chest and kiss the top of her head. "Say the word and we'll come straight home, okay? You are my number one priority," I say into her hair, squeezing her tight.

"I"m okay, Oberon, I promise." She squeezes me back and looks up at me, resting her chin on my sternum. "I just want to start easing back into routine. It'll be good for me."

"Let me fuss over you," I pout, nuzzling her nose.

"You can buy breakfast." She smiles and pecks my lips.

"Deal." I sneak another kiss and release her, opening the front door.

We walk hand in hand to her favorite bakery to get a dozen donuts, then open up the Funeral Home. She settles into the couch, tucks into an apple cider donut, and I round the desk to check my email.

I'm greeted by a brilliant red pomegranate sitting on the coaster I usually set my coffee. A note is tied to the stem.

"What the fuck?" I mutter, reaching out to grab the fruit. As soon as my fingers brush against the rind, the pomegranate starts to wither, the color bleeding away and skin shriveling, rotting in the span of a few heartbeats. I jerk my hand back, heart racing.

"Oberon, what is it?" Liv asks, looking up at me, brows knitted together.

I grit my teeth and grab the note.

Tread Lightly, K. Kennedy

Fuck.

"Oberon?" She gets up to come over to me.

"Nothing, baby. Just forgot I left this pomegranate here." I shove the note into my pocket. She rounds the desk and scrunches her nose.

"Gross."

"Mhmm." I rub the back of my neck, mind racing. Somehow, I've pissed him off. But the fact that he issued a warning at all might be a good sign, if he was truly threatened, he'd have probably done away with me by now.

But 'Tread lightly'? I wrack my brain for what he could be talking about, and with a sickening twist, it hits me.

He has to be referring to Radcliffe and, therefore, the missing and murdered kids. It was all right there in front of me, I just didn't want to see it. Didn't want it to be true.

Keanu is reclaiming his hold on Alder Bridge and the magic community, stepping out from the shadows. And I've stepped directly into his path, with Olivia in tow.

I sink into my desk chair and drop my head in my hands. The thought of telling her, putting this on her after everything she's already carrying, makes me sick to my stomach. But if I want to keep her safe, and maintain her trust, I have to be honest.

I pull the note out of my pocket.

"Liv?"

"Yeah?" She looks up, some chocolate icing on her lip.

I get up and sit next to her on the couch, handing her the note. "I didn't leave a pomegranate."

She takes the note and unfolds it, reading it quickly. "Keanu did," she says bluntly, turning to look at me.

I nod. "He has something to do with the missing students, Radcliffe must have been his informant."

She takes my hand, squeezes it. "Do you want to back off?"

I look down at our joined hands and rub my thumb across her knuckles. I can't put her in danger, but I can't let Keanu continue to get away with murder. And if he had Radcliffe in his pocket, there's bound to be others. There's no telling how far up this could go. Hell, the governor could be in on it, offering up Senators kids for a taste of the Arcanum's power. The glory.

At one point in my life, there was nothing I wouldn't do for them, for Keanu. I gave him everything when all I had to offer was myself.

"He's been unrivaled for a century," I grit my teeth, muscles in my jaw flexing. "He's threatening me because he knows I'm his only equal."

I assumed he left a note because he wasn't threatened, but the opposite is true. He's *very* threatened. By me. He didn't come after me because he's afraid. His appearance at the festival was a warning, a mind game. He thinks by playing cavalier I won't dig deeper, I won't take him seriously. But I learned that lesson a long time ago.

With Keanu, it's always deadly serious.

Liv runs her finger along the cool metal around my wrist. "Does he know about this?"

I shake my head. "No, because if he did, he wouldn't be issuing warnings."

"Then we have an advantage."

The way she says it, so calm, so collected, with so much faith in me, it turns me inside out.

I lean back onto the arm of the couch, dragging her with me so she's laying across my chest, nose to nose. I slide my fingers through her hair and cup the back of her head, connecting our lips in a sweet kiss. She smiles, pulling my bottom lip between her teeth.

"Fuck, Liv. I love you," I moan, tightening my grip and flipping her underneath me, devouring her mouth.

The front door chimes and voices carry down the hall.

"Shit," I hiss, jumping up and adjusting my pulsing cock. I point at her, "Don't move. I'm not done with you."

An elderly couple waits in the foyer. I greet them with a smile and go through the routine pleasantries. They apologize for not having an appointment, but hoped I had some time to discuss their burial plans and commission headstones.

Despite my aching cock, I agree and lead them back to my office. I open the door and expect to see Olivia where I left her, but she's vanished. I walk over to my desk and gesture for them to sit in the chairs across from it, and take my seat after them.

Something brushes against my leg, making me jump. I look down and am greeted by two chocolate brown eyes, sparkling with mischief.

Godsdamn.

"So, Mr. and Mrs. Brennan, have you already thought through your wishes for burial, or would you like me to outline some options?"

Olivia's hands creep up my thighs as they answer, and it takes all of my focus to listen to their words and jot down some notes. She pops the button on my trousers and slowly tugs down the zipper, her hair tickling the exposed skin from pushing up my sweater. I don't dare look, but I can tell she's unzipping me with her teeth.

Blood rushes back into my cock, twitching painfully, desperate to be released from the confines of my boxers.

I try to focus on the Brennan's, but it seems they've thought everything through, and feel the need to walk me through every painstaking detail of not only their inevitable deaths, but their entire lives.

Olivia's hot tongue glides along the outline of my cock through my boxers, that torturous, wicked little thing. She laps at the wet spot by the head, tasting the precum she's already earned. Her fingers tickle along the waistband and she starts dragging it down slowly, inch by inch, until my cock forces itself free, slapping against my stomach.

"We have a few mason's we use for headstone design," I answer, about 5 seconds after they asked the question and turn my monitor to show them examples. "It's a touch screen if you want to scroll," I add, swallowing the moan that rises when she licks a stripe on the underside of my cock from balls to tip.

She takes me into her mouth, lowering her head at an agonizing pace, tongue swirling around the velvet skin.

I fight not to buck my hips or shove her down, she needs to take this at her own pace. But *fucking hell*, it's torture.

"I like this one." Mrs. Brennan pipes up, pointing to an intricate rose design with a Catholic rosary.

"That's a great choice." I smile, "If you're ready, we can finalize your information and I can send off the commission. They usually take a few months to complete—"

My cock-head hits the back of her throat, the muscles squeezing me mercilessly as she hollows her cheeks. She starts to bob her head up and down, and I see stars, my grip on reality loosening as she expertly sucks my cock.

I grab her hair then, holding her still at the tip of my cock.

"You can fill this out," I pull up the official form and pass them the keyboard.

"Ben, you're a doll," Mrs. Brennan coos, accepting the keyboard. "You've made this morbid business such a breeze."

"It's my pleasure, ma'am." I flash my most unassuming smile.

Olivia starts suckling the head, massaging the underside of it with the tip of her tongue.

I can't hold back the growl that rumbles up from my chest and I try to cover it with a cough, but that forces me to let go of her head, dropping her all the way back down onto my cock. I clench my hands into fists, gritting my teeth as my balls start to tighten.

Under normal circumstances, I would never compel someone, but she drives me fucking mad. I grab hold of the Brennan's tethers and tap into the little bit of compulsion magic Gideon taught me when we were kids.

"I'll finish the paperwork, why don't you two head along and get some brunch?" I say, as kindly as I can manage while throwing all the energetic weight I can behind the command.

Thankfully, that glassy film slides over their eyes and they nod, immediately getting up and taking their exit.

As soon as they leave my office, I grab Olivia by the throat and drag her up, throwing her on top of my desk.

"Wicked girl," I growl, leaning over her.

She bats her lashes and licks her lips, innocent as a doe.

I drag her by the ankle to the edge of the desk and step between her legs, which fall open instantly to accommodate me. I push up her dress and tear off her soaked panties, showing them to her. "Is this what you wanted?" I fist my cock, slapping it against her wet, needy cunt.

Her head bobbles like a doll. "Yes, sir."

I ease into her, hissing at the delicious burn of her scalding core, watching her face slacken and a brilliant smile break free.

My gorgeous girl.

I pull most of the way out, then slam into her, over and over again until she's writhing like a demon beneath me, screaming my name. Pleasure overwhelms me, the hungry pulse of her walls blocking out the rest of the world. There is nothing but her, and her perfecting fucking pussy that was made just for me.

I find her clit with my thumb and abuse it, hurtling towards my own climax. But I'll be damned if she doesn't come first.

I'm about to break when I feel that gorgeous shiver in her walls, her orgasm within reach.

"Come on, baby. Come all over my cock like a good girl. I know how bad you want to," I lean down and whisper in her ear, almost immediately being rewarded by her bone-shattering release. The grip of her orgasm finishes me off and I pump her full of my release, biting down on her soft shoulder as I rock against her.

I collapse on top of her, both of us panting for breath.

She licks a stream of sweat from my temple. "Thank you, sir." She grins at me, devilish.

I smack her thigh and lift off of her, grabbing some tissues to clean us up. "You'll be punished for that later."

She feigns horror. "No, please. Spare me!"

I smack her thigh again and yank her up by the throat, nose to nose. "You'll take what I give you and you'll like it."

She pecks my lips sweetly, smiling. "Yes, sir."

I pat her cheek and move away, zipping up my pants and grabbing a donut. "Let's go." I beckon her with a finger and head out the door.

We spend the rest of the day cooped up in the morgue, going over every detail of the missing and murdered kids, looking for anything concrete to confirm our suspicions, but come up empty handed.

Keanu's arrogant, but he isn't stupid.

He wants these kids for something, but are they just sacrifices, play things for the rich and powerful? Or do they offer something more? What's their value to him?

"Oberon!" Olivia waves me over to the desk, turning up the volume on her laptop. A news report fills the screen.

"Two of the missing Folke students were found this afternoon at Edgewood Park, unharmed. They deny any foul play and insist that they were just 'getting away' for a while and are grateful for the community's efforts, but assure that nothing was amiss."

I pause the video, taking a closer look at the kids. They look perfectly fine, not a hair on their heads mussed. But something catches my eye, glittering on their hands. I look down at my own hand, at the onyx signet ring I never take off. They have identical ones on their ring fingers.

It was a marker of the Arcanum, black onyx, a stone of great historical significance, with roots in nearly every culture across the globe, used in equal parts for war and art. I still wear mine as a reminder of the things I've done, the darkness I'm capable of.

It seems that these students have been inducted. Is that why Jacob and the couple are dead? Did they refuse to join?

But these are just college kids, smart ones with gifts from the Source, sure, but they're just kids. With no powerful lineages or money. Although, maybe that's exactly why. The country's greatest minds, lonely and isolated, detached from the real world in a cesspool of greed and power like Folke. Young enough to crave familial bonds, scrappy enough to survive on their own. The whole world at their feet.

"They joined him," she says, zooming in on the rings. "That's why they're still alive."

I nod, discreetly slipping my own ring off my finger, but of course, she catches me.

"You were a part of it, weren't you?" There's no judgment in her voice, only concern.

"A long time ago." I roll the ring between my fingers.

She gently takes it from me and drops it into one of the desk drawers, closing it firmly. "Then it's in the past. It doesn't have any control over you." She takes my hands. "You are the one with the power, Oberon."

I bring her hands to my lips, kissing her knuckles. "Then why do you make me so weak?"

"Because you're not as scary as you look," she teases, taking her hands back to shut off the laptop. "Can we stop at my place? I want to grab a few things."

"Sure, I'll close up here, you go find the cat." I smack her ass when she walks by, earning a surprised squeak from her, then I close down the morgue.

It's freezing on the walk to her place, a cold blast pushing in from Canada. The inside of her house isn't much better considering it's been unoccupied for nearly two weeks. I go check the thermostat and light the fireplace as she goes to make some tea in the kitchen.

A scream rips across the house, making the hair on my arms stand up.

"Olivia?" I shout, running towards the scream.

She crashes into my chest as she barrels out of the kitchen, shaking and crying.

"The fridge, there's, oh my god," she stammers through tears, clinging to me.

I push her behind me and creep into the kitchen, seeing the refrigerator door flung wide, spilling eerie yellow light across the room, and a shattered mug on the floor. I approach cautiously, and what I find sends a chill down my spine.

A severed deer head sits in a pool of its own blood on the middle shelf, a light brown doe, with its eyes carved out in jagged holes and replaced with electric tealights. A gruesome omen. Horrific enough that there's only one person I know who'd come up with something this twisted.

"We have to go," I say, shutting the door. "Get what you need, quickly."

She blinks at me in shock, eyes red.

"Olivia, I will take care of this. We need to get back to my house, you'll be safe there. *Go.*" I push her towards her room and she finally starts to move, dashing inside.

He's fucking with us, fucking with her. Baiting me. We used to love these cat and mouse games, the primal hunt between two predators. But I'm not playing anymore, not with her.

I take the deer head and dissolve it to ash in the trash can, gritting my teeth at the searing burn of my wrist. It takes nearly a whole roll of paper towels to mop up the blood, and I toss them into the fireplace to dispose of them. She comes out of her room with an overstuffed duffel bag and we head out, practically running the five blocks to my house. I can finally breathe when she steps over the threshold and into the safety of my wards.

"What the fuck was that?" she asks, dropping her bag in the hall.

"He's toying with us. Trying to scare you," I answer, locking the door and checking them twice.

"Why? What the fuck did I do to him?" She tugs at the roots of her hair.

"It's me." I put my hands on her shoulders. "He wants me."

She raises an eyebrow. "He wants you to join him?"

I nod, "He never forgave me for leaving. And he doesn't like to share." I can see the gears turning in her head, but I don't elaborate. It's irrelevant.

"So is he mad because we're onto him, or because you're with me?"

"A little column A, little column B. It's a double-whammy of disloyalty in his mind," I shrug, trying not to worry her. But I'm worried. To Keanu, disloyalty is the epitome of evil. He could stand me leaving, so long as I didn't betray him. And if that's his angle, we're in much more danger than I thought.

Meddling and vigilante justice, he can forgive, might even find it amusing.

Disrespect? Absolutely not.

"I didn't realize you came with so much baggage," she teases half-heartedly, dragging me back from my thoughts.

"Over a century's worth," I sigh, pulling her in for a kiss before I take her bag to my, or I guess now our, room.

I order entirely too much Chinese food from her favorite spot and we disassociate on the couch to some horror movies until she falls asleep in my lap.

I pull out my phone and shoot Gideon a text, "He's inducting those kids and now fucking with me and Olivia. I'm running out of patience."

"Meet me tomorrow at Grizzly's. 9 p.m.," he responds a few moments later.

I carry Olivia to bed and tuck her in, turning out the lights before heading back into the living room. I make myself a cup of peppermint tea and settle into my recliner with Olivia's worn copy of "Pet Sematary", but I can't seem to focus on the words.

Thoughts of Keanu and Olivia swirl in my mind, getting hazier as sleep overtakes me.

As soon as Keanu walks into the room, I can tell that I'm dreaming.

I'm sitting at my desk at Folke, surrounded by piles of books and paper. The only light is the green lamp on my desk and a few flickering candles on the mantle.

Keanu strides in, wearing nothing under his black dress robes. His pale skin glows in the lamplight, a collage of hardened muscle and scars, agonizingly beautiful. He crosses the room in a blink and pushes my chair backwards, straddling me.

I run my hands along his muscled chest, feeling the grooves and texture of his skin. He shivers under my touch and grabs my face, pulling me in for a searing kiss. It's all tongue and teeth, two wolves battling for dominance.

I grab his hair in a tight fistful and rip his head back, exposing his long neck to me. Quick as a snake, I bite down on his jugular, tearing through the skin like its paper. Blood gushes into my mouth and down our bodies, slick and boiling hot.

He moans and grinds down onto my throbbing cock, groping my chest, hands slippery with his own blood. My trousers fall open and he's fisting my hardening cock, pumping it slowly. He shifts and starts rocking his dick against mine. I wrap my hand around both of our cocks, stroking them together slowly as I tongue fuck his mouth.

Hands slide down over my shoulders and Keanu looks up, a wicked grin stretching across his face. He reaches out and pulls whoever it is towards him, crashing their lips together in a sloppy kiss. Dark hair falls into my eyes and a familiar moan fills the room.

Olivia.

Keanu climbs off of me and pulls her into his chest, sliding his hands into her hair and angling her head so he can kiss her deeper, covering her exposed tits and face in his blood.

I expect to feel a wave of jealousy, but lust and desperate hunger overwhelm me at the sight of them together.

Keanu lifts her up and sets her on the desk, pushing up her slip to expose her dripping cunt, the blood on his hands leaving a crimson trail of his touch. They turn to look at me.

Olivia beckons me forward with a curled finger, parting her supple thighs.

I wake up with a start, my cock rock hard and tenting my sweatpants, precum leaving a wet spot on the gray fabric.

"Gods, fuck," I breathe, wresting down the raging lust clouding my mind.

My phone vibrates beside me. I pick it up, it's a text from an unknown number.

"I've got lots of tricks up my sleeve, ."

Olivia

We head into work Wednesday morning, battling the miserable mist hanging over Alder Bridge.

I slept like shit last night, and I have a feeling Oberon did too. Things are getting weirder by the day, and I know he's withholding how much danger we're actually in.

But my fear feels distant, dormant. Almost like I'm repressing it before it even happens, my subconscious reacting to trauma it's endured in the past.

More acutely, I'm worried about Oberon. Clearly, he and Keanu have a storied past, and I can tell that it's weighing on him. He puts up a good front, but he's constantly fidgeting with his binder and refuses to let me out of his sight. I get the feeling he blames himself for what happened to me, and for what happened to Leda. He carries a tremendous amount of guilt with him every moment of every day. A person can only do that for so long before they buckle, or break.

We're starting in the morgue today, with two new intakes scheduled to arrive. Oberon swipes his card and pushes open the doors, or tries to. He pushes it about six inches before there's a loud metal scraping, and the door resists opening further.

"Stand back," he instructs before throwing his shoulder into the door. It bangs open the rest of the way, revealing the flipped autopsy table that had been blocking the door moments before, and a completely torn apart morgue.

Every cabinet is thrown open, their contents strewn about the room. Bitter ammonia and bleach saturate the air, multiple gallon jugs of cleaner dumped onto the counter tops and floor. Our coolers are flung open, empty. The computer has been thrown across the room, shattered. Every filing cabinet is tipped over, papers littering the floor and soaking up the spilled chemicals.

Oberon slaps his hand over my eyes, shielding me.

"Go upstairs," he barks, pulling me back towards the door, but I slip away, spinning out of his arms and straight into the remaining autopsy table, and face first with myself.

Panic seizes my chest as I take in the grizzly display. It's *me*, completely naked, bloodied and bruised, with a five pronged antler stabbed in my sternum.

My knees turn to liquid and I fall, a scream tearing out of my chest. Oberon's arms encircle me before I hit the ground.

"It's just a mannequin, love. Shhh, it's not real." He tries desperately to soothe me, but I can hear the pinched panic in his own voice, the terror of reliving his greatest trauma. "It's fake, he's just trying to scare us."

"Well, it's fucking working!" I shout, the now all too familiar tremors setting in.

"I know, I know." He rocks me back and forth. "But I will never let him hurt you. I *will* keep you safe."

"The next time you see this motherfucker, you better kick his ass," I whisper, trying to take deep breaths. My fear has alchemized into anger, into a sharpened blade.

"Come on, we can't stay here." He helps me up and we leave quickly, deciding to go across the street for coffee and the normalcy of the general public.

He orders two mocha lattes with cinnamon, but I can't stomach it. The image of myself stabbed through by a massive antler haunts me, ghost pains radiating through my chest.

A news report rolls across the TV over the counter, the cameras cutting to a press conference with the Chief of Police. There's another missing student: Una Sayyid, a gifted history prodigy.

Beside the chief is a well-dressed man wearing a red silk scarf. His expression catches my eye, his eyes vacant as a fish. The chief introduces him as Idris Poe, renowned professor of American History, and Una's mentor. Idris steps to the podium and begins speaking, but his words fall on deaf ears.

Keanu was standing behind him, jaw set, eyes blazing. He's impeccably dressed in an all black designer suit, tattoos climbing up his throat, looking every bit the danger to society that he is, and staring directly into the camera.

I look away.

"Does Idris Poe ring a bell?" I ask Oberon, who is staring intensely at the screen, his jaw flexed.

"He's a descendant and the owner of the Poe literary estate." His voice drips with malice, his jaw flexing.

"So, Scrooge McDuck money?"

Oberon nobs. "Just Keanu's type."

A stunning blonde woman steps over to Keanu and slips something into his hand. She's wearing an immaculate pinstripe suit with red-bottomed heels.

Oberon tenses. "Cylla," he growls.

"An old friend?" Jealousy quirks in my stomach. She and I are polar opposites, a Victoria's Secret model compared to a swamp witch.

"No," he says pointedly, catching my eyes. "She was my replacement. She's Head of the English Department at Folke, as well as Transfiguration. She looks nothing like that in reality, it's all glamour magic."

I mull that over. There's bitterness in his tone, could *he* be jealous?

"Oberon, were you and Keanu...?"

He rubs his hands over his face, pushes his hair back. "We were partners."

My stomach flips. "Partners in what way?"

"In every way," he sighs, reaching out to take my hands. "But it was codependent, toxic. A relationship built on suffering and greed. He needed to own me, and I needed a purpose. There was never any love there, not real love."

The hurt in his eyes is clear, the toll that the years with Keanu took on him. It's a wound that still smarts and refuses to heal.

"Those years I spent with him are the greatest mistake of my life."

I squeeze his hands. "He took advantage of you."

"I was complicit. He offered me power, and I took it, I *wanted* it. He destroyed my family, and I still went to the ends of the earth for him, killed for him." His hands squeeze mine tighter, lost in his anger. "I became a monster for him."

"And you broke free, Oberon. You reclaimed yourself."

He searches my eyes, maybe looking for judgment or scorn. But I know all he'll see is acceptance.

"I did horrible things, Liv," he whispers, hanging his head.

"You're not a villain, Oberon. You are so much more than that." I brush away a tear that sneaks down his cheek. "You are capable of redemption, my love."

He nods, holding my hand against his cheek.

"I will be by your side every step of the way. I love you."

"I love you too." He takes my hand and presses delicate kisses into my palm and down my wrist.

"We're going to kill that motherfucker." I smile, bopping his nose.

He offers a smile, but it's hollow.

We pay for the coffees and head out into the crisp afternoon, hands intertwined.

I snuggle into his side as we walk, feeling the warmth radiating from him, and it eases some of the anxiety tightening my chest.

We unlock his door, and once we step inside, he pulls me into a tight hug. "You saved me," he whispers. "The hope that one day I'd find you, that I'd see you again, hold you again. It brought me back from the brink. Reminded me of my humanity, the man you loved. I wanted to be him again, no matter how badly it hurt."

I look up at him and smile, rising onto my toes to kiss him, but a yawn interrupts me.

He chuckles, dragging me to the couch and ordering me to lay down, which I eagerly oblige. I drift off quickly, the brush of his fingers through my hair lulling me to sleep.

I wake to strange voices drifting from the foyer. The sun has set and the room is illuminated by a dancing fire and dimmed lamps.

"You got a cat!" a man says, answered by a pleased *breow* from Church.

"Olivia found him," Oberon says.

"I thought you hated cats," a woman says, her voice low and melodic.

"Yeah, well..." Oberon trails off.

I can hear the other man talking sweetly to Church, the cats purr audible from even here.

"She's awake," the woman says casually, making goosebumps rise on my arms.

I hear familiar footsteps and Oberon pokes his head around the corner, meeting my eyes. An absolutely stunning redhead strides past him, clad in black straight leg jeans, a white Sex Pistols tee, and a black denim jacket covered in patches. Her hair is the richest copper I've ever seen, with platinum streaks framing her face. Full lashes and black liner sharp as a knife frame her hazel eyes. A golden locket hangs around her throat. She's so beautiful it makes me want to crawl under the couch.

"Hi, honey," she says, voice like caramel, and sits on the coffee table in front of me. "I'm Ayla." She extends a manicured hand with short, almond nails red as blood.

A bit of my anxiety unwinds. *His sister-in-law.*

"Uh, hi. I'm Olivia." I shake her hand gingerly, unsure of what's happening.

Oberon sits on the couch beside me, placing a reassuring hand on my knee.

"We were good friends back in the day." Ayla inspects the rings on my fingers, tracing her thumb over the crescent moon on my ring finger. "And we will be again." Her eyes flick up to me, a soft smile playing at her lips.

"Darling, don't scare her." The tallest man I've ever seen rounds the corner, ducking under the arch. He's cradling Church to his chest, tickling the cat's belly. He's wearing unevenly rolled Levi's and dirty Chuck's, with a Cobain-esque vintage sweater. I can see the resemblance to Oberon immediately, with the sloped nose and broad shoulders, the striking blue eyes. But Algernon's hair is sandier, and he sports a full beard, as well as round, gold framed glasses.

I look at Oberon, confused.

"They're here to help. And no, I did not invite them." He looks pointedly at Algernon, who's too busy counting Church's toe-beans to notice.

"You were going to anyway," Ayla says, rising and taking the cat from her husband and setting him on the armchair. She opens Oberon's wine fridge and pulls out a bottle of Riesling, making a face.

"Ayla is a *very* nosy seer," Oberon says, noting my raised eyebrows.

She hands the bottle to Algernon. As soon as it touches his fingers, red starts to bleed into the golden color, quickly transforming the crisp white into the signature bloody garnet of Cabernet. She pops the cork and pours four glasses, passing them out, then taking hers and sitting beside the crackling fireplace.

"And Algernon is an alchemist." The muscles in his jaw flex.

"I- what? Like Nicholas Flamel?" I gape at them.

Algernon snorts and flops into the empty armchair closest to his wife, his impossibly long limbs splaying out. "Nick wishes." He grabs his wine and takes a sip. "He may have cracked the code to immortality, but he looks like a wrinkly testicle, so."

I look back at Oberon, unsure if I should be charmed by his odd older brother or terrified.

"Besides me, Ayla and Al are basically enemy number one for the Arcanum. I'd trust them with my life." He takes my hand and brings it to his lips, kissing my palm gently. "We couldn't ask for anyone better on our side."

"You flatter me." Algernon smiles, pleased.

Ayla is staring into the fire, brows furrowed. The men lapse into silence, watching her closely.

Algernon places a hand on her head, nearly covering the entirety of her scalp. "What do you see, kitten?" he asks softly, as if she were sleeping.

She jumps to her feet, narrowly missing her wine glass and making us all flinch.

There's a knock on the door.

"Gideon," Ayla and Oberon say in unison. Oberon seems slightly relieved, where Ayla and Al throw their guards up.

Al goes so far as to pull Ayla into his lap, caging his arms around her short frame.

Oberon holds a finger out to me, telling me to stay put, as if I was going to move an inch.

The idea of hiding under the couch is sounding more and more appealing.

He goes to answer the door and comes back a few moments later, Gideon striding behind him. He's wearing all black, with a charcoal duster and royal blue scarf. If he's surprised to see Algernon and Ayla, he conceals it well.

"We're not supposed to meet until later," Oberon says, sitting close enough to me that our thighs are pressed together. He drapes an arm across my lap like a seat belt.

"Please, little brothers. I won't bite," he says, shooing Church off the remaining armchair and sinking into it, resting his right ankle on his left knee.

Not so easily deterred, Church hops back up into his lap and settles in, definitely leaving gray hairs all over his probably designer trousers. Gideon makes a face, but doesn't push him off.

"A rather pressing matter came up that couldn't wait." Gideon goes on, eyes flicking between his siblings, intentionally avoiding Ayla and myself.

Algernon pulls Ayla closer and she whispers something in his ear that makes him snicker.

"Sane is throwing a party," Gideon finishes.

He could only be referencing Dr. Theodore Sane, the Dean of Folke University. I had only met him once in the past, at orientation for the Forensics Department. He was young, the youngest Dean Folke has probably ever had, but he is one of the most gifted Mathematicians alive. I remember his shock of white hair, his skin like washed marble. His albinism made him impossible to ignore, but it was only a fraction of what made his presence so monumental.

"And that's relevant because...?" Algernon quirks an eyebrow.

"You are on the guest list," Gideon says, his cold gaze landing on me. Oberon stiffens.

"What? I'm hardly a distinguished alumni," I stammer, anxiety swirling in my gut.

"Exactly," all three brothers say in unison.

"You, my dear, are bait." Gideon's lip lifts slightly at the corner, making me want to smack him.

"Absolutely fucking not," Oberon snarls, tightening his grip on me.

"So hasty. She'll be perfectly safe in such a large crowd. You and I will both be there. Right, Ayla?" His serpent gaze slides over to her.

She stares back, unimpressed, then lets her eyes flutter close.

Algernon stares down his older brother, the change in his demeanor jarring. He went from golden retriever to lion in the span of a heartbeat, and their relation becomes glaringly clear. Each of them are as deadly as they are handsome, with hairpin triggers.

Ayla opens her eyes again, looking towards Oberon and I. "You'll be safe," she confirms.

Oberon's shoulders creep down a fraction.

"Why should we go?" I ask, tired of being left out of whatever this insane dynamic is.

"Answers, of course," Gideon says simply, taking a black envelope out of his jacket pocket and handing it to Oberon.

It's a formal invitation to Dr. Sane's home with my name scrawled in golden script.

I look at Oberon, uncertainty plain in his face.

"I don't think we have a choice. We need to know more about his plans," I say, taking Oberon's hand.

He only nods, rubbing my knuckles with his thumb.

"We'll give you guys some space," Ayla says, wriggling her way out of Algernon's arms and getting to her feet. Algernon stands with her, nearly hitting his head on the light fixture.

"Our rental is just down the street. If you need anything," he glances down at the binder on Oberon's wrist, "Call me."

Oberon stands and shows them out, grabbing Gideon by the collar and dragging him with them. He closes the door behind them with a click. He comes back into the room and sinks to his knees in front of me.

"I'm sorry, love. I had no idea—"

"I know, honey, it's fine." I stroke his cheek. "It was, ah, enlightening." I force a smile despite the uneasiness lingering in my chest.

"We don't have to do anything you're uncomfortable with." He takes my hands. "I won't put you in harm's way."

"Then it's settled. It's just a party, right?" I try to muster up as much conviction as possible.

"Right. And I'll be right by your side." His eyes gaze into mine, their stormy blue a sea I would gladly drown in.

I lean in to kiss him, exhaustion settling back over me. He caresses my cheek, kissing me back softly.

"Pasta in the bath?" he asks, stroking his thumb over my lower lip.

"I love you." I grin, kissing him again.

Act 4

Oberon

The following day seems to fly by in nervous anticipation for the Dean's event. We procrastinate getting ready for as long as possible, but around 6:00 p.m. Olivia rises from the couch and heads into the bedroom.

I pour us each a glass of wine and follow, finding her sitting with her legs folded on the vanity, dabbing on concealer. I wrap my arms around her and rest my head on her shoulder, just breathing her in. I linger there while she does her makeup, listening to the thud of her heart, memorizing every millimeter of her tether, of her soul.

Maybe I'm being paranoid, I doubt Keanu would risk causing a scene at such a high-profile event. My brothers are right, he just wants to talk to me. I have to hope that his choice of such a public setting means he doesn't want any trouble, that he's afraid of what I'd do if I had him alone.

Truthfully, *I'm* afraid of what I might do if I had him alone. Part of me hopes I'd eviscerate him, part of me fears I'd fall to my knees and beg his forgiveness.

I release her and step into the shower, trying to wash away the film of anxiety hanging over me. I need to be strong for her, if she sees that I'm nervous, she will be too. I need her to believe that I have this under control.

I step out and find her mostly ready, shimmying into a stunning burgundy satin dress. It fits her like a glove, highlighting every curve and dip of her body, splitting at the peak of her right thigh and spilling the floor. The back is completely open, exposing her smooth skin. I can't resist touching her, feeling the slip of the fabric through my fingers, the warmth of her skin underneath.

"You're a vision," I murmur, admiring her sultry makeup and effortless waves. I twirl a ringlet around my finger and tuck it behind her ear. I see the crystal necklace on the nightstand and pick it up. "May I?"

She smiles, but it doesn't reach her eyes, and turns her back to me.

My poor, anxious little love. I slip the necklace around her throat and clasp it under her hair, then turn her to face me.

"I've got you, love. I promise." I kiss her gently, pulling her closer. She relaxes a bit under my touch, leaning into the kiss. "I love you, Olivia."

"I love you, too." She cups my cheek, brushing her thumb along my cheekbone, then turns to finish getting ready.

I pull on my suit, navy slacks and jacket with a lavender button-down. Keanu always said how much he loved me in black, and I refuse to give him even that much.

There's honk from outside, a black SUV idles by the front door.

The ride is uneventful, both of us trapped in our own minds. I keep a hand on her bare knee, rubbing her soft skin absently.

When we arrive, there's dozens of people loitering on the Dean's front lawn, the who's who of New York. The estate sits atop a gentle rise, surrounded by lush, manicured gardens and age-old tree.

The manor's exterior boasts an impressive facade, constructed with grayish-white field stones, carefully arranged to form intricate patterns. The symmetrical design is punctuated by tall, graceful windows adorned with decorative cornices and delicate wrought iron railings. A grand, pillared portico graces the front entrance, welcoming visitors with an air of opulence.

The driver opens my door, but I stop him before he touches Olivia's, opening it for her myself. I take her hand and help her step out, pulling her close to my side. I feel eyes swivel towards us.

It's impossible to tell if they're lingering on her beauty or my reputation. Probably both.

"Oberon!" Gideon emerges from a group to our left and pulls me in for an awkward hug, no doubt trying to dispel suspicion, marking us as members of this upper echelon of society. He pulls Olivia in and kisses her cheek.

I swallow my displeasure. He's performing for the audience.

"Let's get you two some drinks." He smiles, ushering us into the house, which has even more people inside.

The vaulted ceilings and gleaming hardwood amplify the snobbish chattering, raising it to a dull roar. Gideon guides us to a bar and orders two whiskeys and a glass of red for Liv. The bartender delivers our drinks, and we crowd around a nearby high-top.

A steady stream of people approach to talk to Gideon and regale us with stories of funerals I've hosted. A fair share approach just to make a move on Olivia, which she elegantly deflects. She's conducting herself effortlessly, slipping into her Funeral Director training. Soon, she's a hit, and I have to fight to keep a hold of her hand.

"Quite a charmer, your girl is," Gideon murmurs, turning towards me in a moment of calm. Then, his eyes narrow. "Cylla just arrived."

I look up and immediately catch her yellow eyes over the crowd. Idris is on her arm, his scowl tangible. She narrows her gaze at me, then pulls Idris into the fray, both of them disappearing from my line of sight.

"Let the fun begin." Gideon smirks, taking a long pull of his drink.

A shock of white hair catches my eye, moving toward us in the crowd. The sea of people part, and there stands Dr. Theodore Sane, Dean of Folke University and the School of Old Arts.

He's dressed impeccably in a burgundy suit, bringing out the pinkish violet hue of his eyes. He smiles warmly as he approaches and shakes Gideon's hand, then turns to us.

"Oberon," he says, extending a hand. "It's a pleasure to see you again."

I shake his hand, uncertain. Was he a part of Keanu's plan? He, like Gideon, left the Arcanum behind decades ago, not that he was truly a member in the first place. He'd saved Algernon's life once, and Ayla's. And because of him, they'd been able to save me. In a lot of ways, I owe him my life.

But, still. How well can you really know someone?

"The pleasure is all mine, Dr. Sane." I turn and wrap an arm around Olivia's waist. "This is—"

"Ms. Olivia Hunter." He grins, eyes fixed firmly on her face. Exceedingly formal, per usual. "I believe I knew your father."

Olivia blinks at him. "Really? He only taught here for a few months."

"I never forget a name," he replies, softening. "I was very sorry to hear about his passing. He was an exceptionally intelligent and kind man."

She smiles, a genuine, heartbreaking thing. "Thank you, Dr. Sane."

"I'm afraid I must check on the dinner preparations, but I hope you have a lovely evening and thank you so much for joining us." He claps Gideon on the shoulder, then turns and is swallowed up by the crowd.

I exhale, pulling at my shirt collar. All the competing energies are making me uneasy, clouding my ability to read the room.

"Want to dance?" Olivia slides closer to me, tucking herself against my arm. People have started to gather in the center of the room, swaying to a piano cover of La Vie en Rose.

I look down, her brown eyes hopeful, and I can't say no. I take her by the hand and stroll onto the dance floor, pulling her close. Her body is warm against my chest, her perfume saturating my senses. We sway together, my left hand resting in the gentle slope of her lower back, my right hand holding hers, our fingers interlocked.

The rest of the room fades away; all I can see is her.

I'm transported back to our wedding day, the feel of her pressed against me, love drunk and naive. What I wouldn't give to go back to that, to a time when we could love each other without fear, without persecution. When life was simple and sweet, and we'd never known pain.

Three songs play as we dance together, entranced with one another.

Then, the hairs on my neck rise. I look up, my eyes drawn to him like a magnet, his energy slicing through the weaker souls in the room like an ax.

Keanu Kennedy.

Before my brain fully processes the information, he's moving towards us, a shark through murky waters.

"He's coming," I whisper to her, feigning confidence. I pull her close and move us off of the dance floor, searching for Gideon.

Cylla finds us first, bumping directly into Olivia and spilling a full glass of champagne down her front.

"Oh my gosh, I am *so* sorry!" Cylla cries, tossing her blonde hair over her shoulder and grabbing some napkins to dab at Olivia's dress. I swallow the urge to tell her to where she can shove that champagne flute.

"Oh, no, really, it's alright. Accidents happen," Olivia responds, stepping closer to me.

"Let me take you to the ladies, I'll clean you right up!" Cylla babbles, deliberately avoiding my glare.

I grab hold of Cylla's tether, a thorny stem, and force her a few steps back. "Don't touch her," I growl, pulling Olivia behind me.

"What happened here?" His low voice wraps around us, sucking the air out of the room.

I turn slowly, raising my chin. "Nothing of your concern," I respond, setting my jaw.

Keanu is breathtaking and terrible, in a pitch-black suit dripping with luxury. His bone structure could cut glass, his black hair slicked back. A single, strategic piece dangles over his forehead, curling slightly at the arch of his dark brow. He looks exactly as I remember him, beautiful and cruel.

"I'm glad you could make it, Olivia," Keanu says lightly, eyes trailing from her eyes, down her throat, and into the valley of her damp breasts. "I apologize for Cylla." His eyes flick up at the blonde, flashing with murderous intent, then slipping right back to their usual, although contrived, warmth as they return to Liv. "She can be quite clumsy."

A bell chimes from the grandfather clock by the grand staircase, signaling dinner is served. The crowd starts to herd towards the dining hall.

"Time for dinner." His lips turn up into a wolfish grin, sending my heart plummeting to my stomach. "I'm *starving*." He winks at me, turns, and disappears once again, Cylla vanishing along with him.

"I don't like this," Olivia whispers to me, wrapping her hands around my arm, shaking slightly.

Me neither, but it's too late to turn back. I can't show Keanu even an ounce of fear, or all of this will be for nothing. "Let's get you cleaned up." I kiss the top of her head and guide her outside, where we find Gideon chatting with a small group of professors.

He peels away when he sees us and frowns at the mess on Olivia's dress. He waves his hand and the wine evaporates, leaving her dress good as new.

"Thank you." She offers him a nervous smile.

"I assume you made contact?" Gideon raises a brow at me.

I nod. "I'm going to talk to him after dinner, will you stay with Olivia?" I give him a pointed look, hoisting his tether to gauge his response.

"I'd never miss an opportunity to bask in such delightful company."

"Don't make me regret trusting you," I growl, tugging on his tether enough for him to feel it.

"I won't make that mistake again," he says, looking directly into my eyes. Then he breaks into a lopsided grin, "Let's go eat."

We head back inside and find our reserved spots just in time for the first portion to be placed down in front of us, roasted lemon and fennel salad. We pick our way through all 5 courses, luscious salmon, whipped potatoes, wagyu with vintage wine reduction, swordfish, and brown-buttered lobster. Neither of us have much of an appetite despite the incredible food.

After the final course, Dr. Sane makes a lengthy, heartfelt toast, but I find myself searching for Keanu. He's nowhere to be found. My stomach whirls, torn between relief and disappointment.

Dinner comes to an end, and everyone files back out into the main hall.

I take a deep breath and swallow the rest of my whiskey.

"I'm going to find him," I say, cupping Olivia's face. "Stay with Gideon. I'll be back soon." I kiss her quickly, swiping my tongue across hers, needing to taste her. I break away and look pointedly at Gideon. "Keep her safe."

He nods, his expression unreadable.

I study Olivia's face, the anxious set of her brow, then force myself to turn and walk into the crowd, searching for his tether. The texture of it is burned into my memory; I could find him anywhere in the world.

Keanu is in the study, waiting for me.

I let his tether guide me out of the hall and into the rest of the house, down a long hallway and to a set of white French doors. I see Keanu through the glass, his hands gliding across the grand piano by the window. I let myself in, locking the door behind me.

The music fills the room, the vaulted ceilings lending it a haunting echo. I recognize the composition immediately, Nocturne in C Minor, by Chopin. A favorite of mine.

Keanu looks up at me, his fingers never faltering.

"Did you find her?" he asks, taking me by surprise.

I bristle, desperately trying to maintain control of my emotions. Not that it matters much, he sees right through me. "Not exactly."

"Ah." His fingers slowly come to a halt, and he stands, closing the top gently. "So she found you in another life. Poetic, really." He rounds the piano and approaches me slowly, gliding across the room. "Our story could never live up to something so...honeyed," he murmurs, getting close enough that I can smell his warm cologne.

It stirs something inside me, something between hatred and desire. The tease of an old habit, the ache of a broken bone poorly set.

"This is your only warning. Whatever you want with me, leave her out of it," I snarl, refusing to back down, to give in to him.

He only hums in response.

I nearly jump when I feel his cold fingers brush my wrist, tracing the metal binder.

My blood turns to ice. *Shit.*

His fingers continue up my forearm and over to my side, his touch sliding under my blazer and into the grooves of my muscles, remembering the map of my body. I take a small bit of pleasure in that, knowing he memorized me the same way I memorized him.

But his touch doesn't spark heat like it used to, instead it's been replaced by a validating wave of disgust.

Finally, I'm free.

His hand falls away immediately, his smirk dropping, all the warmth draining from his eyes.

"I have one favor to ask, Oberon," he says curtly, turning to pour himself a glass of whiskey.

"And what makes you think I would help you?"

He swallows the entire glass, setting it down hard enough to rattle the cart.

"I think you know why."

"Enlighten me," I sneer, crossing my arms.

"This alt-right movement poses a threat to us. People are losing their self-control, succumbing to their most ignorant impulses. It needs to end." He sits behind the desk and steeples his fingers, watching me carefully.

"And what would you have me do?"

"Dispose of them, the politicians and capitalists. The system is beyond repair by my own hand, and it's only a matter of time before they set their sights on witchcraft once again."

"Play God, you mean?" I shake my head. "You think wiping out the government will change things?"

"It's a start." He smirks.

"How many times does the cycle have to repeat before you realize that people will *never* change. True justice is impossible, so long as humans have free will."

"That's exactly why *we* need to be in charge, Oberon. Plato envisioned a perfect Republic, we've seen it in smaller communities. You've witnessed it yourself, been a part of it. Guided by Source, we can live in peace."

His voice sounds so sincere, so optimistic, a sliver of my resolve slips. This is how he gets people to follow him, to trust him. Radical optimism combined with near-divine power. Everyone wants to hope for something better, a simple answer. He offers a safe space to surrender.

"You're a fool." I growl. "Is that why you're murdering students? Using the brightest minds and untrained power to construct your new plan for world domination?"

His smirk returns. "Something like that. We are nothing without the youth of the world."

"Humans will never accept you. And you are a fool to think you're any different than they are. You will succumb to the same impulses, over and over again. You will be just another cog in the machine, a flip of the coin. There is no escaping it, Key." I'm almost pleading with him now, begging him to see reason after a century of insanity, of bloodshed and delusion. "You just have to live your life exactly as it is. That's all any of us can do. Control is an illusion, we're all slaves to the same things."

"Except you." His eyes darken, the air in the room grows thicker. "Only you are truly free. And yet you choose to remain subservient, play pretend at being something you're not. You hold the key to change, to alter the wheel of fortune once and for all. You stare at the face of injustice and do nothing." He's angry now, rising to his feet. His energy snaps around him, electric, a faint blue glow bleeding into his aura.

"I don't care what you think, Keanu." I push his energy back, rising to meet him. But the binder stops me from matching him fully, and fear licks at my insides. "I am not a God, and neither are you. I'm done carrying the weight of your world. Stay away from us, or I will end you."

I dig deep and force my feet to carry me to the door even as he tries to hold me, wrench it open, and slam it shut behind me. Exhaustion crashes into me, my wrist bright with pain, but I trudge down the hall and out into the party.

I reach for Olivia's tether, but am met with terrible, all too familiar silence.

No, it can't be. I was only gone for 5 minutes. She was with Gideon.

Like a gut punch, the air is knocked out of my chest. I nearly collapse, my knees turning to liquid, but I force myself outside and down the steps, rage boiling me from the inside out.

My phone pings, and I grab for it, a sliver of hope breaks through the blinding terror.

It's a text from Gideon.

"She's alive. Reconsider, and she will be returned to you unharmed. You have 24 hours."

I stare down at my phone, my heart hammering against my ribs.

Another ping.

"I'm sorry."

"Fuck!" I throw my phone against the house, smashing it. The grass around my feet shrivels and turns black, the smell of burnt flesh reaches my nose.

Gideon betrayed us.

I failed her again.

Suddenly Algernon is there, pushing through the crowd and grabbing me. He's speaking, but I can't hear him over the blood rushing in my ears. He drags me across the lawn, careful not to touch my skin, and throws me into the backseat of a car.

The car pulls away. I can see Ayla watching me in the rear view mirror from the driver's seat.

"She just saw it, Ben," Al says, turning to look at me. "Gideon compelled Ayla when she was looking through the veil. He manipulated her. I thought he'd changed." His jaw clenches, hurt clear in his eyes.

"He lied to us," I grit out, black pulsing at the edges of my vision. My power is consuming me, the binder burning through skin and into muscle, pain radiating into my bones. But I barely register it, the cracking of my heart drowning out everything else.

I failed her again.

"We'll make this right, we'll save her," Al insists, taking the risk and touching my hand. "You won't lose her again."

"We'll end that fucker once and for all," Ayla snaps, eyes like daggers.

Pain swallows me up, the grief like a noose around my neck, smothering me, until I feel nothing at all, the closest I'll ever come to experiencing death.

Olivia

"You are so fucking dead!" I try to scream at Gideon through the tie shoved into my mouth, kicking and thrashing in his arms as he carries me through the empty halls and out of a back door.

He tosses me into the back seat of a black SUV and shuts the door, which locks with a hollow *click*.

He rests his elbows on the rolled-down window and peers in at me, infuriatingly unbothered. "We'll see." He taps on the roof of the SUV, and it pulls away, merging into traffic and swiftly leaving the Dean's house behind us.

I can't see the driver's face, the divider is so tinted it's nearly black, as are the windows. I kick and scream, throwing myself against the car doors and windows until I can barely breathe, my ankles and shoulders throbbing.

I take some deep breaths, willing my heart to slow down and my mind to quiet. I need to focus and put the pieces together.

Gideon betrayed us. The thought is a bitter pill, equal parts rage and sadness for Oberon and for myself. But getting hung up on it won't do me any favors. I need to focus on what's next.

Will they kill me? Recruit me? No, most likely I'm just bait, like the dinner party. Whatever Keanu offered Oberon tonight, he must not have bitten. But with my life on the line, I'm not sure what his choice will be. Will he try to save me? Or avoid Keanu's game altogether and let me die?

A dull ache kicks up in my chest.

Do I want him to rescue me? Put himself in harm's way for me?

I'm not afraid of death, it's one of my closest friends. But a life without him? That's the scariest thing I can imagine.

The car rolls to a halt, and the door is flung open, spilling me out onto the icy sidewalk. A man in a ski mask hauls me up and throws a bag over my head, blocking out the meager light offered by the streetlamps.

I don't try to fight, it will only waste vital energy.

I'm dragged up what feels like an endless amount of stairs, down a hall, and down another endless flight of stairs, pain lancing through me with every bump, before I'm dumped onto the ground.

The cuffs behind my back are released, and the door swiftly shuts behind me.

I rip off the bag and undo the gag, swallowing cold lungfuls of air.

The room around me is sparse, with concrete floors and water stained walls. A single twin bed rests on the floor in the corner with a thin pillow and toddler-sized quilt. A toilet sits in the opposite corner, along with a metal desk and chair. There are no windows, and the door is a solid sheet of steel. I can see a small slit beside it for meals.

My only sources of entertainment are a few worn books stacked on top of the desk and a notebook with a single black crayon.

I pace the room, feeling every corner and divot, checking for the slightest crack in the facade. All I find is a camera in the light fixture and crippling disappointment.

I really am trapped.

"Keanu!" I shout, waving my arms at the camera. "Gideon, you motherfucker!" I run through every name I can remember that's affiliated with the Arcanum, but receive nothing but more ringing silence.

Sorrow claws at my chest, and I'm too tired to fight it off after a while. It engulfs me as soon as I let go, drowning out everything else. I collapse onto the bed, heaving, choking on my tears.

There is nothing in the entire world but misery and grief. And blinding terror.

I feel every second like a barb in my side, constantly reminding me of my predicament. My only measurement of time passing is the never ending cycle of terror, confusion, hope, and despair.

I try to lose myself in one of the books left for me, a cracked copy of Dracula, but can't seem to follow the words.

Stiffness starts to grow in my back and neck, the mattress is barely more than a dog bed. I roll my neck to find relief, but a bright, lancing pain shoots down my spine, spreading out in my limbs. I jump up, twisting and turning to shake the rigidity, but it only worsens.

In the span of a few breaths, I can barely turn my head or lift my arms. My legs feel stiff as boards. With a cold rush of terror, I realize I can't even scream, my jaw locked shut. Even breathing hurts, my rising and falling chest straining against the parallelization creeping through my body.

The door swings open, and Keanu strides in.

"Hello, Olivia darling." His mouth curls up into something resembling a smile, but is too cruel to be called one. He's wearing the same blackout suit he wore at the party, so it can't have been more than a few hours since I was taken.

I try to scan his face, attire, and body language to glean an ounce of information from him, but panic makes my mind turn to soup. The only thought taking any sort of shape is *run*.

But I can't. It's taking every bit of strength and concentration to keep my lungs pumping.

"You're afraid." He draws closer and circles around me, taking in my disheveled dress and tangled hair. "I can smell it on you," he murmurs.

All of my instincts scream at me to recoil.

He moves back around to my front, unabashedly examining the slope of my decolletage, the swell of my breasts. His hand comes up, hanging in the air between us before brushing one of my sleeves off my shoulder to reveal a love bite. The tendon in his jaw flexes, his eyes narrow. His hand travels back up my arm and over the curve of my shoulder, cold as ice, and ghosts over the purple skin.

Keanu's inhuman eyes flick to meet mine. "He's an exceptional lover, no?"

Nausea flares in the pit of my stomach, acrid jealousy crawls up my throat.

"I see why he's so drawn to you." Keanu inches closer, nearly touching me, and drags his nose along the column of my throat, inhaling deeply.

I lash against the spell he's put on me, but can't move a damned muscle.

"Still such a feisty little thing," he tuts with approval. "Oberon always liked a challenge." His lips are a breath away from mine, his dragon's blood cologne clogging my senses. "I wonder if I can still taste him on you," he whispers, breath fanning across my face. He reaches up and caresses my collar bones with the pads of his fingers, then fists the crystal necklace and tears it off, sending beads scattering around the room.

He draws back, shaking his head.

"Although I can see what he finds so compelling about you, you are of little consequence to me. Like Leda, you are simply in my way. Disposable."

My stomach drops, realization dawning. The pieces click into place, and I can't believe I didn't see it before.

He adjusts his suit and smooths back his hair, like he didn't just reveal that he'd *murdered* my past life. "The Raith brothers are powerful, exceptionally so. They could have been Gods if their parents weren't such cowards." Bitterness seeps into his chilled tone. "I knew Oberon was the key. I saw the shadow in his heart as soon as I laid eyes on him. And I was right, for a while. But he always did have that pesky moral compass, no thanks to you." His eyes slide back to mine, reptilian. "No harm will come to you, so long as you cooperate and Oberon submits. You will, however, participate in this evening's festivities. It's Halloween, after all."

Keanu reaches into his pocket, withdraws a popcorn ball wrapped in a colorful orange wrapper with a jack-o'-lantern face, and sets it on the desk. Then, he crosses the room and the door swings open for him. He looks at me over his shoulder. "Get some rest, dove."

The paralyzing spell falls away like a blanket sliding off my shoulders, and he's gone. I grab the popcorn ball and unwrap it, the gnawing in my stomach not caring if it's drugged or that it's the worst Halloween snack on the planet.

I lay back down and nibble on it, feeling like a hamster in a cage. Thoughts are swirling in my head, but they're just hazy, malformations of things. Anything I try to grasp slips through my fingers. Exhaustion steadily takes over, and the room slips into darkness.

I open my eyes and find myself in an unfamiliar place, standing in a doorway. The room is massive, so huge the walls and ceilings disappear into shadows, never ending.

The gleaming hardwood floor stretches out before me, bloody footprints creating a path straight ahead and into the darkness.

A dream, it has to be a dream.

I start to follow the trail of blood down what feels like an endless path, until I start to hear low voices and movement.

Fire erupts to my left, the flames the color of the sky, contained in the largest fireplace I've ever seen, and illuminates the room.

It's empty, except for a black throne resting atop a dais, with a naked man sprawled across it, and a worshiper on his knees before the throne, his feet covered in gashes, dripping blood onto the floor.

I creep closer, and realize that the man sitting on the throne is Keanu, his face contorted in pleasure, a sinful grin on his lips.

"That's it, bear" he murmurs, softly petting the raven hair of the man on his knees.

My stomach drops.

The worshiper is Oberon, eagerly swallowing every inch of Keanu's cock, moaning with pleasure, his feet a gruesome mess.

I open my mouth to call out to him, and the room twists, sending me careening down into the black abyss of shadows.

I slam into the ground and look up to see a hauntingly familiar sight. I'm at the bottom of a grave, staring up at the night sky.

Oberon leans over the entrance and peers down at me.

I try to reach out to him, but I'm paralyzed, terror freezing my limbs.

He winks, then shovels the first pile of dirt into my grave.

The lock on the door clicks with a dull thud, jarring me out of my fraught sleep. It swings open with a horrible screech, revealing Gideon on the other side. He steps inside and shuts the door behind him, flicking on the overhead light.

I flinch at the sudden brightness but refuse to acknowledge him, overcome by the pounding of my heart.

Just a dream, it was just a dream.

"You must think I'm a monster," he says after a beat, pulling out the chair by the desk and sitting down, elbows braced on his knees.

I glare and keep my mouth shut, very much not in the mood for his guilty conscience.

"I wouldn't have brought you here if I thought you'd be in danger." He drags his hand across his face. "Keanu won't hurt you."

"And why should I believe anything you say?" I snap, propping myself up on my elbow.

"Because he won't make the mistake of killing you twice."

So, he knew.

"It doesn't matter if he kills me. Keanu sealed his fate." I flop back down onto the pillow and turn away from him.

"I love my brothers, Olivia. Everything I've ever done is for them," he says quietly enough that if he hadn't addressed me directly, I'd assume he was talking to himself. "We spent our entire lives in the shadows, hiding what we were out of fear of the small-minded. Al and Ben didn't experience what life was like before the farm. They were isolated from it all, all the hatred, the abuse." He draws in a breath, shaking his head. "They deserve better. All the kids like us deserve better."

"Why are you telling me this?" I look back at him, moved despite my callous intentions.

"Because you need to understand why I'm doing this. Key has his own motives, those I cannot speak to. But all I ever wanted was to protect my brothers and leave them with a better world than I inherited."

"You say that like you're going to die."

"The day will come when I have to betray Keanu, and it'll probably be sooner rather than later. I'm not naive enough to think I would survive it. Hell, Oberon might kill me himself when he comes for you." His gloomy eyes flick to mine. "Just, tell him that I did my best." He stands and walks across the room.

"Gideon." I sit up, wanting to say something and soothe the horrible hurt lurking behind the storm clouds in his eyes, hating that after everything he's done, I believe him. But the words don't come.

"Won't be long now." He smirks, the icy mask slipping into place, and flicks off the light, pulling open the door and locking it behind him.

I try desperately to fall back to sleep, to disappear into the quiet of my subconscious, but it refuses to come. Hours pass in maddening silence. Hunger tears at my insides, making me feel unsteady and foggy.

An indeterminate amount of time later, the slit in the wall creaks open and a slip of fabric is pushed through, followed by a small amber bottle. I wait with baited breath to see if food or water will be pushed through, but no such luck.

I stand up and the blood rushes to my head, spots dancing in front of my eyes, and I slide back to the ground. I keep my forehead pressed to the cold floor until the spinning ebbs and my vision returns, then crawl over to the delivery.

It's a sage green slip, with delicate lace details and floral embroidery, soft as a petal and familiar as a dream.

I pick up the vial and turn it in my hand. There's a handwritten label stuck to it: 'wear me'. Carefully, I unscrew the top and waft the air above it, immediately recognizing the herby, floral scent. Lavender.

I step out of my heavy dress, tossing it onto the bed. I can't believe that I thought it was beautiful once. I decide to remove my old underwear as well, the unwashed feeling making my skin crawl.

The slip slides easily over my head and down my body, fitting better than I expected. My breasts are concealed enough, and the hem reaches to my knees. The fabric feels like cool water against my skin, the relief of clean clothes taking the edge off my anxiety, if only for a moment.

I pick up the perfume and sniff it again, as if I could detect caustic chemicals or drugs by scent alone.

I dab some on my wrists, behind my ears, and under my arms. I even run a few drops through my hair. I set it down onto the desk, and the door swings open.

Gideon is standing there, in his usual suit and a cerulean scarf, flanked by three masked figures. They're all dressed to the nines, with ceremonial daggers strapped to their sides.

Gideon's eyes widen for a fraction of a second when he sees me, before freezing over again. "It's time, Olivia," he says, extending a hand to me.

For a moment, I consider bolting, but then a masked figure throws a bag over my head and I'm swallowed by darkness once again. I feel Gideon's hand wrap around mine, far gentler than I'd expect, and we start walking.

"Is that Gin's scarf?" I whisper to him.

He doesn't falter, just squeezes my hand. "Make sure she doesn't mourn me."

My heart pinches. I squeeze his hand in acknowledgement, and we lapse into silence.

After what must be at least 10 minutes, I hear a heavy-sounding door being pushed open and the murmur of voices. There's an intake of breath, and then heavy silence.

I'm led up a small set of stairs, and then there's arms around me, lifting me into the air. I'm dropped onto an ice cold slab. The embalming table floats into my mind, Oberon's hands all over me, the strong and steady feel of him. Tears well, but I swallow them down.

Hands start grabbing my arms and legs, pulling them wide against whatever table this is. The image of myself impaled on the embalming table startles me and panic seizes me.

I try to fight against them, kicking and slapping and writhing, but it's no use. I'm strapped down in seconds, so tight that I can't move even a fraction of an inch.

The bag is ripped off of my head, and I scream.

A massive chandelier hangs above me, lit by what seems like a thousand candles. Masked faces loom over me, men and women wearing 5 piece tuxedos and designer gowns. Devils, clowns, goats, wolves, the horrible, haunting masks swirl in my vision, the room tipping violently to the side. I scream again, only for something hard to be forced into my mouth. I realize with horror that it's a ball gag.

A man in a gleaming, bone-white deer skull mask leans over me from behind. The massive antlers cast long shadows in the candlelight, like reaching fingers.

I recognize his cologne immediately.

Keanu lifts the mask off of his face and grins down at me, leaning in close enough that I can feel his lips on the shell of my ear.

"Happy Halloween," he purrs.

I scream around the ball gag, the sound coming out a strangled gurgle, forceful enough to arch my back off the marble slab, but the restraints have absolutely zero slack. I can already feel tingling numbness spreading through my fingers and toes.

Keanu stands and straightens his mask, facing the room of people. There's only about 10 of them, all of them standing around me in a circle. A twisted, sadistic funeral. *My funeral.*

There's a massive black throne at the end of the room, flanked by the largest midnight black stag I've ever seen. It's full body is taxidermied in terrifying realism except for its eyes, which have been replaced by glimmering rubies.

"Friends, thank you so much for joining me this evening. This is a big night for us, a night where we reclaim what was lost and step through the Veil." He walks around the altar, looking each guest in the face. "Once again, Death will be our servant, and we will be unstoppable."

A cheer goes up from the disciples, some even sound a little choked up.

"You all are a part of my inner circle, my most trusted companions. My family. I would gladly kill or die for any of you." He touches each of their chests as he walks by, palm flat against their hearts.

A woman in a rabbit half-mask falls to her knees, grabbing onto his ankles. Her blonde hair falls over her shoulder, and I realize it's Cylla.

He pulls her up gently and cups her cheek. "My love for you is endless." He lifts his mask and kisses her softly, then moves on to the next person, leaving her shivering and whimpering, thighs squeezed together.

If I wasn't so terrified, I'd roll my eyes.

"Tonight, we will complete the circle." He turns back to me. "With the help of our dear friend, Olivia."

I curl my hands into fists and stick up my middle fingers.

A surprised laugh flows through the disciples, but Keanu doesn't react. Instead, he steps up onto the marble table like it's a single stair and places a patent leather boot on my sternum.

I can see my tear-stained reflection in their gleam.

"I've been exceedingly patient with you, Olivia." He applies pressure, the air slowly wheezing out of my lungs. "Whether you are alive or dead, he will come."

My heart drops to my knees, the room tilting once again as my brain starts to go fuzzy from lack of oxygen.

He lifts his boot and hops down, agile as a panther. He approaches a man in a hawk mask, and I notice the blue scarf around his neck. Gideon.

"Will you do the honors of starting the ritual?" Keanu asks, touching his masked forehead to Gideon's.

"I'd be honored." Gideon places a hand on Keanu's shoulder, then turns and grabs a long, blood-red rope from the wall.

Oberon

"Take it off!" I yell, slamming Algernon into the wall hard enough to knock picture frames off the wall.

"I will! Just calm down!"

I can't stand the pity in his eyes. I feel like a poorly contained thunderstorm, rage pushing at the edges of my skin, desperate to escape. The binder has been burning continuously since Olivia was taken, struggling to contain the surge of power chasing my anger.

I will turn this city to fucking ash if that's what it takes to find her.

Ayla grabs my shoulders and pulls me away from Al, attempting to guide me to the couch, but I shake her off, more harshly than I intend. I hate feeling like this, unmoored. A rage spiral, a tornado kicked up inside me, shredding any rational thought. It takes me back to those weeks after I lost Leda, when I was nothing but anger and grief. When I wanted nothing more than to *leave*.

"We don't have time for this. Do it," I growl, holding my arm out. Black veins spider from the charred skin around my wrist, dried blood and carbon dust are caked onto the metal, taking away its shine.

"You have to calm down," Algernon says, holding his hands up. "Or you'll lose control. You can't help her if you let your power overwhelm you. You'll just be another threat."

I sink onto the couch and drop my head in my hands, rage evaporating once again into despair.

"I've always been a threat to her." My heart is an anchor, dragging all my organs down, tearing through muscle, cracking bone, destroying me from the inside.

"That's not true." Algernon sits beside me. "You've had control for decades. Don't lose it now, not when she needs you the most."

But I failed her when she needed me most before. Was I so arrogant to think that this time would be any different? That'd I'd have what it took to stand up against not only one of the strongest witches alive, but the second greatest love of my life? The man who gave me something when I had nothing, who showed me what power tasted like? Who taught me to not fear my gift, but embrace it, wield it.

The love Keanu and I had was ugly, violent, greedy. Truthfully, it was more of a sick obsession than love. But the thought of killing him, really killing him, sits like a stone on my stomach.

No matter how much I loved Keanu, it pales in comparison to my love for Olivia, and the love I had for Leda. For Keanu, I would kill. For Olivia, I would die. The difference is fundamental and affirms what I'm about to do.

A sharp gasp tears through the thick silence in the room. Algernon is on his feet in a blink, running over to wear Ayla stands leaning against the fireplace, a hand pressed to her forehead. He lowers her down to the ground and pets her hair, ensuring she doesn't accidentally hurt herself when the vision fully takes hold.

It's not often that vision hits her like this, but I notice her locket on the table, her own, removable, blocker.

A low groan slips through her teeth, every muscle in her body rigid with pain. Her eyes are alabaster white, lashes fluttering like a sleeping child.

Blood has begun to drip from her left nostril, which Algernon swipes away with his thumb.

The love my brother has for his wife is never in question, hasn't been since they were teenagers, but it's moments like this that it becomes brilliantly clear. My energetic, slightly unhinged brother is beside himself with love for Ayla, out of his mind with it.

He loved her from the moment he saw her, over a century ago. He had told me that night that she would be his wife one day. It took over 50 years, but they got there.

Leda and Ayla had been close as sisters. They got drunk together on dandelion wine under the moonlight and danced until they collapsed. Algernon and I would carry them home, tuck them in together on the couch because we knew they'd want to share coffee and complain about their hangovers in the morning.

Together, Ayla and Algernon helped me leave the Arcanum and gave me a safe place to land when my world split apart for a second time. They were the only family I had for decades, until Olivia walked into my life.

A fresh stab of grief fills my chest and I have to look away from them, from the tender way he holds her, the way she leans on him with complete trust.

Ayla's vision subsides and she sags into his arms, gasping for breath.

"Tomorrow night, Halloween. They're doing a ritual." The words rush out of her, wobbly with tears. "We have to go or..." She trails off, her head lolling onto Al's shoulder, unconscious.

He scoops her up like she's weightless, her small frame fully encapsulated in his long arms. He sets her into a recliner and tucks a blanket around her, softly kissing the top of her head before turning back to me with a heavy sigh.

"It's going to hurt," he says, looking down at the binder.

"I deserve it," I respond, holding my arm out to him, at his mercy.

He shakes his head and sits on the coffee table, placing my wrist on his lap. "So melodramatic," he teases. "Just, don't kill me alright?"

"Doesn't matter. I can just bring you back." I offer a meager smile.

He grabs a thin book of poetry from the stack beside him and hands it to me. "Bite down."

"Seriously?" I take the book, looking at him incredulously.

"Your call." He shrugs, then focuses his gaze on the binder.

Blinding pain rips through my arm, stabbing down to the marrow. It hurt like hell when he first created it, but that was a flu shot compared to this unholy torture. I shove the book into my mouth and bite down, swallowing the scream tearing at my lungs. It isn't long before darkness starts to creep into my vision and I black out.

It goes on for an hour as Algernon rewrites every cell from his patented gold hybrid material back to skin matching my DNA.

I fade in and out of consciousness, the pain unbearable. But finally, blessedly, it ends, and a tsunami of sensation crashes over me.

My power has been bound for so long that I forgot what it felt like in all its glory. I can sense every heartbeat, every intake of breath. I can trail my hand along the dozens and dozens of tethers that zigzag through my field of vision, every life within 100 meters at the tip of my fingers.

My brain feels like it's splitting in two, the stimulation agonizing after so many years of silence. But it's exhilarating too, and a wicked grin breaks out on my face.

Algernon watches me warily, and grimaces at the smile on my face. "Ben, are you sure you can handle this?"

I crack my neck. "What's our plan?"

"Raise hell," Ayla says, lifting her head and grinning back at me. "You're so much more fun like this."

"Maniacs, both of you." Algernon rolls his eyes, but cracks a smile.

We spend the next few hours deliberating and coming up with the bones of a plan. Securing Olivia's safety is priority number one, then take out as much of the Arcanum as we can. The more that are left alive, the more likely they are to regroup.

Algernon and Ayla will distract the disciples and protect Olivia while I make my move for Keanu. Whether I manage to kill him or not, it'll be me that suffers the consequences. If things go south, they can get Olivia out, and that's all that matters.

If we can dismantle the Arcanum at the same time, so be it, but her life matters more. I'm not interested in saving the world, just my girl.

Suddenly I feel nagging at the back of my brain. Someone's crossed through my wards.

There's a knock at the door.

Al and I look at Ayla, but she shrugs.

"I don't know *everything*."

I get up and answer the door, shocked to see Dr. Theodore Sane standing stiffly on my door mat.

"I believe I may be of some assistance," he says, removing his sunglasses and black hat, his violet eyes meeting mine.

Algernon appears behind me. "Teddy!" He exclaims.

The Dean breaks into a smile. "Algernon, my dear friend."

Al pushes past me and the two men embrace, clapping each other on the back.

"Impeccable timing, as usual." Al grins, holding him by the shoulders at arms length. "We could very much use your assistance."

"And I, yours." Theodore glances at me. "If you'll have me, of course."

"And how do I know you aren't working with the Arcanum?" I cross my arms.

"Because I would never let harm befall my students. I want my school back. Folke is a place for learning, for community, not malicious scheming.

Folke must move out of the Arcanum's shadow, and the only way to do that is to destroy the head of the snake." His sincerity sings along his snow white tether. Despite his calm expression, I can feel his rage as if it were my own, his hurt and guilt.

"The more the merrier," I concede, stepping aside to let him in.

We fill him in on our plan, and he provides the location and access to where Keanu is operating from, the Catacombs underneath the school. Sane will get us in and to the right place without interference, and we'll handle the rest.

Like Ayla, Sane can see into the future, using formulas and numerology to predict outcomes with near 100% accuracy. There's probably about a million other things he can do, but math was never my forte.

The day ticks by slowly as we prepare, our patience worn thin by anxiety.

Finally, the sun begins to set.

Olivia

T he doors open with a boom, flying off their hinges and shaking the marble beneath me.

Everyone screams, each of the disciples dropping into a defensive position. Three move to flank Keanu: Cylla, Idris, and a third I don't recognize.

Only Gideon remains motionless, holding the red rope in his hands.

I see Keanu straighten his spine, and know exactly who just arrived.

"Ah, the guest of honor," Keanu says, shedding his mask and walking around the altar, raising his arms in welcome.

I try to angle my head to see Oberon, but can barely move. Something touches my wrist, making me jump, then glossy copper hair falls into my periphery.

"Ayla!" I mumble through the gag.

She winks at me and flips the catch, removing it from my mouth. "Stay low and quiet," she whispers, then moves to start working on my restraints.

"Traitor," Oberon snarls, and I see Gideon flinch.

I ignore the flare of pity for him. He deserves to be called that and more.

"Spare us your hypocrisy, Oberon," Keanu says lightly.

One of my wrists pops free, then the other, and I prop myself up onto my elbows, not being able to resist turning to see him.

Oberon stands in the doorway, dressed in a black button-down and slacks, looking every bit the Grim Reaper, my God of Death. Algernon stands beside him, also dressed in all black, looking tall and deadly, eyes flicking around the room.

Oberon's eyes flick to mine, locking our gazes together. My heart flutters at the relief plastered on his face. I want to run and tackle him, kiss him until the sun freezes over, but then Keanu takes a step forward, and his gaze slides away, hardening once again.

"State your terms," Oberon growls, crossing his arms over his chest. The lack of any metallic glint catches my eye, as I'm sure it does Keanu, and I gasp. His binder is gone, leaving only a ring of scar tissue behind.

He has his full, unbridled power.

The thought sends a thrill through me, electric adrenaline that makes my heart hammer in my chest.

If Keanu is surprised, he hides it well, barely even glancing at the scarred skin where the binder used to be. Instead, he smiles even wider, his teeth snow white and sharp.

"I want what I always have, what *we* always have." His eyes darken and he continues to stride toward Oberon. *"Everything."* The word booms around the room, bouncing off the walls and vaulted ceilings, making my ears ring.

Bitter hatred rises in my throat. I could slap him for looking at Oberon like that, like he's something to eat, to play with. Like he's still *his.*

Oberon is mine, but more importantly, he's his own.

He'll never be anyone's weapon again.

The chandelier above my head starts to sway. At first, I think it's a trick of the light, but then a drop of gold lands on my nose. Definitely not the light. The chandelier is melting, thick ropes of gold reaching down toward me like vines.

Ayla frees my ankles, and I pull them up to my chest. The streams of gold reach the marble and start to solidify, forming a massive golden birdcage around me.

I reach out to touch the solid bars. Immovable, impenetrable.

I look back at Algernon, and he flashes me a wink.

Keanu rakes his eyes over the cage, furrows his brows a bit, then frowns. Apparently, gold is something he can't manipulate.

"Our little bird in a cage. What are you protecting her from? The only one who wants violence is you." Keanu clicks his tongue when neither of the brothers respond. "I see you want a fight, Raith's." He signals his disciples. "Then a fight you shall have."

The room erupts with magic, the air turning to highly charged static. They throw everything they have at the brothers, but Algernon throws his hands up and deflects every move with a solid wall of air, or what was air a second ago. Now it looks like a fun house mirror, conjured out of, well, thin air, distorting the room in a sickening spiral.

Someone throws a marble bust, shattering the mirror, but Algernon had already moved on to his next trick. He drops to his hands and knees, his fingers splayed wide.

Oberon has disappeared amidst all the chaos.

The disciples rush forward, but before they can reach him the marble floor turns to liquid, just long enough for several of the disciples to sink to their ankles or fall flat on their faces.

Algernon lifts his hands and the second his skin breaks contact with the ground, it solidifies back into stone. Screams rip through the air as the marble crushes all the bones in their hands and feet.

Several gunshots ring out to my left and I whirl to see Ayla shooting down the trapped disciples in an orderly fashion. *Holy shit.*

Cylla rushes at me, fire licking up her arms and at the ends of her hair. I scream, and another gunshot goes off beside my head, throwing the room into ringing silence. I look over my shoulder and see Ayla, her gun pointed directly at Cylla.

She falters, but doesn't stop, until Oberon lunges from the shadows. He grabs Cylla by the flaming hair, unflinching, and whispers something in her ear. She screams as the fat and tissue melt from her body, her face becoming shriveled and dry, all of her beauty and youth sucked away in an instant. He releases her, and she crumbles to the floor, a pile of leather and bones.

A swarm of identical masked men stumble forward and reach for Oberon, blending together and apart like a head spinning kaleidoscope. They circle him, jeering.

One of the clones backs up to the birdcage, and I notice his cloak snag on a jagged sliver of gold.

I've never thrown a punch before in my life, but I have approximately one second to act before he moves and is lost in the illusion. I bring my knee up to my chest, my legs shaking, and donkey kick him as hard as I can in the kidneys.

Pain sings from my ankle, up my leg, and into my back, but the disciple lets out a small, startled cry, and that's enough for Oberon to lock onto him.

Oberon's hand strikes out like a snake, grabbing the third attacker's face. The other bodies dissolve into nothingness, just a trick of the light. Oberon crushes the man's skull between his hands, reducing it into ash, leaving a headless, twitching corpse behind.

It's a horrifying massacre, ruthless and calculated. A clean sweep of the inner circle of the Arcanum.

I should be appalled by Oberon's cruelty and the intensity of his power. But then he looks up at me and winks, and all I feel is a breathtaking rush of love and arousal.

The three of them work so quickly that the fight is over in a few moments, and everyone but the three brothers, Keanu, Ayla, and myself are disposed of. Keanu hadn't made a single move to stop them.

Keanu starts clapping, slowly, then faster, and the room starts to shiver, building in intensity until it's impossible to stand, throwing everyone to the ground.

I hold on desperately to the bars, and I feel the marble shake and crack, my brain rattling in my head.

Keanu points to one of the large tapestries on the wall and sends it flying across the room at Oberon, where it wraps him up like a straitjacket, squeezing hard enough that his eyes bulge.

It lasts only seconds before the fabric disintegrates to ash, and Oberon spreads his arms wide. That horrible inky blackness eclipses the whites of his eyes, tendrils of darkness spider webbing across his face and hands. The tips of his fingers start to gray, then blacken, like necrotic tissue. He grins.

Apparently, they both have a flair for the dramatics. I almost chuckle, but then the disciples start to rise.

Keanu tries to freeze them in place, but he is no longer their Master. They start calling out to him, crying for him, begging to be released, to be saved. But he appears to be unmoved.

His feet lift off the ground as he draws his hands together. Blue light glows between his palms, steadily growing brighter and brighter. Lighting crackles inside the sphere of light.

The undead disciples desperately try to grab at his feet and legs, but he's just out of their reach. They climb on each other like animals, like a grotesque scene from The Walking Dead.

Keanu rolls his shoulders, then spikes the sphere directly at the tangle of bodies. It's like they're struck by one of Zeus' fabled lightning rods. I can see their skeletons reflected in the blast, and then the light is gone, leaving only ash and teeth where 8 people stood, along with the sickening smell of burnt flesh.

He floats back down to the ground, looking eerily calm.

"No more bodies to play with, Oberon," he sneers, raising his hands to create another ball of kinetic energy.

A fresh wave of fear courses through me, shattering the glimmer of hope I was desperately clinging onto. I watch my love with bated breath, praying to whoever is listening to spare him, just this once.

Keanu launches the cannonball of power directly at Oberon, who lunges to the left, but is too slow. It hits him squarely in the stomach, sending him flying backwards and into the wall with a nauseating crack.

Algernon rushes Keanu, but Keanu is faster and flies onto Oberon, who lays on the floor in a broken heap, motionless.

Keanu grabs him by the throat and lifts him off the ground, that blue light spilling from his hands and spreading under Oberon's skin, its frightening glow emitting from his slack mouth.

I'm too stunned to cry, every sound in the room vanishing as ringing fills my ears. My vision narrows to a single pinpoint, Oberon's vacant eyes.

Three gunshots cut through the din, and I wrench my eyes away to see Ayla standing in the middle of the room, gun pointed at Keanu.

Disgusting blue-black blood pours from the bullet wounds in his back, and the kinetic energy in his hands flickers as he registers what happened.

That fraction of a second is enough time for Gideon and Algernon to tackle Keanu to the ground and pin his hands. Algernon withdraws a spiked golden collar from his pocket and clasps it around Keanu's throat, the point stabbing into his skin. He rails against their hold like a rabid dog, screaming as blood soaks his shirt collar.

Oberon stirs on the floor, his fingers rolling into fists. Slowly, he pushes himself onto his knees and rolls his head up, pale, but alive.

His eyes lock on the massive stag standing behind Keanu's throne, and I see the corner of his mouth lift up a fraction.

A horrifying groan rips through the air, rendering everyone silent. The stag turns its head with a sickening crack, looking straight at Oberon.

"Fucking Christ," Algernon mutters, mouth hanging open.

Even Keanu looks stunned.

The stag leaps off the pedestal, turns, and barrels straight toward him. Keanu throws up his hands in an attempt to stop it, but the stag is too quick. It gores him through the center of his ribs and lifts him into the air, pinning him against the wall, trapping his arms. Blood flows freely from the gaping hole in his sternum, coating the stag in viscera. It drips down onto his throne, a strange blue against the onyx stone.

Oberon steps around the stag and peers up at Keanu, who's drowning in his own blood and weakly trying to pull the antler from his chest. Oberon pats the stag on the shoulder tenderly, and the beast takes a few steps back, withdrawing its antlers and dropping Keanu with a meaty thud onto his throne.

Despite the softball-sized hole in his chest, Keanu recovers enough to stand, chest heaving. His skin is deathly pale, but his eyes glitter when he turns to Oberon.

"Turn my own Familiar against me, eh? Couldn't stomach the kill yourself?" He takes several steps forward. "You were a coward then, and you're a coward now. You and I both know that you can't kill me. But *I* killed you *and* pretty Leda. One day, I'll have precious Olivia, too, unless you're willing to trade your love for your life. For power beyond your wildest imagination." Keanu smirks, stepping closer to him, their chests nearly touching.

"I can see how badly you want this," he breathes, eyes searching Oberon's stoic face, unflinching despite the revelation of the truth behind

Leda's murder. "How badly you crave...power." Keanu reaches out to touch him, but Oberon catches his wrist in a vice grip, knuckles white.

Then, Oberon laughs, the sound so sinister it sends a chill down my spine. "You, Keanu, are a speck of dust. An insignificant thing." Oberon grabs him by the throat and lifts him into the air. "What could you possibly know about power?"

Keanu opens his mouth to argue, eyes flashing with rage, but then screws up his face in confusion, then pain. His body rapidly disintegrates into a pile of charcoal black ash before he even has time to scream.

We all freeze, held hostage by staggering shock.

In a blink Keanu was gone, dissolved to nothing. Eviscerated.

He underestimated Oberon, and it cost him his life.

Oberon slowly sinks to the floor, kneeling in the ashes of his enemy, his past lover, and hangs his head.

Algernon pushes through the shock and rushes over to me, grasping the bars of my cage and muttering something under his breath. The chandelier melts back down, leaving a glimmering pool of gold around me.

I scramble off the altar and to Oberon's side, gathering him in my arms, tears finally forcing their way up and out of my throat.

He turns and crushes me into his chest, burying his face in my hair. "My love, I missed you so much," he breathes, voice raspy and shaking. "Are you alright?" He leans back and cups my face, inspecting every millimeter. The blackness fades from his hands and face.

Tears roll down my cheeks, and I smile. "I'm perfect."

He flashes me that lopsided grin, the one that turns my heart to mush, and crashes his lips against mine. I can taste the salt and ash on his skin, feel his pain in the desperate way he parts my lips with his tongue, drinking me down. I could drown in him, I'd let him eat me alive so that we'd never be apart again.

Out of the corner of my eye, I see a cloud of ashes start to rise from the ground and off of Oberon's clothes, swirling gently. I turn my head and see Algernon guiding them with his hands over to a black marble urn where Keanu's throne once rested, the stone pieced together with rivers of gold. He funnels the ashes inside and seals it with a marble cork, then bathes the top in liquid gold, which quickly hardens to seal the ashes inside.

Oberon turns my head back towards him. "He will never hurt us again," he says, emotion heavy in his voice.

"I'm so proud of you." I put my hand over his heart. "I love you, Oberon."

Moisture collects on his lower lashes, and a flush creeps into his cheeks. "I was so afraid to show you...me. What I was truly capable of." He looks at the scar on his wrist, red and angry but healing.

"It was incredible." I gently brush my fingers along his arm. "You're incredible."

He pulls me in for another kiss, this time much softer. "I love you, Olivia."

"I hate to break up the moment, but what are we going to do about this?" Algernon calls out.

We turn and see him standing beside Gideon, who's wrapped up in the red rope he held earlier. Ayla has the gun pressed against his temple, her mouth set in a grim line.

Gideon's expression is impossible to read, somewhere between pride and discomfort.

Oberon sighs.

"I think you should forgive him," I whisper quietly enough that only Oberon can hear.

He looks at me skeptically. "Why?"

"He's a victim too. And he loves you," I touch his cheek. "He deserves forgiveness too."

Oberon stares at me for a moment, then stands with a groan and walks over to his brothers. He nods at Ayla to lower the gun. She rolls her eyes, but drops her hands to her sides. He unties Gideon and takes a few steps back, then hauls off a wicked punch straight to Gideon's jaw.

"I should let her shoot you," Oberon growls, shaking out his fist and crossing his arms.

Gideon clutches his already bruising face, wincing. "I would."

"Never forget that I didn't. And that it is solely because of Olivia's kindness." He points at me. "Betray her trust, and I will not spare you a third time."

Gideon looks back and forth between his younger brothers, then over at Ayla and I, and back.

"I have so much to learn from you two," he says after a few moments, looking thoughtful. "I'm not sure where all that compassion came from, but it certainly wasn't me."

Algernon snorts, trying to stifle a smile.

Someone clears their throat, and we all turn to see Dr. Sane standing in the doorway, arms crossed.

"Gideon, with me," he says coolly.

"Now, if you'll excuse me, I have to grovel for my job." Gideon bows dramatically, then walks out behind Sane, dropping his mask at the door.

Oberon walks back over to me and offers a hand, pulling me to my feet.

"Home?" He asks.

"Home."

Oberon

I'm sliding the slip off her shoulders before we even get all the way through the front door, my hands all over her. I can't believe she's really here, under my fingertips, alive and well. Safe.

She drags me down in the foyer, undoing my belt and fisting my cock through my boxers.

Our tongues battle for dominance, the kiss bruising and intense, never getting enough of each other. Desperate for more, more, more.

She pulls out my throbbing cock and straddles my hips, dragging the pulsing head through her wet lips, shivering as pleasure lights up her nerves. Slowly, I sink into her liquid heat, relishing the sinful stretch. We moan into each other's mouths, tasting each other's pleasure, refusing to part for even a second.

She's here. I'm here. We're here together. And safe.

"Fuck, Liv," I growl, grabbing the silk fabric bunched at her hips. "This looks exactly like Leda's wedding dress." I drag my rough hands up her delicate curves and wrap them tightly around her neck. "You'd make such a pretty little bride." I bite the soft spot under her ear, earning a breathy moan, and massage away the sting with my tongue.

Her pussy spasms around me, my words pushing her closer. She tries to rock against me, needing friction, release.

I buck my hips up, hitting that spot deep inside that makes her scream. I fuck her fast and hard, the head of my cock spearing her cervix. Our bodies slam together as we battle for every scrap of flesh and pleasure the other has to offer.

Olivia's nails dig into my shoulders, drawing blood and leaving angry red marks across my skin. I bite her hard enough to bruise, marking her. *Mine.*

Her orgasm crests, squeezing me and pulling the air from my lungs, coiling so tightly it's unbearable. A punishing snap of my hips rips her apart, her orgasm dragging her under, screaming.

She collapses onto my chest, blind and boneless, but I continue to rut into her ruthlessly as she twitches and shakes with aftershocks.

"You're mine, precious. My body, my cunt, my mouth." I glide my tongue up her cheek, making her shiver. "My tears, my screams. All mine."

"Yes, yes!" She babbles as she bounces on my cock, devoid of coherent thought, dizzy with joy as her second orgasm looms.

"Give me one more, pretty girl. My perfect little wife. One more."

She comes again, her pussy releasing a scalding gush of liquid as my cock wrenches the orgasm out of her with brutal force. I hold her in the air, pistoning my hips in and out of her abused pussy. She can do nothing but take it, swept away in a torrent of bliss.

"Olivia!" I cry her name as my orgasm overtakes me, slamming her down onto my cock as I fill her up. My body trembles with aftershocks, quivering uncontrollably as pleasure saps the energy from my bones. "I love you so much, Liv," I say, cupping her face and kissing her deeply, warm and sweet, wiping away her tears with my thumbs.

"I love you," She pants, too weak to do anything but smile like a fool.

"So, is that a yes?" I smirk, tucking her hair behind her ear and searching her face.

"Was that a proposal?" She teases.

I stroke her sweaty cheek with the back of my knuckles, growing serious. "You've been my wife for a century, I want to finally get the chance to enjoy being your husband."

Her heart rate picks up.

"Olivia Hunter, my fierce, compassionate, lifelong love, will you marry me?"

There's a single moment of agonizing hesitation before tears well in her eyes, and she bobs her head yes. Relief loosens the last threads of tension in my body, and I pull her down to kiss her, savoring the velvet of her lips and the heat of her tongue. *Mine.*

My cock starts to stiffen again inside her as we kiss, and that minx wiggles her hips in acknowledgment, swirling my cock through her sopping cunt. She smiles against my lips, full of mischief and joy.

I hold her tight against my chest with one arm and flip us over, pressing my weight down onto her, feeling every inch of her skin against mine. I rest my forearms on either side of her head, peppering kisses all over her blushing face as I slowly start thrusting, dragging my cock along her tender walls.

She quivers underneath me, flushed and sweating, warm and loose. Ripe for another round.

"My wife," I coo, nibbling along her jaw, lapping at the bruises I left across her skin. Her taste is salty and sweet, decadent. "I can't wait to marry you again, make you mine."

"I'm already yours," she mewls, grinding against me and making an obscene, incredibly erotic squelching sound, desperate for me to move faster. *Greedy girl.*

But there's no reason to rush now, we've got all the time in the world. Eternity. She'll be with me until the world ends, and we perish together, slipping into sweet oblivion, in love and complete.

I start moving my hips a fraction faster, groaning as her walls clamp around me, refusing to let me go and pulling me deeper with every thrust. She was made for me, and I for her.

"Tell me about your dream wedding, love," I say, wanting to hear the words from the lips of an angel strangled by pleasure.

"I want—" a moan interrupts her as I tilt my hips upwards, hitting that sweet spot that makes her back bow. "I want to be in nature...the for...the forest or something." She can barely string words together as I grind into her, scraping every inch of her hot cunt with my rock-hard cock.

"What else?" I encourage as she loses her train of thought. I can hardly blame her, the need to fuck her deeper, harder, saws away at my control.

"Black dress," she pants, digging her nails into my shoulders, the sting making my cock throb. "Red wine...cheeseburgers."

I can't help but laugh and pause at that. "Cheeseburgers?"

"Mhmm, please don't stop," she whines, puffy lips pouting. She bucks her hips into me, making her tits bounce beautifully.

"I think I'll stay just like this," I smirk, the squeeze of her muscles flexing making me drool. "Keep going, baby."

She continues rocking her hips against me, the gears turning as she tries to chase her orgasm while stringing together a coherent thought.

"Handfasting," she manages, grabbing my scarred wrist. "Just us."

"Would you like a ring?" I ask, lifting her hand off my arm and sucking her ring finger into my mouth, swirling around the digit with my tongue. Little does she know, I already have one. Leda always took hers off before bed, it was the only thing of hers that I still had. It only seemed right that it should be returned to its rightful owner.

She shakes her head, her cunt clamping rhythmically around me, her orgasm looming. "I just want you."

"Sweet girl." I grin. I reward her by relinquishing my control and slamming into her, fucking her hard and deep. I dip my fingers between her legs and start massaging her hot, swollen clit. "Now, come for me."

She obliges almost instantly, her big doe eyes rolling back as her pussy squeezes my cock so tightly I'm afraid she might rip it off and keep it for herself. She screams with a wicked smile across her face, and I love her so much I can barely breathe.

I manage a few more delicious thrusts before my orgasm takes hold. I pull out and pump my cock over her stomach, splashing her with rope after rope of scalding release.

She looks gorgeous covered in my come, a sinless darling fucked within an inch of her life. Marked by a monster.

Finally spent, she sags into the ground, her eyes fluttering closed.

"Bath, please," she murmurs, lazily drawing her finger through the pools of semen.

I chuckle. "Course, baby."

I draw her a bath and get her settled with wine and a book. Church hops up and lays on the edge of the tub behind her head, purring and attempting to make biscuits on the ceramic.

After a few minutes, I go into my closet and pull down a small, well-worn safe. I dial in the code, Leda and I's wedding day, and it pops open. Inside is some cash, my mother's Grimoire, and a green velvet ring box. I take out the ring box, my chest swelling, and flip it open.

It's a gold ring, carved with delicate botanicals, set with an emerald the size of my pinky nail haloed with white diamonds. Leda always said it was a bit much, but her eyes lit up every time she put it on. Nothing's too much for my love.

I close the box and head back into the bathroom, kneeling down beside the tub with the box behind my back.

"Hi, baby." She smiles at me, setting her book aside.

"Hey." My heart melts at the soft way she's looking at me, the corners of her perfect mouth tilted up. I pull the box out from behind my back. "Change your mind?"

Her mouth falls open.

I open the lid, and her eyes widen, and her hand comes up to press against her chest.

"Oberon, oh my god. I can't accept that." She meets my gaze, tears gathering at the corners of her eyes.

"Well, that's unfortunate." I grab her hand and slip the ring onto her finger, a perfect fit. "Because you're mine, whether you like it or not."

She stares at it in awe. Tilting her hand to watch the emerald glimmer in the candlelight. Suddenly, she reaches out and grabs my face, dragging me over the edge of the tub.

I catch myself before I fall in and kiss her eagerly, laughing. "I love you," I murmur against her lips, grinning like a fool.

"I love you, too," she replies, nipping my bottom lip.

I strip down, and we spend the rest of the evening languishing in the tub, making love and plans for tomorrow, November 1st. Our wedding day.

We head out just before sunrise, when the air is still quiet and heavy with dew, nothing but bugs and animals stirring.

She's wearing a black slip with a corseted waist. It's short, stopping a little above mid-thigh, with delicate ruffles and a lace underskirt. I put on a black silk shirt, leaving it loose and unbuttoned past my sternum, goosebumps rising as we walk in the chilled air.

I have a perfect spot in mind that's a few meters into the forest behind my house, with an ancient willow tree and full cypresses. This time of the year, a blanket of colorful leaves cover the ground, and a gentle mist swirls through the underbrush.

The intricate Handfasting rope is draped around my neck, a thick braided cord of pumpkin orange, deep maroon, and midnight blue, adorned with gold charms and dried herbs, anointed with my mother's special rosemary and basil oil blend. I'm also carrying a picnic basket, with two bottles of wine, one being a sparkling red to toast with, the other a rich cab to savor, along with a ceremonial dagger, and a vial of clear liquid.

Olivia's carrying a woven blanket, with Church burritoed inside, and some beeswax candles anointed with the same oil blend.

It doesn't take us long to reach the spot, and it's even more breathtaking than I imagined, although it's a challenge to look anywhere but at her heart-stopping smile.

I create a salt circle around the perimeter and lay out the blanket, while she lights the candles.

We join hands under the cool shade of the willow tree as the sky turns pink.

My heart hammers in my chest, excitement stealing my breath. I try to remember the speech I rehearsed, but my soul speaks instead.

"Olivia, I have loved you for more than a hundred years, and I'll love you for however many more I have left. You are my reason for being, my reason for breathing. I promise to always be your hero, and protect you from pain." I feel tears start to rise, clogging my throat. "I can't promise that there won't be hardship, but I can promise that you'll never have to face it alone. I will be by your side in this life and the next."

Tears run down her flushed cheeks, making her chocolate eyes bright. "I never thought I'd find love like in the story books. It always seemed so impossible, too perfect for ordinary life. But no life is ordinary, and you've ensured that mine will always be extraordinary. You are my great love, my soulmate, my person. And I will always be a safe place for you to land. I will always love you, not in spite of the broken parts and shadows inside of you, but because of them."

We're both crying now, holding onto each other's hands for dear life. I take the silver dagger from my belt and hold it out to her.

"Traditionally, witches conduct a blood bond before Handfasting, a physical bond to coincide with the symbolic one."

Her eyes widen a fraction as she takes the heavy dagger.

"We don't have to do this if you don't feel comfortable, but—"

She opens her left hand to the sky, and drags the blade across the satin skin of her palm, parting her flesh easily, crimson blooming in the wake of the blade. She grimaces slightly in discomfort, then passes the dagger back to me.

"There's no half-way with you, my love." She smiles.

I drag the blade across my own palm, and press my wound against hers. Because of the ceremonial blade, it won't heal for at least a few hours.

I sheath the dagger and take hand-fasting rope from around my neck, and we start binding our arms, winding it snugly and securing it at the ends. I murmur an old spell under my breath, one that my mother taught me when I was a child. A spell of endless, unconditional love, one of companionship and closeness. A bond built on friendship, trust, and loyalty.

"Olivia, will you be my wife?" I ask, my cheeks sore from smiling.

"I will." She squeezes our bound hands. "Oberon, will you be my husband?"

"I will, today and every day." I pull her in and capture her lips in mine, sealing our vows. Our tear-streaked lips feel damp and salty, the warm kiss reminiscent of a comforting autumn dawn.

The blood bond sizzles to life between our palms, warm and tingly, spreading up our arms and into our chests, settling comfortably around our hearts.

I lift her into my arms and carry her to the blanket, laying her down gently, our bound arms resting over her head. The kiss deepens, heady and raw, our tongues delving into each others mouths, savoring the taste of this moment.

I skate my hand down her side, the silk cool to the touch against our heated skin, and dip my fingers between her legs. Her dripping pussy unfurls for me, soft as the petals of a rose. I slowly ease my fingers into her, drinking down the precious moans that fall from her lips.

I pet her clit gently and she squirms beneath me, tilting her hips into my touch.

"My needy little wife," I purr into her ear, my lips brushing softly against her skin.

Her back arches against me, her hand wandering over the planes of my torso, making goosebumps rise on my skin.

"Don't tease me," she whines, tugging lightly on my hair before tucking it behind my ear.

I chuckle and remove my hand from her warm center, unsheathing the dagger at my hip. I bring it up to her chin, the tip barely touching her skin. I feel her bound hand tighten against mine, our fingers twined together, warm blood still pulsing between our palms.

I drag the tip slowly down the column of her neck, feeling her tether fizzle with excitement, her heart rate kicking into double time. Because of the blood bond, every ounce of pleasure she feels, I feel too, along with every ounce of pain,

The knife cuts easily through the thin fabric of her dress, slicing it quickly down the middle, leaving her gorgeous curves on full display for me.

She gasps as the cold air rushes across her heated skin, turning her pink nipples to hardened buds.

I drag the tip of the knife back up the swell of her stomach and between the valley of her breasts. I press gently into the curve of her left breast, just below her heart, coaxing droplets of ruby blood to the surface.

Her pain quickly morphs into pleasure, and she arches into my caress, panting.

I turn the blade onto myself and make a cut in the same place, four cuts actually, an oblong diamond, the closest I can get to an 'O'.

Olivia raises her trembling hand and presses her finger in the blood dripping down my chest, smearing it across my skin. Then she touches her breast, leaving a crimson trail across the velvet skin. She suddenly reaches up and grabs me by the throat, dragging me down on top of her, slamming our mouths together in a fervid kiss.

I drop the knife and unbutton my trousers, freeing my aching cock from its confines. I plunge into her with one thrust, nearly collapsing from the blistering pleasure, doubled by our bond.

She's so hot and ready for me, her walls already shivering with tension.

I thrust slowly, wanting to feel every inch of her perfect cunt. To feel every bit of my *wife's* perfect body and soul. It's bliss, making love to her, coaxing those pretty sounds from her lips, wringing orgasm after orgasm from her goddess-like pussy.

"Oberon," she cries, grasping at my chest, dragging her fingers through my blood. "Please."

I can't stop the rumble that rises from my chest and I snap my hips forward, forcing her up the blanket. I pound into her, my body and soul demanding her orgasm, her submission.

Her walls start to tighten, squeezing my cock in that bone-crushing vice grip.

"That's it, baby. Come all over your husband's cock," I growl, grabbing her face with my free hand to force her eyes to meet mine. "Gods, my little cunt feels so fucking good."

I feel her orgasm crest with those final words and crash down onto her, dragging me over the edge with her. I grind into her, prolonging our joint climax for as long as I can.

We collapse into a puddle of sweat, blood, and cum, panting heavily. She kisses me sweetly, and giggles, exhaustion and joy settling over us both.

She sits up as best she can with our hands bound and grabs the sparkling wine, popping the cork. She pours a generous amount into her mouth, some trickling down her chin and onto her chest.

I grab her and lick up the trail of wine, then open my mouth wide for her to pour some in, which she happily obliges.

I turn and fish the vial out of the picnic basket, and hold it out to her.

"What is that?" she asks, taking it and holding it up to swirl the liquid in the yellow sunlight.

"Algernon's Elixir of Life," I answer simply.

"Swear?"

"Swear." I smile.

"Forever's a long time," she says, popping the cork and taking a sniff.

"And not nearly long enough."

"You won't get sick of me?"

I look down at the still bleeding 'O' carved over my heart. "Never, my love."

"Promise?"

"I'd pinky promise, but my pinky is currently bound to yours by enchanted rope and our blood."

She smiles, bright and beaming, then pours the elixir down her throat in one swallow.

I feel her tether change, get thicker and stronger, as immortality takes hold. It shouldn't feel any different to her, but it's clear as day to me.

"Less climactic than I thought," she says, patting herself down to check for any physical changes.

"I'll give you climactic." I smirk, before wrapping my arm around her and dragging her back to the ground with me, capturing her wine-sweetened lips in mine.

My Olivia, my Leda, my life, my wife.

It's a perfect morning with her, and that was more than enough to be grateful for a lifetime.

Finis.

Bonus Chapter

Keanu, Winter, 1921

Oberon has avoided me for months, although I suspect his reasoning has changed. Still fear, but of a different breed. A fear I can work with.

I step out of the shower, wrapping a towel around my waist, and approach the mirror. I smooth my dark brows, brush the longer top layer of hair back and off of my forehead, smoothing the shorter sides to lay flat. To keep myself focused, I've taken to the gym, and my new body is a marble testament to that work. I've never even a particularly muscular man, more height than anything else, but now, I rivaled even Oberon, although he's considerably broader than I am.

Just the thought of his bear-like shoulders has my cock tenting the towel.

Poor Oberon had a tough day today. Some dimwit trespassed onto campus in pursuit of one of my students, and stumbled across the absolute last professor he would want. Oberon laid him out without a second thought, killed him instantly, failing to consider that he'd never killed anyone before.

He'll adapt.

A solid knock on my door jolts me from my thoughts.

"What?" I stalk over to the door and pull it open, not caring that I'm almost completely naked.

Gideon blinks but manages to keep a straight face. "He's not doing well."

"What do you mean?" I turn back into my room and drop the towel, stepping into a black pair of trousers and throwing an undershirt over my head.

"He's still sitting in the courtyard. Hasn't spoken, hasn't eaten. He's frozen."

"And why are you coming to me about this?" I ask, coy, pulling on my shoes.

Gideon huffs in frustration. "Because you two are twin flames or some stupid shit like that. You've got the same foul attitude."

I bark out a laugh, although the words strike a chord deep in my chest. *Twin flames*. I like the sound of that.

"I'll handle it," I wink, getting to my feet. I make the quick walk out of the Manor and across to the Main building.

It's eerily quiet, not a soul in the building besides those trapped in the relics displayed here. The courtyard is at the center of the room, just behind the pyre, completely walled in by glass. I can see Oberon sitting on the edge of the fountain, his head in his hands, moonlight spilling over him.

Ash dusts his shoes and trousers, is raked through his black hair. *Gods*, I must've missed that detail where he rendered the predator to ash. Killed is a damn understatement.

Pride wells up inside me, and I make my way towards him. He doesn't look up when i open the glass doors and cross the cobblestones. Doesn't look up when I crouch in front of him.

"My prince," I murmur, gently sliding my hands beneath his to cup his jaw and tilt his head up. "Your heart is so heavy."

His eyes search my face, heavy lidded and watery, following the arch of my eyebrows, the slope of my nose, the bow of my lips. Heat sparks behind them, the hunger of an animal that's spotted an escape.

"I can make the pain go away," I whisper, wiping his tears with my thumbs. "Can I take your pain away?"

His chin dips, the smallest nod of consent, and I lean forward, pressing my lips to his cheeks, tasting the salt of his tears, the chalky ash of what he'd done. I ghost my lips across his cheekbone and his brows, down his nose, to the other cheek. His skin is cold as ice and he shivers slightly underneath me.

I move to pull away when his hand flies into my hair and yanks me back, slamming his mouth on mine with an intensity that makes my head spin. There's no love or affection in the way his tongue fucks my mouth, or the way his teeth tear at my lips. It's all rage, raw hunger, madness, and it snaps my resolve like a bird bone.

I give every bit of ferocity back to him, matching him lick for lick, bite for bite, until neither of us can breathe, every ounce of air stolen straight from our chests.

I drag him onto the ground with me, feeling his heavy weight crush me against the cobblestones, their chill a welcome balm to the burning under my skin. I tug his shirt over his head, dragging my hands down his broad chest and strong stomach. His skin is so hot it's like he's about to burst into flame, beads of sweat already collecting in the valleys of his throat. I flatten my tongue against his collarbone, lapping up every salty bead of moisture I can find. He fumbles with my shirt, eventually just tearing it down the middle so he can press against me, heart to heart.

"Key," he pants, his granite hard cock grinding into my hip as he ruts against me, so fucking needy.

"How long has it been since someone's touched you?" I purr, reaching between us to begin unbuckling his belt, the metal loud against the stone in the quiet courtyard.

"Too long," he grates, moaning in relief when my hand wraps around his scalding flesh.

Fuck me, he's even bigger than I thought.

"I'll never leave you without, Oberon." I capture his lips again, sucking on his lower lip as I slowly start pumping his cock.

"Gods, fuck," he hisses, letting his head fall into the crook of my shoulder as he thrusts into my hand. He starts pawing at my pants, grasping my aching cock and squeezing it.

"Ah!" I exhale, pleasure shooting through me, making my cock throb in his grip.

He unbuttons my pants and pulls my cock out, the cold air doing nothing to sate the heat radiating from it. I pull out his cock as well, our shafts sliding against one another, slick with precum and burning.

His mouth finds mine against as we thrust our hips in time, rubbing our cocks between us, the friction making my head spin.

"Fuck, I knew you'd feel good, but this," I pant, reaching around to feel his ass muscles flexing with effort.

"Everything you wanted, *prince?*" He mocks, biting down on my shoulder, sending a bolt of arousal between us.

"You wanted it too. Stop fucking lying." I snap, slapping him hard enough to hurt my hand, earning an angry grunt. "I can *feel* how bad you wanted this."

"Shut up." His hips start to stutter, his voice sliding down an octave. I can feel the muscles bunching under his skin, his release close.

Mine.

"Make me," I purr, reaching between us to wrap a hand around both of our cocks, amplifying the friction. My own release is barreling towards me, but I'll be damned if I come first.

"I will fuck that arrogance out of you," his hand wraps around my throat, making my already tired lungs burn.

"I can't wait for you try." I give our cocks another hard squeeze and send us both over the edge, painting our stomach with cum, mixing our releases together as we rut through it. Our cries echo off the stone and glass, ringing back at us.

Oberon drags his fingers from my belly button to my sternum, collecting our combined seed, and feeds his fingers into my mouth. I greedily suck them dry, my eyes fluttering closed at the heady flavor.

Then he rolls off of me and onto his back, glistening chest heaving as he tries to catch his breath, a fucking God. A God marked by me. Brought to his knees *by me*.

There is nothing more intoxicating than that, than this.

He looks over at me, a slow smile stretching across his face.

"I hate you," he chuckles, pushing his damp hair out of his eyes.

"How much?" I smirk, propping myself up onto my elbows.

"Enough that I'll make you wait until we get back to your room before I fuck you." He tucks his cock back into his pants and zips them up before getting to his feet. He doesn't offer me a hand, just grabs his discarded shirt and walks out of the courtyard.

I sigh and get to my feet, tucking my own cock away and shedding the tattered remains of my shirt. I scoop some water from the fountain and wash off my chest, even though all I want to do is run after him like a love drunk puppy.

I have to retain some semblance of control, although now I suspect it'll be much, much harder than I thought.

When I reach my bedroom door, I can hear the shower running. I follow the trail of discarded clothes into my bathroom, where I'm met with an unobstructed view of Oberon's naked body, glistening and lathered with my preferred dragon's blood soap.

The bathroom is completely open, with a grotto style shower made with onyx and smokey quartz. A claw foot tub rests in the center of the room, and candles litter nearly every flat surface, the flickering light mixing with the steam to lull even the most tightly wound person into relaxing.

I've had many a lover join me here, but none so beautiful as Oberon. Every muscle flexes and ripples as he glides the soap over his skin, taking care to massage out the tension along his shoulders and back.

A voice in the back of my head reminds me that he could kill me at any moment. Could realize what I'd done. But I could kill him too, and he knows it, based on the way he's tracked every footfall from the moment I crossed the threshold of the bathroom.

My cock jumps in anticipation. Finally, an even match.

I shed my clothes slowly, taking my time, before approaching him. I glide my hands through the suds on his back, relishing in the way his muscles jump under my touch. He turns around to face me, nose to nose, and starts massaging the soap onto my skin, working my shoulders and chest into putty. I can't help but moan in delight, the tension flowing out my body and down the shower drain.

His cock nudges mine, growing harder by the second as he moves down my arms and around my back, working the knots at the base of my spine.

"You know I'm a man of my word?" he murmurs, dipping his head to graze his nose along my throat.

I nod, not trusting myself to speak without whimpering for him.

His hand slides lower, the suds turning his touch to silk. He dips his fingers between my cheeks and finds the place I've ached for him most, starting to massage it gently. Another breathy moan escapes me as he teases me.

"I never expected you to submit so easily," he sneers, sending a flare of embarrassment through my chest.

I let the shame awaken my power as I wrap my hand around his rigid cock, letting the energy shoot tingles down his shaft and into his balls.

"Oh *fuck*," he pants, his knees starting to shake. I crank it up to just shy of painful before I relent, his eyes glassy and his jaw slack.

"Submission is an illusion, prince," I grin, drawing him up to a sloppy kiss, water pouring down our faces and across our bodies.

He pushes his tongue into my mouth, at the same time pushing his middle finger past the tight outer ring and into my ass, the stretch sharp and exquisite. I collapse into him, grasping his shoulders as he works his thick finger deep inside me, quickly inserting a second.

"Could have fooled me," he purrs, massaging my prostate in a way the makes my eyes cross and legs turn to jello. With his other arm, he reaches down to caress the back of my thigh before scooping me up into his arms, securing my legs around his waist and spreading me open for him.

I slide down further onto his fingers, feeling his knuckles brush against my skin. He walks forward to press me against the warm stone and pulls his fingers out, leaving me gasping around the emptiness. But they quickly slip back inside, this time with additional soap and a third finger. I grit my teeth against the stretch, but the warmth of his skin and the water helps me loosen for him.

"That's it," he breathes, tucking his head under my chin to lap at the water collecting on my collarbones. He fingers me at a steady pace and I forget to control my reactions, moaning lewdly into the open air like a cat in heat.

I reach between us and start stroking his mighty cock, tracing my thumb over the thrumming veins and velvet head. I feel his mouth fall open against my neck, his breath hot, and double my efforts, matching my strokes to the tempo of his fingers.

His mouth finds mine in the steam, drinking down my whines of pleasure and winding the coil between us to the breaking point.

"I won't beg," I pant, although we both know that's a lie. "There's plenty of whores around here that'll sit pretty while I ride them."

His teeth bite at my lower lip, the muscles in his shoulder bunching with agitation.

The jealous type, hm?

With a jolt of surprise, he drops me to the floor, his fingers vanishing. Then his hand is on the back of my neck and he's steering me to the bath tub and bending me over the edge of it.

"So jeal—" a sharp slap to my left cheek steals the words from my lungs, a ripple of warmth arching along my spine.

"What did I say about the attitude?" He hisses, lining his cock up with my wanting hole.

"But it's one of my best features," I tease, glancing at him over my shoulder. Fuck, the sight leaves me breathless, him towering over me, huffing with anger, cock red and ready to split me in half.

"I don't think so, pretty boy." He spits on my asshole and presses his cock forward, the head pushing through without mercy. "This is your best feature." He doesn't pause once to let me adjust, just sinks deeper and deeper until I feel like his cock is in my throat, the pain bright but bearable. Finally, after what feels like an eternity, his hips lay flush against my ass.

I'm gasping for air, keening like a whipped dog as he drags his hips backwards, then snaps them forward, spearing me on his length. He grunts with pleasure, the sound low and animalistic, and I know he's about to tear me apart.

He fucks me like a savage, a madman, blistering my ass until I'm crying out, begging for release, begging for mercy, begging for more. And I know I'm not the only one being carved up with pleasure, I can feel it in the tremor of his hands, the grating gasps for breath, the sloppy thrusts as his orgasm hunts him down.

Oberon reaches around and starts pumping my cock, unraveling the last of my sanity and hurling me over the edge and into a mind-shattering orgasm, sparks of blue shooting from my fingertips and toes, pinpricks of electricity dancing along my nerves. He follows right behind me, biting hard onto my shoulder to contain whatever prayer was about to come out of his mouth as he pumps me full of scalding release.

He shivers against me as the pleasure bleeds from us both, leaving behind a rawness that feels like an open wound. He steps back and slides out with a wet *slap* making my cheeks heat at the way I must look to him, stretched and dripping.

Just when I'm about to stand up, I feel his fingers caress the underside of my cock and balls, up to my asshole, collecting the seed that's escaped and pushing it back inside, his touch gentle, almost reverent.

"Can I stay?" he asks, voice soft as he touches me.

It feels so good, I almost say yes.

"No." I straighten up and push his hand away, moving back under the stream of water to clean myself up. "I'll call you when I want to see you again."

He narrows his eyes, but for once doesn't argue. Just grabs a towel and his clothes and leaves the bathroom. A few minutes later, I hear the main door slam shut.

The shower echoes in the empty apartment as the last of him is washed from my skin. A deep pang of anxiety makes my gut twist, memories long repressed flooding back. Loneliness gnaws at my mind, a black and sludgy thing.

Sending him away was the right choice, the smart choice. So why does it feel like he left with half of my soul?

Memento te Aurum

It took us two weeks to get from Boston to Alder Bridge, NY. Two grueling weeks hopping train cars, crossing forests, and driving horses. Two grueling weeks with my parents relentlessly pestering me: 'Are we there yet?'

I've seen it in my dreams for months now, a farm out in rural New York, with rolling hills, ancient oaks, and an endless starry sky. A safe-haven for people like us.

My father, James, says we're blessed. My mother, Paloma, says we're chosen.

I always felt relatively indifferent on the matter. It gets me into trouble, and out of it.

My mother is a mind-reader, and a powerful one at that. With a single touch, she can see into your soul, the secrets you keep hidden even from yourself.

My father is attuned to the weather. He always knows when it will rain, or snow. He can bring down lightning and hail, make the streets flood and the pipes freeze. He can also make flowers bloom, but he never seems to have that inclination.

I can see into the future. Most often in dreams, sometimes in blinding flashes of knowledge that bring me to my knees. I have no control over it, I can't will them to come, I can't *look* into the future. It just lingers there, humming like a bothersome gnat. Always present, but out of my reach.Tools are the only way I can purposefully peek into the future, but those are muddy and vague at best.

This is why we're searching for Alder Bridge, for the Guild of witches that reside there.

In my dreams, it's safe, full of people with gifts like me that live peacefully and work together. A community of equals. A family.

I tried to go without my parents, to escape their cruelty, to escape their life of fleeing from town to town. See, they could never use their gifts for good.

My mother would mingle at parties, eavesdrop at the market, whatever she needed to do to figure out who was the wealthiest in town, and then a "natural disaster" would run them from their home. Maybe lightning set their roof on fire, or a strong wind blew a tree into their living room. Anything to make them evacuate, to clear the way so they could rob the family blind.

As a young girl, I would ask them why, and the answer was always the same. Because they could, they were entitled to it. Because they were blessed, and others were not.

I could never wrap my mind around it, and then the Universe showed me a way out. A safe-haven. So, I scrimped and saved, prepped and planned, and bid my time. But I didn't even make it out the front door before Paloma caught me and stole the truth from my own mind.

I saw an opportunity for salvation, they saw an opportunity for power.

My parents had always thought they were destined for greatness, blessed by the Universe with immeasurable gifts for some divine purpose. They believed it made them better, more worthy, than those without gifts, and had often expressed how weary they were of living among the "weaker" population.

I think they're absolutely insane. A lion is no more important than a fish simply because it has fangs. We all have our roles to play.

Early morning sunlight pours through the gaps in the trees, lighting the end of the trail leading to the Raith farm. As we approach, we're greeted by an invisible field so strong it burns my eyes, like a repulsive stench.

"What the hell is that?" Paloma asks, wringing her headscarf in her hands.

"I was about to ask the same thing," a low voice comes from behind us. We whirl around.

A teenage boy stands there. He's maybe a year or two older than myself, 17 at the most, with his arms crossed. A very large rifle is slung over his shoulder, along with two gray rabbits tied to his hip.

"We're looking for Absolon Raith," James says, moving to stand in front of my mother, his arms crossed over his chest.

The boy looks us over, his eyes a warm bluish-green. His hair is a sandy brown color, fading to white blond where the tips reach towards the sun. A scratch of blonde stubble lines his jaw, and a deep tan gives his cheeks a ruddy, impish look.

"Why?" His gaze snags on me, his eyes traveling around my face, undoubtedly stuck on my nest of unwashed copper hair.

"That's none of your business, boy," James sneers, the breeze kicking up to a steady gust.

"Oh, no?" The boy smiles, foxlike. "My name is Algernon Raith, Absolon is my father. And this is our land you're trespassing on, sir."

Something in the back of my mind prickles at his name.

Paloma nudges my father aside and steps gingerly towards Algernon.

I've always known that my mother was a beauty, with shiny brunette waves and tan skin, eyes rich and as brown as a cup of espresso. There was nothing she couldn't flirt her way out of, or into.

"We're just looking for a little help, and we think your father might be the only one able to save us," she says, sashaying towards him.

To my surprise, and profound pleasure, Algernon appears to be unmoved by her charms.

"Save you?" His turquoise eyes flick back to mine, an eyebrow quirking up.

"We're like you," Paloma purrs, reaching out to touch the bare skin of his forearm.

Algernon catches her wrist in his gloved hand before she can touch him and lowers it back to her side.

After a moment of deliberation, he nods. "Follow me." He strides past us and through the barrier, the shimmering shield parting for him.

We hesitate, but fall in line behind him, with me bringing up the rear.

"It's a ward," he clarifies, picking through the woods until we reach a well-trodden path. "Keeps out anyone that isn't granted permission, and let's us know if anyone comes close to the property."

"Can you teach us how to do that?" My father asks, catching up to walk by Algernon's side.

He chuckles. "If my father welcomes you in, we can teach you anything you could possibly want to learn."

My father glances at me over his shoulder, a warning. None of that knowledge is for me.

Algernon leads us to an enormous log cabin, surrounded by a dozen or so smaller cottages and endless rows of crops and flowers. Animals graze openly across the property, both livestock and pets. We see a handful of people beginning what must be their morning chores. They pause to watch us curiously, all of them greeting Algernon warmly while glancing sideways at us.

When we reach the steps, the large front door swings open, revealing an older man with dark hair and the build of a grizzly bear. Beside him is a gorgeous blonde woman, who bears a striking resemblance to Algernon, and two other boys. One, with raven-black hair, looks to be around my age, 15, and the other looks to be in his twenties, the angles of his face severe.

"Al, you were supposed to be hunting rabbits," Absolon says good-naturedly, coming down the steps to embrace his boy.

Algernon mutters something in his ear and his almost comically thick eyebrows shoot up. He looks over at us, surprised, but unguarded.

"Welcome to Raith Farm. My name is Absolon, and this is my wife, Sophia." He gestures to the blonde woman. "You've met Algernon, and these are my other sons, Gideon, our eldest," The older boy nods stiffly in our direction. "And my youngest, Oberon." The dark haired one stares down at his feet.

"I'm James Abbott." My father shakes his hand firmly. "This is my wife, Paloma." My mom does a small courtesy. "And my daughter, Ayla."

Their eyes fall to me, and a wave of insecurity closes my throat. I've been wearing the same drab brown dress for days, and haven't brushed my hair in even longer. I probably look like a wild changeling, or a forest goblin.

"She's the reason we're here," James says, grabbing me by the arm and positioning me between this bear of a man and himself. He places his hands on my shoulders, a sham of tenderness. "She saw this place in a dream and knew it was safe."

"In a dream?" Sophia cuts in, walking down the stairs towards me.

"Yes." James shakes my shoulders. "She has prophetic dreams, and visions. A fortune-teller."

Sophia snorts, and tucks a stray strand of hair behind my ear, her touch cool and feather light. "Divination, darling?"

I nod, tilting my chin up. "Tarot is my specialty."

Gideon's eyes fix on my face, his eyes narrowing, but Algernon elbows him hard in the ribs and he looks away.

"And I can—" Paloma starts, but Absolon holds up a hand and silences her.

"Your abilities are irrelevant to me. I could sense the magic before you even crossed the border." His eyes land on me, then slide back to my parents. *Sense the magic?* "What matters to me, and this Guild, is the content of your character. We take care of our own here. We live off the land and nurture it, growing our relationship with Source."

"Source?" Paloma asks, visibly miffed that she was interrupted.

Absolon smiles. "You have much to learn, Abbott's. Gideon, come," he says, keeping his eyes trained on us as his oldest descends the stairs.

Gideon stops beside his father, gray eyes flitting back and forth between our faces.

"Gideon has a penchant for Psychomancy, manipulation of the mind," Absolon starts, placing a hand on Gideon's shoulder. "I'm going to ask a few questions, and do not bother lying. He'll know."

I notice my father's shoulders stiffen, but his expression remains neutral. My mother's fingers tangle with mine, her grip tight enough that her rings pinch my skin.

"Do they come with negative intentions?" Absolon asks, gaze narrowed at my father.

Why not ask me? I think, petulant. *Maybe I mean them harm.*

My mother digs her thumb nail into my palm, sending a flare of pain up my arm.

Gideon's eyes, now a burnished gold, flick towards me then down to our clasped hand, and my stomach hollows out. *Oh shit.*

"No," Gideon says after a beat. "They have no ill will towards us."

"Have they spoken truly?"

Gideon's gaze pauses at my mother, his brow furrowing slightly. "They embellish, but speak true."

"Are they decent folks?"

I almost laugh, but manage to bite my tongue. But of course, Gideon catches it.

My father's a dick, but we're not bad people. I think, hoping he can hear me. *We have nowhere to go.* Paloma's grip loosens, pleased that I vouched for them.

His brow lifts, but he concedes. "As decent as any of us, Father."

"Very good," Absolon smiles. "Relax, you've passed. All are welcome here, so long as you contribute to the Farm and cause no harm."

We all breathe a sigh of relief.

"Come, let me show you to one of our vacant cabins."

Coming June 2024!

Acknowledgements

This book has been a long time coming. It started when I was barely old enough to read, creating stories with crayons on printer paper. It walked alongside me through adolescence and a Creative Writing degree. Every experience, every scrap of an idea, every tangle of words led me here, to Alder Bridge.

I'd like to thank the many people who have supported my love of books and writing, from family, friends, teachers, to strangers on the internet and beyond.

Thank you to the authors and their stories that inspired me.

Thank you to Kara, who has been my biggest cheerleader and best friend for over 20 years. I couldn't have dreamed this big without you.

Thank you to my mom, who gave me the greatest gift a parent can give: a love of books.

Thank you to my love, Hunter, for being my forever Beta-reader, my guinea pig, and my rock. This book (and Oberon) wouldn't exist without you.

And thank you, precious reader, for giving my baby a chance.

About the Author

Alice Greene is a former gifted kid from Upstate New York with a love of all things spooky, magical, and literary.

With a degree in English Literature and a passion for storytelling, Alice's writing style is a toothsome blend of angst, dark humor, and whimsy that explores the shadowy recesses of the human heart.

Today, she lives in South Carolina with her husband and pets.